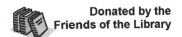

The VIGILANTE POETS of SELWYN ACADEMY

The VIGILANTE POETS of SELWYN ACADEMY

KATE HATTEMER

Alfred A. Knopf 🐎 New York

THIS IS A BORZOI BOOK PUBLISHED BY ALFRED A. KNOPF

All rights reserved. Published in the United States by Alfred A. Knopf, an imprint of Random House Children's Books, a division of Random House LLC, a Penguin Random House Company, New York.

Knopf, Borzoi Books, and the colophon are registered trademarks of Random House LLC.

Visit us on the Web! randomhouse.com/teens

Educators and librarians, for a variety of teaching tools, visit us at RHTeachersLibrarians.com

Library of Congress Cataloging-in-Publication Data
Hattemer, Kate.
The vigilante poets of Selwyn Academy / Kate Hattemer.—First edition.
p. cm.
Summary: "When a sleazy reality television show takes over Ethan's arts academy, he and his friends concoct an artsy plan to take it down." —Provided by publisher
ISBN 978-0-385-75378-4 (trade) — ISBN 978-0-385-75379-1 (lib. bdg.) —
ISBN 978-0-385-75380-7 (ebook)
[1. Reality television programs—Fiction. 2. Arts—Fiction. 3. Schools—Fiction.
4. Creative ability—Fiction. 5. Friendship—Fiction. 6. Family life—Minnesota—Fiction.
7. Minnesota—Fiction.] I. Title.
PZ7.H2847.Vig 2014
[Fic]—dc23
2013014325

The text of this book is set in 13-point Perpetua MT.

Printed in the United States of America

April 2014

10 9 8 7 6 5 4

First Edition

FOR GEORGE

A PREFACE-SLASH-DISCLAIMER FROM ETHAN ANDREZEJCZAK

Just call me Ethan.

You're reading this first, but I'm writing it last. I'm at a corner table in this low-rent Starbucks a few blocks from my house. I had planned to write this on the living-room couch, but I have triplet sisters, and they are four years old.

"Ethan," said Olivia, "sit on the floor."

"Now," said Lila.

"It is time for Candy Land," said Tabitha.

"No. I'm writing." I made my dad's working-from-home face. "I'm *busy,* girls."

The face worked about as well for me as it does for him.

Lila said, "Please."

Olivia said, "Please!"

Tabitha said, "Please. Or I will bite you."

I said, "I call the blue piece."

Starbucks may have provided a refuge, but I can't say I'm upset my time here is ending. Farewell, barista with the

1

mongoose tattoo. Farewell, double-shot mocha Frappuccino with extra whipped cream. Farewell, the daily smirk I got when I asked the former for the latter. Today is Labor Day, and tomorrow we'll start our senior year at Selwyn Academy, Minneapolis, Minnesota.

We, by the way, equals me and my friends. Jackson, Elizabeth, Luke. Jackson and I have been friends the longest. Back in middle school, we were quite the pair. I hadn't had my growth spurt yet (little did I know I never would), and he'd just discovered his passion for computer science. Together we redefined the upper limit of the seventh-grade awkwardness curve. We were best friends by default.

Luke, meanwhile, was the most popular prepubescent on earth. He was impossible to dislike. That's not hyperbole: I tried. I have a strict policy of holding automatic grudges against people everyone likes. But Luke had a mouthful of braces and said "awesome" all the time, and he was totally genuine. He liked everybody and he assumed that everybody would like him back.

How did he become friends with us? Well, he chose us. He chose us at a Saturday-morning math contest called Minne-MATHolis. Jackson and I were on a team with Luke and this kid called Miki Frigging Reagler. (Okay, this kid *I* called Miki Frigging Reagler.) We finished up and went out in the hall.

"Hey, we're the only ones done," said Luke. This happened a lot when you were on Jackson's team. "This is the best part—"

"I KNOW!" said Miki F.R. "We need to catch up, Luke. I've got so much to tell you—"

"—since all the adults are occupied elsewhere—"

"—about this hilarious thing at Jenna's party—"

"—and we are left to our own devices—"

"—which involved suspenders and a case of pop—"

"—alone in a university hallway—"

"—and do you want to go hang out by the water fountain down there?"

"—and when will such an awesome opportunity come again?"

"I can do a flip around the stair railing," I said, seizing my opening.

"No way," said Luke.

I could, and did. It was the one perk to being an eighty-pound thirteen-year-old.

"That's awesome."

"I can do that," said Miki F.R. It was apparently not that easy, even if you *were* trained in ballet, jazz, hip-hop, and contemporary. He bumped his head and went to sulk in the corner.

Luke and Jackson and I performed various feats of rail-somersaulting, head-standing, and pencil-throwing. We also told horrible math jokes. "Got one," said Luke. "What did the zero say to the eight?"

"'You're gonna get fat,'" said Jackson.

"Uh, what?"

"'Because you eight more than me.'"

Luke and I were laughing so hard we were crying. Jackson seemed much funnier with Luke around.

"Not what I was thinking," Luke finally managed to say.

"Which was?"

"'Nice belt.'"

I went home wanting just one thing: to be friends with Luke. And then it turned out that I *was* friends with Luke. It was a miracle.

Four years passed, and we hung out all the time. Jackson's cousin Elizabeth, who lives down the street from him, would come over too. We were a pretty tight foursome. We all went to Selwyn, a highbrow arts school where I belonged to the Untalented caste.

Then junior year happened.

Early this summer, I didn't know where I should start this thing. Life's not a TV show, with easy divisions between seasons and episodes. When *did* stuff begin? I couldn't decide.

Enter tricolon. I'm sort of obsessed with tricolon.

It's a rhetorical device. It means "the succession of three elements." I came, I saw, I conquered. Government of the people, by the people, for the people. Get it?

If you are sophomoric, like all the male juniors in BradLee's English class, let me tell you that yes, "tricolon" and "colon" are related words. We were all sniggering, and then Jake Wall said, "So it's like, *plop, plop, plop?*" BradLee couldn't help laughing. And then he sat on his desk, clutching his forehead, after he explained tricolon crescens. That's when the elements are progressively longer or more intense. Plop. PLOP. *PLOP.*

I've dumped several tricolons into this narrative. I could blame it on my indecisiveness. I could give you a Wikipedia-sourced essay on the importance of threes in the literary tradition. Or I could tell you that the memory of those plops, back when BradLee was just our earnest and embarrassable teacher, and Luke sat laughing next to me, and Maura Heldsman flinched at the sudden sound, her mind spinning off in pirouettes—well, I could tell you that some days, that memory was all I had.

Remember: this is not a novel, not a memoir, not produced by anyone with artistic skill. It's just about what happened last year. It's about reality TV, a desperate crush on a ballerina, and a heroic gerbil named Baconnaise. But mostly it's about my friends. Please remember: not art, just life.

ONE OF THE WAYS I COULD POSSIBLY BEGIN

I was in a locker.

Perhaps you have some questions for me.

Where was the locker?

It was in the math hallway. The hallway also contained TV cameras and reality stars and the love of my life.

Was the locker locked?

We'll get to that.

Oh, and by the way, WHY? Why, in the name of God-slash-Buddha-slash-Zeus, in the name of all things holy, WHY, why why why? *WHY* were you *IN A LOCKER?*

Yeah. That was going through my head too.

It started because I'd been stuck at school all afternoon. Usually I'll catch a ride home in the Appelvan, the child-molester vehicle (white van, tinted windows) that's piloted by my friend Jackson Appelman. But Jackson couldn't drive me because he had to whiz off to the University of Minnesota for an emergency meeting; the chess players were trying to secede from the Board Game Society, and there was some major civil unrest to be quelled. The bus wasn't an option since I needed to stay after for bio help night. My mom had been my last resort.

"Would you pick me up at three-thirty?" I'd asked her before I left that morning. The Appelvan was already sitting in our driveway. Either Jackson or Elizabeth was honking to the rhythm of "Glory, Glory, Hallelujah."

"Ethan, it's *January*. The school year's halfway over. And you still can't remember to tell me these things the night before."

"You could just get me a car."

"How could I entrust a car to a kid who can't remember to ask for a ride?"

Obviously, a car would solve that issue, but it wasn't a good time to point that out.

"The triplets have dentist appointments this afternoon. I won't be able to get you till afterward."

When she'd be battle-scarred and weary. The honking changed to Beethoven's Fifth, the ominous one. Dun-dun-dun *DUN*. "So what time?"

"Five? Five-thirty? Six?"

"Crap. Fine. Bye."

Bio help night, which left me unhelped, was over at three-thirty. I had way too much time to kill, so I figured I'd go sit by my locker in the math hallway and get some homework done. That should tell you how bored I was. Quiet had slammed down on the school, and Luke had walked home, and Jackson was at the U defending Fort Sumter from the chess rebs, and there was nothing else to do.

The corridors were deserted, as dusty and dim as if there'd been some apocalyptic zombie invasion that I had missed. That *would* happen. I'd be playing with Baconnaise, my gerbil pal, and only notice that the world as we know it was ending when those rotting undead hands slunk over the windowsills. I'd have already lost my chance to stockpile canned goods, but it wouldn't matter because I suck at running and the zombies would catch me instantly. But maybe they'd throw me back, like a minnow. Because they eat brains, right? The jury's still out on how big my brain is. My mom, say, has a higher opinion than my teachers.

At least I think she does.

I got so embroiled in my zombie fantasy that I forgot where I was going. I'd ended up near the English rooms. I thought I'd say hi to BradLee, but his door was locked, his room dark. Homework it was. Gurg. I preferred to do homework in the six minutes between class periods. I'm a junkie for the adrenaline rush.

But I resigned myself to my fate, and plopped down in the math hallway, and transferred my phone from my back pocket to my front pocket lest I butt-dial my grandmother again. I got into the zone with some history IDs. And then I heard footsteps. Not just footsteps, but wheels, gurneys, loud adult voices, shrill teenage voices, a cacophony, an approaching horde.

Was it Thursday? It was Thursday. Crap. Cat-piss. Porcupines. I was a cretin. Zombies, this brain is not up to par.

Thursday was the day, every Selwyn student knew, that *For Art's Sake* did its filming. That's the kTV reality show. They'd chosen a school (our school) and they'd chosen contestants (not me). Every episode, they had some artistic challenge and someone got kicked off. The last person standing would be crowned America's Best Teen Artist. The kTV security people do a sweep every Thursday at three-thirty to kick out the non-anointed, but I must have missed them with my daydreaming meander through the English hallway.

Why not just leave? Walk past them? Tell them I had to grab something from my locker, that I was just on my way out . . . ?

I present a tricolon of justifications.

1. This was January. We live in Minn-ee-*soh*-dah. If I left, I'd have to wait on the front steps freezing my butt off, and I don't have much butt to spare.

2. I was scared of Trisha Meier, the woman who hosted the show. She was an actress from LA, and she was very glamorous, and she wore tight pants. No matter what the emotion, she managed to show all thirty-two of her teeth.

3. There was this girl. This girl named Maura Heldsman. She was a contestant, a ballerina, a preternaturally gifted and exceedingly cute ballerina, and I had been in love with her for— hold on—two years, five months, and twenty-one days. I didn't want to be dismembered by Trisha, but I *really* didn't want to be dismembered in front of Maura Heldsman.

Besides, I was avoiding Maura. In the latest episode of *For Art's Sake,* she'd flirted with the person I hate most in all the world, Miki Frigging Reagler. He's a musical-theater twerp who tap-dances up the aisle to turn in tests, who thinks he'll be the best thing to hit Broadway since *Cats.* Which he quotes, frequently. There are many things in this world that nauseate me—sitting in the backseat while my dad drives, watching the triplets eat sardines, doing both of these simultaneously—but Miki F.R. tops the list.

I know what you're saying: "Who *is* this girl to cheat on the likable and upstanding Ethan Andrezejczak?" You should know that this was all one-sided. It was possible Maura knew my name—she'd never proven she didn't—but that was it. In fact, she was dating Brandon Allster. I told myself that Brandon was just practice. Maura was destined to end up with me.

The noise was getting ever closer. I panicked. I tried a couple classroom doors. But they were all locked, the teachers long gone, and there was Trisha Meier's piercing laugh—*henc! henc! henc!* The film crew would only be passing through the math hallway, I figured. I just needed to get out of the way for a minute.

I put my books in one empty locker, and I leapt into the one right next to it. I wrenched my fingers through the slats and I slammed shut the door.

The whole entourage turned the corner. I contorted my neck and squinted through the slats so I could see. They ground to a halt right in front of me.

"I've got a great tagline, Trisha," said an eager voice. I identified the source: Damien Hastings. Damien, another LA-actor type, was Trisha's co-host. He had ultra-gelled hair with frosted tips like the Backstreet Boys circa 1999 and he was obviously as terrified of Trisha Meier as I was, although he showed it by kissing her ass.

Trisha didn't respond.

"Ready? Ready?"

No response.

Damien put on a stagy voice. "'The theater department isn't the only place you'll find drama at Selwyn.' Get it, Trisha? T-Dawg? Get it?"

"Brandon," said Trisha. "Maura. Come here." Brandon, who sings opera, jogged into my limited field of vision. Maura separated herself from the crowd with that toes-pointed-out glide of hers. She looked only slightly less spacey than she usually did in English class.

She was very close to me.

"Makeup, check; hair, check. Looks good," said Trisha. Truer words never spoken. "You two know the basic outline?"

"I'm stringing him on," said Maura.

"She hooked up with Miki and I know it," said Brandon.

I was getting interested despite myself. Sure, I was jammed in a half squat, and the coat hook was boring a hole into my spinal cord, and my air supply had the scurvy stench of ancient brown-bag lunches. But it wasn't all that bad. I couldn't wait to tell Luke and Jackson and Elizabeth. *Nobody* got to watch the episodes being filmed. I was like a secret agent.

* * *

"We're fixing the lighting, Trisha," someone said. "It'll be a minute."

"Fine." A burly cameraman moved right in front of my locker. All I could see was half a polo shirt and a hairy biceps. Trisha's voice suddenly changed. "Well, *hello,* you." I was pressing my face so hard against the slats that I was going to get corrugated, but I couldn't make out who she was talking to.

"Hey there."

"Just *happening* to stroll by?" Trisha trilled a little laugh.

"Exactly." The voice was a pleasant, gravelly, tenor rumble.

"Would you like to stay and watch a scene or two?" I didn't need to see Trisha to know that her hand was on one hip, her head saucily canted to the side.

"Oh, just passing through. Have to get home; I've got pounds of grading—"

BradLee! It was our English teacher! He hadn't been in his classroom, but he must have had a meeting or something.

"We're ready, Trisha," said the cameraman in front of me. I jumped and hit my head on the shelf. It clanged. I held my breath.

"All right, kiddos," said Trisha in the fakest voice possible. "Let's get this done. Maura, Brandon, go where Ken tells you."

Ken was apparently pointing right at my locker, because that's where they went. If I'd had goblin fingers, I could have reached through the slats and touched Maura's hair. This was getting freaky. Nightmare scenarios ran through my head. What if my quads gave out and I toppled through the door? What if the cameraman could see my eyes glinting through the slats? What if Brandon started kissing Maura and I couldn't restrain my wild virile jealous rage?

"Take some deep breaths," said Trisha. I did too. "Remember, there's only one winner! Only one trip to LA!"

"Only one spread in *La Teen Mode!*" said Damien.

"Only one scholarship," Maura muttered to Brandon. The winner got a lot of glitzy crap, but also a hundred-thousand-dollar scholarship to any arts college. That's what most of the kids were gunning for.

"Makes this seem a lot more real, doesn't it?" said Brandon.

"Chop-chop!" called Trisha. "Stop talking. We're ready. And, action."

"Look, Brandon," said Maura, suddenly enunciating, "can't we talk later? I've got to get to the studio. This week's challenge—"

"This can't wait. Listen. I was rehearsing my aria in one of the practice rooms, and I went out to see if Miriam would accompany me on the piano."

"Miriam? Help someone? Are you crazy?"

"She was all, 'I need to keep my fingers fresh, I have to perform Bartók's *Allegro Barbaro* in three hours.'"

"Whatever."

"Yeah, what a prima donna," said Brandon.

"Good, good," murmured Trisha Meier. "Keep going. Get to the point, Brandon."

Brandon took a deep breath. I figured out what was going on. They'd been having the conversation somewhere else, and Trisha was just making them do it over. For the light, probably.

"Then I overheard Miki. He was bragging. He said he'd hooked up with you."

"He's lying. Why would I hook up with him? I hate him."

"Really?"

"Do you trust me?"

"I trust you."

"Well, I trust you too. And I didn't do *anything* with Miki."

Trisha interrupted. "*Bor*-ing."

"Maybe I should kiss her?" said Brandon. Maura winced. She was in profile to me now, her elegant swan neck and her little chin and her thin, straight nose all flowing upward to the bun that rose from the crown of her head.

"Where's a scriptwriter when you need one?" said Trisha.

Guess reality TV has some downsides.

"Any ideas?" she said.

Damien jumped up like a puppy. "We need a *visual*. So I was thinking, you know bridges?" He paused as if requiring some assurance that Trisha Meier did, indeed, know bridges. "There's this thing where couples put padlocks on bridges. To, like, lock their love."

"Surprisingly," said Trisha, "that has some potential. Ken, fetch me a padlock."

"It's a European custom," said Damien airily. "When I went to—"

"Spare us the details." Ken trotted back with a padlock that I bet he'd taken off the locker of some fool who hadn't closed it. Trisha handed it to Brandon. "We'll want to finish with a close-up shot of the lock clicking shut."

"I can *see* it," said Damien. "We zoom, it clicks, it's shut, their love's eternal. The music swells—"

"Shush," said Trisha. "Maura, Brandon, improvise as best you can. And, action."

"Maura," said Brandon. He lifted the padlock. "You and me. We're locked together."

"Oh, Brandon," said Maura.

"Look into his eyes," hissed Trisha.

"Together forever," said Maura. She put her hands over Brandon's, and they looked into each other's eyes and then down, bashfully, as they threaded the shackle through the hole. She glanced up at him and he gazed down at her, tears glistening in his eyes.

"Us," he whispered. The lock clicked shut.

"Cut," said Trisha. "Not bad. Let's get moving."

They left.

And that is how I ended up stuck in a locker.

The problem with situations that give you time to think is that you don't want to think when you're in them. Like when we train for the zombie invasion by running laps in gym. My dad claims running is meditative, but personally, my running meditations all concern how I'm about to vomit a lung right out of my chest. And it'll lie there on the track, gelatinous and pulsating, and the gym coach will be like, "Andre—er, Ethan! Pick it up!" And I'll be like, "The lung? Because I have this *thing* about touching my own internal organs." And he'll go—

Anyway. I was in a locker, and I had a lot of time to think. After half a year in BradLee's English class, I was getting used to asking, "What's the deeper meaning?" Hmm, let's see. Boy meets girl. Boy contracts huge crush on girl. Boy gets imprisoned in locker by girl as girl professes eternal love to other, hotter boy. Basically, I was helpless and passive and pathetic. Then there was the part about how "locking away" is a phrase usually applied to lunatics or felons. And about how I'd watched the whole thing and it'd taken me till half an hour later to start fantasizing about leaping out of the locker and telling Maura I was the one who truly loved her. If my life had been a poem, I could have analyzed the shit out of it.

Before these depressing thoughts, however, I'd determined the recipient of my save-me text. I had three options, which I submit in order of how little I wanted to text them.

1. *Elizabeth*. Elizabeth is a very competent person. She'd pulverize that lock. However, she would also laugh like a banshee and post pictures online.
2. *Jackson*. Jackson would first feel the need to calculate how many possible combinations there were for a Master-brand padlock. Then he'd formulate an algorithm for the best way to guess the combination. Then he'd start guessing.
3. *Luke*. It had to be Luke. Luke wouldn't mock me, Luke hated math as much as I did, and Luke would bring a crowbar.

I could hear him coming down the hallway before I could see him, because he was rattling like an escaped convict.

"Marco!" he yelled.

"Polo," I said weakly. I could see him now. He slung his backpack to the floor with a jangling thud.

"We got a bolt cutter, we got pliers, we got a pry bar—"

"What'd you do, raid a Home Depot?"

"But the first thing I want to try is a good old-fashioned hammer. Prepare thyself."

All I could see was his forearm. The ropy muscles tensed. I closed my eyes. The blow reverberated right into my teeth, like biting into ice cream. I opened my eyes to see Luke inspecting the lock.

"Almost," he said. "Take two." He hit it again. "One more." It shattered. The pieces fell to the floor with an anticlimactic tinkle. I stumbled forth into the light.

"Should I ask?" he said.

"I don't think I'm quite ready to talk about it."

"The ordeal too recent, huh?"

We walked companionably to the main hall. He didn't press me for details but instead started going on about his latest idea, which was all about long poems and censorship and protesting *For Art's Sake*'s intrusion into our school. (More about that later.) I nodded along. There were footsteps and I cringed, but it was the janitor.

"Mr. Miller," said Luke, saluting him. "How's it going?"

"Well, hey now, Luke." He didn't know *my* name. Granted, I didn't know his. "You didn't hear a noise, did you? I thought the TV guys had left, but—"

"Maybe coming from the math hallway?" said Luke.

"That's what I thought."

"We were just there. It looked deserted."

"Hrm."

"All right, Mr. Miller. Take it easy."

"You too, Luke."

My mom's minivan was just pulling into the circle. She rolled down the passenger window and leaned all the way over. "Luke Weston! How *are* you, honey?"

"Hey, Mom," I said.

"You heading home, Luke? Want a ride? Front seat's open!"

"It's your son, Ethan," I said.

"Thanks, but I'll walk. It's just a couple minutes."

"Yep, great to see you too," I said.

"You sure? That backpack looks heavy."

I got into the front seat. Luke stuck his head in the window and looked back. "Lila? Olivia? Tabitha?"

"LUKE!" they screamed with joy.

"How are my favorite four-year-olds?"

"I'm the oldest," said Olivia.

"You're still four," said Lila.

"But I'm a bigger four than you."

"We just got our teeth cleaned."

"Except for Tabby," said Olivia. "She bit Dr. Pohlman."

Tabby had her entire fist in her mouth and was staring out the window, sulking.

"Tabby doesn't like Dr. Pohlman," explained Lila.

"He doesn't like her either," said Olivia. "He said only little girls with clean teeth got to pick from the treasure chest."

"Then he said she'd get cavities."

"No, he said he *hoped* she'd get cavities."

Tabby looked like she was about to bite Olivia. Luke must have noticed too. "All right, girls, see you!" he said hurriedly. "Bye, Mrs. Andrezejczak. See you tomorrow, Ethan. Call me if you can't figure out the calc. I already know I can't."

"Thanks," I told him.

"Don't mention it," he said, grinning.

My mom pulled away, shaking her head. "You're so lucky to have Luke as a friend."

She didn't even try to hide the fact that she liked Luke better than me. I stretched out my stiff legs. "Yeah," I said. "Best friend I've ever had."

ANOTHER OF THE WAYS
I COULD POSSIBLY BEGIN

Let's leave the locker debacle shrouded in the mists of the future. Rewind, if you will, to the beginning of that week.

We were back to school after the holidays. The school year was turning out like an ill-constructed burrito: a few bites were interesting, but most were just rice. All our teachers' jokes had started to seem recycled. Even the kTV cameras seemed normal. Yeah, it was still thrilling to watch Maura Heldsman on *For Art's Sake,* but it was an established thrill. It was part of what we did. There was no longer much self-consciousness in the act of flipping to a big national station and seeing the scene shift from Laguna Beach to our own quirky Minnesotan school.

Last period that day was BradLee's junior-senior English Lit class. I'd been there for a few minutes, deep-breathing to recover from the trauma that is AP Biology, when Luke stalked in from his journalism class.

"Another piece rejected," he said. He slammed down next

to me without taking off his backpack. We technically didn't have assigned desks, but you know how it goes. Day one, the territory gets peed on. Days two through forever, the seats stay the same.

"Another?"

"That's three in two months." His long legs were splayed out and his arms crossed. Jackson came in from his math tutorial and sat down behind me. I canted around so we could face each other. There was still some time before the bell, though BradLee had an annoying habit of starting class as soon as everyone arrived. He could occasionally be deterred, but you had to demonstrate through body language that you'd flip your shit if he dared disrespect your six minutes of freedom.

Jackson was updated. "You're arts editor," he pointed out. "You're honcho number two. Who's doing the rejecting? June?" She was the editor in chief.

"Supposedly," said Luke. "She claims there's no space. But I kept pushing and she told me that Mr. Wyckham is the one making the call."

"The call on space?"

"The call on me."

"Ah," said Jackson. He set his briefcase on his desk, dialed the Fibonacci sequence to unlock the clasp, and removed the stapled stack of paper he used for English notes. As a matter of principle, Jackson doesn't buy notebooks. He hates the corporate idea of repackaging cheap commodities for extreme profit. Drink bottled water around him and live to regret it.

"The call on you? What's that supposed to mean?" I said.

"There isn't supposed to be 'controversial material'"—

Luke did the bunny-ears thing—"in the *Selwyn Cantos* this year."

"This year?"

"That's preposterous," said Jackson. "It's a *newspaper*. Controversy is news."

Elizabeth rushed in at the bell. I waved, but she'd long held that English was her chance to hang out with other people. "With my normal friends," she said. I didn't think to ask Luke what was so controversial about his story until BradLee had started us on a warm-up. We had to identify rhetorical devices in phrases he'd projected onto the whiteboard.

For God, for country, and for Yale. "Tricolon," I wrote. I barely resisted drawing a little heart by the word. I loved tricolon. "What was the article about?" I wrote on a piece of scrap paper. As soon as BradLee was hawkishly strolling the other half of the classroom, I flipped the note to Luke.

And murmuring of innumerable bees. "Onomatopoeia," I wrote. Actually, I tried to write it. I knew it started with an *O*.

Luke passed me the note. "It was on *FAS*." Abbreviation of *For Art's Sake.*

"A review?" I wrote back.

When I next glanced over, Luke had abandoned the warm-up and was scribbling a long screed. Luke's rangy and tall. He has brown hair that looks like it chose to be brown; it's that rich, nutty brown girls have, not the boys' brown that's just there in the absence of any other color. His eyebrows are straight and his eyes are a complementary chocolate, and in a totally heterosexual way I'll say that he's pretty cute.

Not that I was thinking about Luke's attractiveness in English class. Nope, I was working on the warm-up. *He took his hat and his leave.* Zeugma.

He finally gave me back the note, and then looked up at the board with feigned concentration just as BradLee circled back to us. It is a truth universally acknowledged that English teachers excuse all sorts of malfeasance in anyone who can write like Luke Weston. BradLee for sure knew something was up—he's not dumb—but he didn't call us out on it.

"It's a review, but it's mostly editorial," Luke had written. "I tried to suppress my snideness. I may not have been totally successful. I questioned why the school's allowing the show when it's just a big moneymaker for kTV. Whatever percentage the school's getting has to be piddling. Pocket money. Blood money, more like."

BradLee glared at me. I casually draped my arm over the note and stared at the board with a face that exuded intellectual curiosity. It must have worked because he started pestering Rummica Fitzgerald.

I kept reading. "I didn't even write about how I feel disenfranchised, marginalized, shut out. This school used to be about the arts. It used to be the best place to go if you were serious about both arts and academics. And now it's about venerating the *FAS* kids and congratulating ourselves because we're getting national exposure. It's changed everything."

I threw the note over my shoulder to Jackson. I knew he'd been craning to see it. Either BradLee was eyeing me or I was paranoid. *Her home was a prison.* Duh, metaphor.

Jackson passed it back. He'd drawn a graph. The x-axis was labeled *craptasticness of FAS*. The y-axis was labeled *$$$*. The line pointed due northeast: perfect, positive correlation.

"I believe the word is *craptasticity*," I wrote. Luke heaved a sigh. I tried to fake some more outrage, but he saw right through me.

Because sure, I agreed with him. But I didn't really care that much. Not in English class, at least. The desks were arranged in a two-tiered circle, and across the room from me was this girl. This girl named Maura Heldsman. You might have heard of her. Usually, I would care more about how much *For Art's Sake* sucked for Selwyn. And usually, I'd care a *lot* more about Luke's disappointment.

It was just hard to concentrate. Given the surroundings.

BradLee gave us the answers for the warm-up. "New unit starts today, guys," he said. "We'll begin with a brief lecture on our main topic." Yay, I thought, a lecture. Selwyn is too cutting-edge to have many lectures, and that means I spend my life listening to people who don't know anything—i.e., my classmates. In a lecture, the one who knows his shit is the one who's doing the talking. Very logical.

I admit, however, that lectures make it easier to zone out. Especially when Maura Heldsman is within five yards.

"Ezra Pound called it a 'tale of the tribe,'" said BradLee, gesturing with vim, "which can encompass an entire culture's values and history."

Oops. Speaking of zone-out, I'd missed the entire topic. I wrote down "tale of tribe" anyway.

"Langston Hughes called its author the 'bearer of the light.'"

Damn, I'd missed the *it* again. "Bearer of light" went into my notebook. Then Maura Heldsman yawned. Her yawn was as delicate as a cat's, as delicate as every other motion of that dancer's body of hers, sinewy and light, poised in the seat, toes out.

"And in fact, it's a pseudo-epic. The epic is the vision; this is the re-vision—revision and *re*-vision, a true 'sighting again' . . ."

I wasn't in the same room as Maura Heldsman often. I felt like I had to soak her in, to make the most of my scant time. Maura was a secondary satellite that lessened my gravitational pull to everything else clamoring for attention in my world: Luke, Jackson, BradLee's lecture. She didn't know who I was. But if I was an Etch A Sketch, she operated the stylus. When she was nearby, the magnetic fuzzies of my consciousness all rushed to her.

She also inspired the creation of really bad metaphors.

"And so in a postcolonial . . ."

I gave up on BradLee. I couldn't follow his thread and I let it trail away. He led the class through the labyrinth without me. I was lost down a dead end, entranced by a girl.

Luke suddenly sat up straight and started writing, fast. It startled me out of my trance. He was supremely focused on BradLee, writing every word that came from his mouth. I refocused my attention, but it was too late.

"And that, class, is why we will be spending the rest of this quarter on the long poem."

I titled my half-assed page of notes "Long Poems," and then added a parenthetical note: "(wah)." How long, I wondered, is long? A page? More than a page? I tried to find someone to exchange commiserative glances with, but Luke was still writing intently, and Jackson was staring down at his crotch, surreptitiously playing (let's hope) one of the math games he'd written for his graphing calculator.

"Now that you all understand the term 'revisionary mythopoesis,'" said BradLee, "we'll go ahead and get started on our main author, Mr. Ezra Pound." He clicked around on his computer until an old photo came onto the projection screen: a man from a side angle, with an artistically tormented expression, a fabulous mustache, and big hair. *"Ecce homo,"* said Brad-Lee. I'd studied Latin for five years now, which meant that I could, on rare occasions, actually translate something. *Behold the man.*

"The true *auteur* of revisionary mythopoesis," said Brad-Lee. The index of words I understood was steadily dropping. I subtly inclined my head toward Luke's notes, but he'd flipped the page and was writing busily. I would have tried Jackson's notes, but they didn't exist. "Here's a representative story. In 1919, Pound published 'Homage to Sextus Propertius' in *Poetry* magazine."

Jake Wall guffawed.

"Se*xtus* Propertius, Mr. Wall."

Hey, I had heard of Propertius. Maybe. All those Latin names sounded the same.

"Who's Propertius, by the way?"

"A Roman poet," I said, hoping that BradLee would think I'd been paying attention all along, also hoping that he would not ask me for more details.

"Good. So then"—phew—"a classics professor wrote to the magazine, calling Pound 'incredibly ignorant' of the Latin language."

Jackson poked my back with his pen. That morning we'd had a wretched test on Ovid. Incredible ignorance of the Latin language was near and dear to our hearts.

"He said there were scores of errors in 'Homage.' Can anyone guess Pound's response?"

Luke's hand shot up. "I bet he said it wasn't supposed to be a translation."

"Exactly," said BradLee happily.

"And that he wasn't pleased with the editor publishing the letter of a persnickety, picayune Latin professor."

"You must be the modern-day incarnation of Pound," said BradLee. "Nailed it. Pound wrote a response to that effect, which was *not* published. Possibly because it began with the imprecation, 'Cat-piss and porcupines!'"

I wrote that down. My notes already blew serious chunks. The addition of cat-piss and porcupines would not make them much worse.

"Even in 1919, Pound was rejecting the artistic mores of the time."

BradLee kept talking. His full name is Bradley Lee; I always wondered how such a smart guy could have been spawned by such half-witted parents. He turned thirty earlier this year, though he looked more like twenty, and he could have passed for fourteen if he'd gotten rid of his red-blond "beard." (Peach fuzz.) His favorite shoes were Keds, but in an ironic way. He was the type of guy to have a favorite punctuation mark. It's the interrobang, which combines the exclamation point and the question mark: ‽ As in: could anything possibly be dorkier than having a favorite punctuation mark‽

Though I'm rather fond of the semicolon.

The bell rang. Elizabeth and her normal friends shot out. I'd wanted to leave at the same time as Maura, but she wafted out of the room while I waited for Jackson and Luke.

"I'm going to write a long poem," said Luke. At the end of the day, the hallways are so crowded that it's like being swept along a river. A highly trafficked, piranha-infested river; if you make any unexpected movements, you'll probably get whacked by an instrument case.

"Why?"

"Weren't you listening to BradLee?"

"No," said Jackson and I simultaneously.

"Pathetic."

"I was trying," I said, "but circumstances conspired to defeat me."

"'Circumstances' meaning 'the rack of one Maura Heldsman,'" said Luke.

"She doesn't really *have* a rack," said Jackson.

We had been over this many times before. It was an occupational hazard of being in love with a ballerina.

"Why does our every conversation return to Maura Heldsman?" Luke asked.

"You're the one who brought her up," Jackson told him. He keeps a mental recording of every conversation so he can note your every inconsistency. It's both useful and highly irritating.

"We're the oppressed," said Luke. "I will be the bearer of

the light." He started talking faster. "Talk about postcolonial. Talk about minimal cultural authority. That's us. We were a beautiful indigenous society until kTV came in." And faster. "They're just like the British in India, the Belgians in the Congo. It's all for their own gain, and they justify themselves with the smug belief that their culture is superior. It's exploitation, and they're paying us just enough that we don't mind. So we go along with it." Now I knew what he'd been scribbling in his notebook. Luke works through ideas first on paper.

"What does that have to do with long poems?" said Jackson.

"Weren't you *listening?*"

"No!"

We'd reached the tributary of the journalism hallway. "I will reappropriate our culture. See you dolts later." He negotiated the turn and floated away.

"A long poem," I said.

"The only thing I *like* about poems is that they're short."

"Cat-piss and porcupines."

THE THIRD WAY I COULD BEGIN, AFTER WHICH I WILL BEGIN (I PROMISE)

Roll the tape back even further. Early September. First week of school. It was the third day, during Morning Practice, when the PA system went off.

"All students and faculty are to immediately report to the auditorium for a special announcement. Thank you."

Luke had a theory that the secretary had a fetish for splitting infinitives on the loudspeaker. I thought that was bullshit but she sure wasn't helping my quest to disprove it. I put down my trumpet, wiped the spit from the corners of my mouth, and left the practice cubicle.

It's hard to imagine now, but as I joined the stream of students, I don't think I was curious about what we'd hear. I was just relieved that Morning Practice was interrupted. Morning Practice is a ninety-minute period after first bell when all of us run off to our respective studios and ply our respective trades. It's one of Selwyn's best recruiting tools, although they never mention to prospective parents what a school sounds like when a hundred instrumentalists are practicing at once. Sometimes I make myself play trumpet, and sometimes I go draw. Those are my two majors. I am mediocre at both.

I ran into Luke on the way, and we saw Jackson and Elizabeth waiting for us in front of the auditorium. Jackson and I exchanged smiles. We both considered Morning Practice a painful experience. He spent the time working on lighting design for *Giselle,* the upcoming dance performance. This task bored the crap out of him. (Literally, as he'll tell you if you ask. I suggest you don't.)

"I can't *believe* they're interrupting us," said a girl who was still wearing a paint-splattered smock. "I was entering my *flow.*"

Her friend was noisily sucking on an oboe reed. "I know, right?"

"Like, this time has been placed upon the altar of Art," said Elizabeth, catching my eye. "How dare they defile her temple?"

"I have made a sacred commitment to my Muse," I said, "and she shall not, uh, be cool with this."

Elizabeth dropped the Valley-girl voice. "This *is* annoying."

"You're allowed to think that, because you're good at what you do." In fact, Elizabeth is crazily good. She's an art major, like me, but she specializes in graphic design. Not many Selwyn alumni can actually make a living in an artistic field, but she's going to end up designing book covers or posters for hipster bands. "Yep, it's the poseurs I can't stand," I added loudly. Oboe Sucker gave me a disgusted look.

We shuffled into the auditorium. I still couldn't believe my luck. Instead of being trapped with my trumpet in a cubicle that reminded me of an insane asylum, with its padded walls and intimations of despair, I got to sit with my friends in these amazing, soft, velvet seats. Selwyn poured money into the auditorium. The lighting and sound systems are top-notch, and there are lushly pleated velour curtains and even those little boxes for royalty. And the seats are seriously more comfortable than my bed.

Elizabeth got out a sheet of paper. She'd recently become so sick of us going "That's so predictable" that she'd started making us write down predictions.

Jackson was first: *Installation of video-game kiosks within soundproof practice studios; recognition of gaming as artistic major.*

"You wish, Jackson," said Elizabeth, peering over his shoulder. Jackson wields a controller with the precision and grace of an orchestral conductor, but his genius, like Vincent van Gogh's, has been unrecognized in his lifetime.

"One of these days they'll see the light."

I hoped not. That'd just be another art form I sucked at.

Luke: *New program to bring art to low-income kids and their families.*

"Could be, could be," said Elizabeth.

"Because nothing makes a homeless guy feel better than Rachmaninoff," said Luke.

My turn: *New fund-raising drive.*

"Lame," said Elizabeth.

Luke read it. "That shouldn't count. That's like predicting that at some moment between five and eight tomorrow morning, a large fiery orb will appear in the east."

The teachers began applauding forcibly and shushing us, and eventually everyone noticed that Willis Wolfe had walked onstage. You'll recognize the name if you happen to be obsessed with the eighties sitcom *Mind over Matter* and its blond, rugged star, the one with the blindingly white teeth. Teeth the color of baking soda, of laundry detergent. That's our principal.

"Blah blah *fantastic* blah *tremendous* blah-di-blah," said Willis Wolfe. He never says anything worth listening to. I could see his evil toady, Mr. Coluber, waiting in the wings. A prediction so obvious nobody wrote it down: Vice Principal Coluber would deliver the special announcement.

"Blahing blah blahity *awe-inspiring.*"

Elizabeth had clearly spaced too. She was rubbing the edge of the prediction paper between two fingers as if she were making a dreadlock. Elizabeth has a fantastic, tremendous, awe-inspiring head of dreadlocks. She's half black. Obviously not the half that's kin to Jackson "Wonderbreadface" Appelman.

"And here's Mr. Coluber, your vice principal, who spearheaded this initiative and is here to give you the news," said Willis Wolfe.

"Told you," I said before remembering that I hadn't told anyone.

"I take back the low-income idea," said Luke. "Coluber's too slimy."

"Guess it's not so predictable after all," said Elizabeth smugly.

"Fund-raising fund-raising fund-raising," I said.

We shut up when we saw that we were being stink-eyed by Mrs. Garlop, the old hag who doubled as our calculus teacher.

Mr. Coluber tapped the microphone. The drama kids finally shut their traps, an occurrence to be savored. "Good morning, Selwyn," he said unctuously. Coluber is a skinny, tall guy. His eyes are hyper-focused and his hair has receded into a heart shape, which is the only thing about him that signifies he has a heart. "It's nothing you could possibly guess," he said. When he's not wearing a tie, he leaves the top button of his shirt undone so tendrils of chest hair poke out. "It's one of the most exciting things to come to Selwyn Academy." He thinks he's hot stuff, you can just tell.

"Spit it out," said Elizabeth.

"The Kelvin Television network, known to you as kTV, of course"—there was a dramatic pause—"is"—pause—"filming a new reality show right here at Selwyn!"

I think Luke was the only one of us who knew this was a bad idea from the start. He began to shake his head, as slowly as windshield wipers on the drizzle setting, while Coluber told us about how they'd hold auditions to choose contestants, the best Selwyn had to offer in dance and music and drama and writing and visual art.

There'd be a challenge every episode, and every episode one of the nineteen original contestants would be kicked off. I mean, asked to step down. "Sometimes the decision will be made by the judges and sometimes by the American public and sometimes, ladies and gentlemen, by *you*. And the prize? Oh, do we have a prize."

It was here that the daydreams started. I was just sentient enough to see that everyone was glazed over in reveries before I was swept into one too. The American public would discover me. I'd be the hero of a new generation of teenagers trying to make it in the arts: the Guy Who Cross-Hatches. Or, if I decided the route to stardom lay with my trumpet, the Guy Who Lip-Buzzes.

And of course the hero would need a love interest. This was reality TV, after all. The producers would look around for a slim, sassy brunette. A girl as talented as I was. Maybe a dancer? Yes. A ballerina. Perfect.

And the romantic tension would build, and at last during the season finale I would take Maura Heldsman in my arms and bend her backward—her back is extremely bendy—and there would be a kiss, a long kiss, a kiss to build a dream on—

Luke elbowed me.

I shut my mouth, which had gone somewhat slack, and blinked.

"Selwyn is lost," he said. "Lost to kTV."

Life slid back into perspective.

I wasn't going to be on this show. I was so skinny I had to buy skinny jeans to look normal. The stuff topping my head was more akin to underbrush than human hair, and my nose was the size of my elbow and about the same shape too. Nope, not gonna be on kTV.

To be honest, I barely belonged at Selwyn. When we were in eighth grade, my mom got a call from Luke's mom. Mrs.

Weston told her about this arts school down their street, where the academics were outstanding and the arts were *superb,* and, career prospects or no, it could be life-changing, life-*affirming,* to be exposed so deeply to the arts, didn't she *agree?* And my mom, a forty-two-year-old with three newborns she couldn't tell apart, talked to my dad and said something like, "If he's with Luke, he can't go too wrong, and this makes the whole choosing-a-high-school thing a lot easier for us, which, given that the entire house is covered with a scrim of regurgitated breast milk, is an important consideration." And my dad was like, "Yeah."

I wasn't a total philistine. I'd played trumpet since second grade, and in the pre-triplet era my mom had forced me to practice every day. (After their extraction I woke up a baby every time I touched the thing, which made for a convenient reason to leave it in its case.) And I'd always liked drawing. Nobody realized how intense Selwyn would be, but I survived. So did Jackson, who turned out to be okay at tech theater. Elizabeth and Luke thrived.

But I sure wasn't going to be on kTV. And I knew exactly who would be.

I started looking around for those kids, to see what faces looked like as destiny unfolded before them. The piano prodigies, catbitches and a-holes every one, were glaring at each other. And there was Kyle Kimball, a serious actor who likes Shakespeare and, I've noticed, actually *gets* Shakespeare. He was trying to look nonchalant. Being a talented actor, he did look nonchalant. But Miki Frigging Reagler was bouncing in the springy seat, wearing the kind of openmouthed grin that he usually reserves for the last stanza of "All That Jazz," when he's simultaneously licking his thumbs and conga-kicking.

He'd be on the show. They'd love him.

I already knew where Maura Heldsman was. She had a blank look on her face, which wasn't unusual, but her friends were giggling excitedly. Then it struck me: she'd be on TV. I'd get to watch her. It wouldn't be creepy, because everybody else would be watching her too.

I was sort of excited for this thing.

Thus it began. Nothing was inevitable, although by the time I was peering through locker slats to watch Maura Heldsman being filmed for national TV, it sure seemed that way.

After the assembly, Luke ranted for a while: Selwyn sold out, reality TV sucked, et cetera.

"So are you going to try out?" said Jackson.

"*Me?*" said Luke.

"You're easily the best writer in the school."

He was frowning. I was on tenterhooks. This makes me sound like a horrid friend, but I did not want Luke on that show. I'd be so jealous.

"The prize sounds pretty cool," said Jackson. "All that scholarship money."

"True," said Luke.

"And an agent."

"Yeah."

"And national exposure. You'd be famous. You'd have cool friends."

Luke gave his head a quick shake, like a dog just out of a pond. "God," he said. "Who do you think I am? Of course I'm not trying out. That'd go against everything I stand for."

Phew.

"I already hate that show," he said. He started ranting again. I tried to nod along, but I'd already decided I was cool with it. Why?

1. I wasn't going to be left out. Luke wouldn't audition. Elizabeth said she couldn't be bothered. And Jackson wasn't exactly the TV type, unless there was a historic change in public opinion, I guess: "We've had enough of washboard abs. Give us a boy who knows HTML."

2. Maura. Screen. Me. Couch.

3. Seriously? Most importantly? I didn't think it would change my life. I would keep doing the things I did. I'd fool around in the math hallway, throwing magnets onto the ceiling. I'd zone out on the various appendages of Maura Heldsman in English. I'd survive Latin, maybe survive calculus, do okay in history. I'd torment my sisters until I got bored and tried to ignore them, at which point they would torment me. Luke and Jackson and Elizabeth and I would chill in the Appelmans' den (unsurprisingly dubbed the Appelden), where, with Baconnaise on my shoulder, we'd play our favorite video

game, *Sun Tzu's Art of War,* murdering legions of Mongols while talking about whatever Luke was into, which could be Kierkegaard or *Fight Club* or sabermetrics. This reality show would be kind of cool and kind of annoying. Lots of things in life were like that. It just wouldn't matter that much.

That's called *irony,* guys.

CHAPTER ONE

O Selwynfolk! In days of old,
Ideals were high and art was bold.
In that primeval solitude,
We sketched and sang, our crafts pursued.
But now, we watch TV. We're screwed.
                    — THE CONTRACANTOS

After the fiasco that was my introduction to long poems and revisionary mytho—uh, mythowhatchamacallit—I knew I had to pay attention that Friday when BradLee lectured on Ezra Pound again. Despite any stunning reason *not* to pay attention that may have been sitting across the U of desks, pointing and flexing her feet.

"Pound and the Imagists decided on three principles," said BradLee. I perked up. I could get behind anybody who knew the importance of threes.

"First, direct treatment of the subject. Second, use of no word that doesn't contribute. And the third has to do with rhythm. Instead of writing like a metronome"—BradLee beat his desk—"'*All* the *world's* a *stage* and *all* the *men* and *women merely players*,' Pound wanted to use rhythm the way it's used in a musical phrase. Can anyone explain that?"

Rummica Fitzgerald raised her hand. She would. She plays the flute, and she likes everyone to know that she *gets* music, she's *one* with it, melody is her *soul*. Rummica said, "There's still a beat, but there might be four sixteenth-notes or just one quarter note."

"Excellent," said BradLee. "So there could be four quick syllables in a beat or one longer one. You guys need any of that repeated?"

Of course we suck at taking notes, so he had to say the whole thing over again.

"Pound later described his method of 'luminous details,'" said BradLee. "Instead of abstractions and adjectives, he selected crucial details. Revealing details. Honed, chiseled images. He didn't want commentary or philosophy."

BradLee scrawled *luminous details* on the board.

"He wanted good art. He wanted beautiful art. 'Beauty in art reminds one what is worth while,' he wrote. 'I mean beauty, not slither. I mean beauty. You don't argue about an April wind, you feel bucked up when you meet it.'"

BradLee flipped on the projector. "Here's an example of an early Imagist poem. Pound stepped off a train in the Paris Underground, and he saw one beautiful face after another. He worked on this poem for a year, class." There it was:

> *The apparition of these faces in the crowd;*
> *Petals on a wet, black bough.*

Beauty, not slither. Luminous details. I don't even like poetry and I just stared. Everyone was either spacing out or awestruck, which looks basically the same, but I knew Luke was
on the awestruck side too.

We'd planned to hang out later at the Appelden, so I went
home for a couple hours. "I'm going for a run," my dad announced.

"Not outside," said my mom. "The wind chill's negative six."

"Treadmill?" said Olivia hopefully.

"Guess so," said my dad.

"EARTHQUAKE BABY TIME!" the triplets shouted as
one.

"Come with us, Ethan," ordered Tabitha.

I complied. It was Friday afternoon; it wasn't like I had
anything better to do. And Earthquake Baby is a tradition.
While my dad moved the ironing off the treadmill, the girls
arranged me on the dining-room floor.

"Good morning, baby!" said Olivia.

My dad ratcheted up the speed. The room began to shake.

"EARTHQUAKE!" they shouted.

"You are supposed to cry, baby," Olivia told me.

"Wah!"

"Shut up, baby," said Tabitha. "I will feed you breakfast.
Down the hatch!" I automatically opened up, assuming her
spoon would be empty, but then I gagged.

"What the heck? What *was* that?"

"Babies can't talk," said Olivia.

42

"Okay, but what was in that spoon? Do I need to call the poison hotline?"

"It was Barbie hair," Lila informed me.

"No, it was breakfast," said Tabitha.

"And besides, babies can't talk," said Olivia.

My dad had reached cruising speed. The floor was really vibrating. "EARTHQUAKE!" they yelled again.

"Mommy!" I wailed. "Want my mommy!"

"We are in charge," said Olivia.

"Mommy got tilled," said Lila.

"Was she lying in a field or something?" I shot my dad a look, but he was too busy gasping for air to appreciate my quick wit.

"No, dummy," said Tabitha. "She was in the house. The ceiling fell on her head. She got tilled."

"You mean killed."

"That's what I said. Tilled."

I wiped the spittle off my face. "Daddy! Want my daddy!" I cried.

"Daddy got tilled too."

"Did he drop dead of a heart attack?"

"Not funny, Ethan," managed my dad between huffs and puffs.

"And before they got tilled," continued inexorable Olivia, "they said that you had to do everything we say."

"EARTHQUAKE!"

"Maybe we should evacuate."

"You are a baby. You are not allowed to talk."

Go ahead and dog-ear this page if you're the type of person

who'll be like, "Why does Ethan spend all his time with his friends instead of in the bosom of his family?" After enough seismic activity to flatten San Francisco several times over, I struggled to my feet ("BABIES CAN'T WALK, DUMMY!") and headed to the Appelden.

CHAPTER TWO

We <u>were</u> an artists' colony,
Not some outpost of kTV.
We saw the world through the same lens,
Together scorned all mindless trends,
As tinkers, tailors, soldiers, friends.
                    — THE CONTRACANTOS

I guess you already know that Jackson Appelman is eccentric. He's also persistent. He makes these resolutions—e.g., on Thursdays, he takes notes in binary code—and then he sticks to them. Even when they turn out to be stupid. Do you know what it takes to write "long poem" in binary code? Here ya go: 01101100011011110110111001100111001000000111000 00110111101100101011101101.

Both his eccentricity and his perseverance come straight from his parents. Case in point: when they were first married, the Appelmen adopted a beagle named Pickles, and then decided to name all their future pets after condiments. And they like pets a *lot*. Twenty-five years later, most of the normal

names have been used up on dead animals and they're down
to the dregs.

Three pet names that work:

1. Chutney the Angelfish.
2. Wasabi the Ferret.
3. Baconnaise the Gerbil—my suggestion: my
   favorite condiment for my favorite Appelpet.
   Baconnaise is the man.

Three pet names that are just unfortunate:

1. Fish Sauce the Cat.
2. Catsup the Other Cat.
3. Honey Mustard the Golden Retriever. Seems
   like a cute name, right? Well, try yelling "Honey
   Mustard" every single time you're trying to get
   him to go outside or eat his dinner or remove
   his snout from your crotch. You can't call him
   "Honey" and you can't call him "Mustard,"
   because those are both among the dear
   departed who now reside in the necropolis next
   to the basketball hoop, and all three Appelmen
   get teary and sentimental if their names are
   accidentally mentioned. Frigging annoying.

Jackson resents that his dad's name is Jack (get it?), but I
think he should be grateful that he didn't end up as Pesto, or
Watermelon Rind Preserves.

*   *   *

That night in the Appelden, Luke and I sprawled out on the old camelhair couches. I was giving more attention to Baconnaise than to anyone else. He likes to chill on my neck, but if I forget to give him the occasional finger-stroke he'll make a break for it down my shirt. Luke was petting Honey Mustard, who was purring like a cat.

Jackson sat in front of one of the computer monitors playing *Sun Tzu's Art of War,* using one of his lesser avatars so he wouldn't compromise his über-powerful guy. (He only plays that guy under conditions of total focus: between midnight and 4 a.m., parents asleep, the only light being that which emits from the screen.)

"Luminous details!" said Luke. "I'm obsessed with luminous details. I don't know how Ezra Pound exists in the same world as the kTV people."

"He doesn't," said Jackson. "Pound's been dead for like forty years."

In my Baconnaise haze, it took me a minute to orient myself in the conversation. Oh, right, English class. *Petals on a wet, black bough.*

"The sentiment stands," said Luke. "He cared about art for art's sake. The kTV people, conversely, name their show *For Art's Sake* yet care about nothing but money. It's immoral."

Baconnaise, roused by the voices, was now running laps around my neck.

"It's not supposed to be art," I said. "It's entertainment." There he was, ranting on about *For Art's Sake* and Pound again.

"Cat-piss, Ethan. It's all *about* the arts. We go to an *arts* academy. That's the whole premise of the show, kids trying to make it in the *arts*. But the kTV people don't care about art at all."

"I get it." I yawned. I couldn't help it. Baconnaise felt the tautness in my neck and paused, alert. I ran my pinkie down his spine. He's the smartest gerbil I've ever met.

"Elizabeth wants to come over," said Jackson, looking at his phone.

"So invite her over," said Luke.

"I did."

"So why are you telling us?"

"Luke, snap out of it," I said. "It's a stupid TV show. They'll be gone next year."

"You think they're going to settle for one season? This is minting money."

"It's high time you learned some tricks, buddy," I told Baconnaise. "Pretend my fingers are a tightrope." He navigated it no problem.

"Someone should put a stop to it. It's ruining our school. Selwyn's becoming a kTV colony. An outpost in the wilderness, for them to observe and profit off. It's disgusting."

"Did you ever talk to Wyckham about your article?" Jackson's fingers were tapping the arrow keys with a pianist's dexterity. A horde of invading Mongols bit the dust. Duh, I thought. *That's* why Luke's still upset. I felt like an imbecile for forgetting.

Luke sighed. He grabbed a tuft of Honey Mustard's fur and tugged. "No."

"Why not?"

"Because Wyckham's a charlatan."

"Define for the masses." That was me.

"A mountebank."

"Um."

"A fraud."

Elizabeth came in, almost blinding me with her highlighter-yellow sweatpants, and fell onto the other couch. "Talking about Wyckham, are we?" she said brightly.

"How'd you guess?"

"It's the particular blend of revulsion and impatience. Like you're hungry, but there's a big old hairy wad of gum on your fork."

"He's not trustworthy," said Luke.

"That's because he's Coluber's pawn," said Elizabeth.

I tried to exchange a look with Jackson, but he'd turned back to *Sun Tzu's Art of War*.

"Exactly!" said Luke.

This was the look I'd wanted to give Jackson: *Crap. Elizabeth is going to second all of Luke's anti-administration, conspiracy-theory, paranoia-sparked thoughts about why his article wasn't published. We'll never have a normal conversation around here.*

"I mean, half the faculty are his pawns." Elizabeth flopped onto her back, as gracelessly as a dying fish, and shoved her hands through her hair so her dreads fanned out behind her.

"It seems worse with him."

"That's because he's giving Coluber power over the *Selwyn Cantos*. Which is—slash would be—the only free expression left for us."

"Wow, I'm so glad you're here," Luke told her. This was why he was so well liked. He thought stuff like that, and then he said it. I imagined telling Maura Heldsman what I was thinking. She'd walk into English. *Maura, I'm so glad you're here. I needed someone to stare at while this strand of drool bridges the gap between my mouth and my notebook.* Baconnaise cuddled up in my Adam's apple and I felt sorry for myself.

"There's an unspoken rule that any article written by a page editor is published. Plus, this was good."

"Let me read it," said Elizabeth.

Luke gave her the printout. Meanwhile, I rummaged in Mr. Appelman's knitting basket and found a length of yarn. "Baconnator," I murmured, excavating him from his warm little knoll, "it's time for circus camp."

"You've got to do something," said Elizabeth seriously. She folded the article into an airplane and winged it back to Luke. "You're the only one who sees this situation clearly."

"*Thank* you," said Luke.

Jackson dispatched a sinister cadre with two keystrokes. I tied one end of the yarn to the couch leg, just a few inches above the floor. Baconnaise wavered, but managed a four-inch walk. "Not bad, not bad," I whispered.

"I'm going to write a long poem," Luke was telling Elizabeth.

I'd heard this one before. Now Baconnaise could handle eight inches of tightrope without one tremor or false step.

"Long poems are *the* way for the oppressed to voice their identity, to reclaim their culture. And we are the oppressed."

Elizabeth was listening intently.

"We've been denied our voice. I want to reclaim it. I want to present *our* culture, *our* milieu, *our* Selwyn. I'm going to play up the neglected characters. Those of us who aren't pretty enough for the show."

I glanced up from the floor. I've already explained about Luke. As for Elizabeth—I mean, usually I think of her as my friend, as Jackson's utterly asexual cousin, and honestly, I rarely even remember she's a girl, but, like, objectively speaking, she's got keen eyes and wild hair and some not insubstantial curves in the chesticular region.

It wasn't prettiness that kept Luke and Elizabeth from *For Art's Sake.*

"I'm going to deflate the ones who've sold out."

"Please deflate Miki Frigging Reagler," I said. "Pop him like the hot-air balloon he is. If I have to walk into bio one more time and see him practicing his shuffle-ball-change . . ."

"This will be the anti-*FAS.*"

"Very cool," said Elizabeth.

"Hey, speaking of *FAS.*" I motioned to the TV with my head. I couldn't move my hands because Baconnaise was negotiating a three-foot tightrope.

"Groan," said Elizabeth. "Friday night. Nine p.m. It's time for the requisite viewing."

"Must we?" said Luke, even as he pulled the remote from Honey Mustard's mouth.

"We've bought in," said Elizabeth. "As has the entire school. You might love it, you might hate it. But you watch it."

*   *   *

You know the lock scene? The one that made Maura look so sweet, Brandon so romantic? I couldn't believe what they did to it. I was appalled.

This episode started the same way they all did, with a long zoom onto the three judges, Trisha Meier and Damien Hastings and our principal, Willis Wolfe, sitting at a shiny table on the Selwyn auditorium stage. Trisha made some irritating joke about how cold it was, and Damien jockeyed for airtime with his own dumb joke about moving the school to "Cali."

They talked up the prizes. They brownnosed their sponsors. "Remember," said Trisha Meier, "these ten young artistic geniuses are fighting tooth and nail to win an all-expenses-paid trip on Amber Airlines. . . ."

Insert product placement. Trisha misused "literally" twice. Willis Wolfe kept plugging the importance of arts education. Damien shook his gelled head like a pony.

"Besides a guaranteed signing with an agent, the winner receives a trip to LA and a spread in *La Teen Mode*," he said. "Also, a scholarship of one hundred thousand dollars, redeemable at any arts institution and provided by Collegiate Assets, *the* way to help *you* save for school."

A lot of product placement, a lot of commercial breaks.

They explained the format every week, clearly assuming that all viewers were morons. (Granted, we'd chosen to watch *For Art's Sake*.) They'd started with nineteen contestants. When they were down to three, the show would conclude with a live finale.

Cut to the hallway, where Brandon was talking to Miki Frigging Reagler.

"Sorry, man," said Miki F.R. "When I see something I want, I take it."

"What happened to the dude code? Bros before hos?" said Brandon.

Unsurprisingly, Miki F.R. broke into song. "When you got it, flaunt it. . . ."

This other girl, Kirtse Frumjigger, scuttled over. Analogy: Kirtse is to musical theater as a cockroach is to leftover pizza. She joined in. Brandon stomped off when Kirtse and Miki F.R. started harmonizing.

Luke muted it. I kowtowed in thanks.

"I thought Maura and Brandon locked themselves together," said Elizabeth. I'd finally told them all what I'd seen and, more reluctantly, how I'd seen it.

"Probably coming up," I said, shrugging.

Now they were showing Miki F.R. and Kirtse with their heads pitched together in that obnoxious a cappella bffs-in-harmony way, like the vultures in *Jungle Book*.

"Unmute," said Elizabeth. The hosts were about to announce the challenge.

"This week," said Trisha, "you must use art to express anger. Rage. Fury. Ire."

Luke groaned. "Can we please turn this off?"

"Shouldn't you be taking notes for your poem?" said Elizabeth.

"Good idea," he said.

Kyle Kimball, the Shakespeare kid I like, was biting his lower lip and nodding thoughtfully. Miki F.R. was doing a little snap-and-bounce as if he couldn't wait to begin. Maura Helds-man looked vacant.

Luke scribbled all throughout the commercials. The shot reopened on my locker.

"Hey!" I said. "It's me! I'm on TV! Baconnaise! Look!" I crawled up to the screen and held him close.

"Move your big head, Ethan," said Elizabeth.

I couldn't see anything through the locker slats anyway, but I knew I was in there. "My debut," I told Baconnaise.

"Doesn't look like it," said Elizabeth. The image had shifted to the dim backstage. There were two people, their figures indistinct. Now Elizabeth was the one peering at the screen. "I think that's Maura."

Jackson deigned to turn from his video game. "Certainly bony enough," he said.

"*Slender,*" I said indignantly. "Svelte. Slim."

"But I can't cheat on Brandon!" said one of the figures.

"Definitely Maura," said Jackson.

I dropped Baconnaise.

"He'll never know," said the other figure.

Now we were back to the locker.

"I didn't do *anything* with Miki," Maura told Brandon.

Return to the figures backstage. They started groping each other. Ew.

Locker. "I trust you," said Brandon. He held up the pad-lock. "You and me. We're locked together."

Backstage. The faces were sucking at each other. We're talking vigorous make-outage. The slobbery sort you'd expect from Honey Mustard, not a reasonably inhibited teenager.

"Oh, Brandon," said Maura.

"Oh, Miki," said Other Maura.

"Together forever," said Romantic Maura.

"Don't tell Brandon about us," said Wanton Maura.

"Us," echoed Brandon as the lock clicked shut.

Elizabeth wordlessly handed me Baconnaise. I sat, stunned and anguished, on the couch. Maura Heldsman was *not* a two-timer. Or was she? What the hell was happening?

Baconnaise nipped at my chin as we watched the contestants attempt to express rage through art. Andy elicited nails-on-a-chalkboard noises from his cello. Adelpha threw paint onto a canvas while screaming like a peacock. Kyle and Josh ranted via monologues, Kirtse and Miki F.R. ranted via show tunes. Miriam bashed the keyboard. Brandon and Scarlett shrieked out some arias. Maura just danced. Then she told the camera, "I'm not here to make friends."

"Predictions," said Elizabeth after they all performed. "Who's getting cut?"

"Miki F.R.," I said.

"What's with you guys and your inability to distinguish between predictions and wishful thinking?" Elizabeth said crossly. "Come on, Ethan."

"Fine. Andy. That cello piece sounded like a cat in a disposal."

"No way," said Luke. "Andy's the hottest guy on there. They need the eye candy. It's going to be Josh."

"Scarlett," said Jackson. "She's a really good soprano."

"Jackson, bud, that means she'll *stay* on the show." That was me.

"Let me elucidate," said Jackson. "She's good, so her voice is kind of scary and unhuman. And besides, her nose is off-center."

I'd never noticed before, but that was definitely why I felt my OCD kicking in whenever I looked at her face.

"This is my *least* favorite part," said Trisha. Yeah, right. They'd narrowed it to two, and she could barely repress her grin. "Josh, that monologue was sickeningly overwrought. But Scarlett, frankly, my dear, your aria hurt my ears."

Scarlett started to cry. The cameras zoomed in.

"Scarlett, I'm sorry, but—"

Trisha looked at Damien and Willis Wolfe so that they could deliver their catchphrase.

"THAT WASN'T ART!" they chanted in unison.

Trisha bid us farewell. The show cut to commercials. Woe ensued.

CHAPTER THREE

In what is still the recent past,
We Selwynites made art to last.
On fields of beauty we'd purport
To touch the world: our contact sport.
For art is long and life is short.
                    — THE CONTRACANTOS

We have a rotating schedule at Selwyn: daily Morning Practice, plus five of your seven classes. That next Monday, English dropped, and I didn't see Luke until math, right after lunch.

I liked calculus. Scratch that. I hated calculus. But I liked calculus *class*. The only other class Luke and I had together was English, where BradLee and Maura Heldsman, in very different ways, made it hard to goof off. But Luke and I both loathed math, and Mrs. Garlop was not only a harpy but also a terrible teacher. We had to get Jackson to reteach us everything before the tests. Jackson had hit calculus before he'd hit puberty. Now he was doing an independent study with a tutor. He didn't even use numbers anymore.

Mrs. Garlop always had her harpy radar out for Luke and me, so we usually pretended to pay attention. Sometimes we even volunteered to do a homework problem on the board, usually with Jackson's elegant and clearly un-Garlopian (rhymes with fallopian) strategy. But for me, the calculus was a façade. The real subject of the class was hanging out with Luke.

We were rotating line segments around axes and determining the area of the shape thus formed. Luke was crabby, I was heartbroken.

"I wrote another review Friday night," he said, meticulously shading his rotated shape.

"For the *Selwyn Cantos*? You know they're not going to publish it."

"As one final test. It's a pure review, no editorializing. Just a summary of what's been happening on the show."

"So we take the integral of *this*," I said loudly. Mrs. Garlop was sniffing around our desks.

"And then raise it to the power of the derivative of *this*," said Luke. She went to go help Rummica and Missy.

"Um, no, we don't." (If you haven't taken calculus, Luke was spouting nonsense. Also, don't.)

"I took it to Wyckham this morning. Didn't even stop at June. And I made it as difficult as I could for him to reject it. I basically said, 'Hi, I'm your arts editor, I'm number two here, I wrote this, I need it for my page, I just wanted your approval.'"

"And?"

"He took one look at the lead and said no. He said, 'If you've got blank space, here are some ads for advertising. Maybe next issue.'"

"So it'll go in next issue."

"Andrezejczak. Are you listening to me? Instead of publishing my review, we are advertising *advertising* in this godforsaken newspaper. They aren't even ads. They're ads for ads. They're like those benches that say, 'See, You Looked! Bench Ads Work!'"

"Well, they do. Because I always look."

"Not even going into the fallacies of that statement. So ten times three is seven, moving from base four to base six, of course, and if you take the natural log of pi—"

"You sound like a moron."

"She's buying it."

Mrs. Garlop had moved away from us again.

"She just doesn't want to explain it again. She thinks we're hopeless."

Though that was probably good for our relationship with Mrs. Garlop. Once she gave Luke a detention for asking a question that betrayed her befuddlement with the finer points of calculus, and for that reason she put "insufferable arrogance."

"I think the administration has put the kibosh on any meaningful discussion of *For Art's Sake*," said Luke.

"Probably Coluber."

"Definitely Coluber."

"Or maybe it's part of their contract with kTV, that the school can't criticize the show."

"That's even worse!" Luke was gesturing with his pencil.

"At least the administration has *some* justification for censorship. They own the presses, provide the paper, pay the advisor. But it violates all our First Amendment rights if we're being censored by an unethical TV network that's just throwing sops of entertainment to the American public at the smallest possible cost so that they can keep the biggest chunk of adver— YES, L'HOPITAL, I LOVE YOU AND I LOVE FINDING THE DETERMINATE QUOTIENT OF LIMITS!"

He started scribbling random mathematical symbols. Mrs. Garlop gave us a crocodilian smile and circulated back to poor Rummica and Missy.

"Tising revenues," he said.

"L'Hopital's rule is totally irrelevant here."

"If I've learned anything in calculus—which is debatable—it's that L'Hopital's rule is always relevant."

The only thing worse than calculus is discussing calculus with Luke.

"Ethan, I know *you're* not in favor of the show."

Because of Maura, he meant.

"They're really screwing her," he said.

"Yeah."

"Although, perversely, it might be good for her chances of winning. The more drama she generates, the less they can afford to kick her off. She's the one who keeps people watching."

"Yeah."

"But it's just gross, what they're doing to her."

"And to Miki F.R."

"I admire your sense of fair play," said Luke. "And your feminism. Sure, Miki's being portrayed as promiscuous too.

But come on, Miki *is* promiscuous. And he wants everyone to know it. Your friend is in an entirely different situation."

"Not my friend."

"Your lover."

"Rotating around the x-axis would get us, uh, like, a doughnut. Not my lover."

"No need for precision between best friends. We both know there's no action going down."

"*She* has action going down."

"Ethan. Ethan Solomon Andrezejczak. You didn't believe all that, did you?"

"Believe the stuff that *happened*? Of course I did. I *saw* it. It *happened*."

"You are so naive."

I hate being called naive. Probably because it's true. I said, "She did that stuff."

"They edit crazily well. Reality TV is not reality."

"Integrate from one to five. We're going to have to do u-sub."

"You know how all your experiences are seen through the filter of your own particular vision? How everything you perceive may or may not be true because of this filter applied over your senses?"

"Hey," I protested.

"Not you in particular, you in general. Everyone has a filter, a different filter. That's why it's so hard to figure out what the real story is. Or whether there's a real story at all."

"Don't go all philosophical on me. We *definitely* need u-sub."

"Does u-sub have anything to do with U-boats?"

"What does *u* equal? We're never going to be able to integrate something so complicated without u-sub."

"Or U-turns?"

"Frick, Luke. Help me, okay?" Why did Mrs. Garlop only lurk behind us when I was the one talking about math? I actually made sense. "What does *u* equal?"

"You equal gullible. Because kTV made up that stuff. They found tiny unrelated bits of footage, and they put them together to make a story line. To *create* a story line. Which is exactly what you're doing. You're holding like three pieces of a big jigsaw, and you think you know what the whole picture looks like."

I thought about that while Luke doodled a giant infinity symbol.

"How would you know? You're holding three of the pieces too."

"Nope, I've got four. Because I read up on reality TV."

"Are you freaking kidding me? You're lecturing me because you spent some time on the Internet last bell?"

"Yep. I pulled a WiTSOOTT." ("WiTSOOTT" is Selwyn slang, an acronym: Wikipedia The Shit Out Of That Thing.)

"Ugh."

We finished the math problem. We probably got it wrong.

"Let's go talk to BradLee," I said.

"You think it's to that point?"

"It's to that point."

"Are you just saying this because Maura Heldsman was portrayed as all trampy?"

"Of course not," I said piously. "It's because your articles were rejected. Because we're being censored. Because we're being oppressed! Like the long poem stuff. We're the indigent, I mean, indigenous people, and the corporation—"

"So yes. It's because you can't take seeing Maura with other guys."

"Yeah."

Luke and I split up to suffer through our last two classes: bio and American history for me, French and creative writing for him. At last the final bell rang and we met outside BradLee's empty classroom. He was sitting with his head in his hands, either tired or woebegone. Unsurprising, as he'd just taught three sections of freshman English.

"Mr. Lee," said Luke.

"Mr. Weston," he said.

"We need to talk to you about something important."

Here's what Luke explained, as I nodded along:

1. Mr. Wyckham had rejected his two articles for the *Selwyn Cantos* for no clear reason.
2. We suspected there was some censorship going on.
3. We were worried that kTV was taking over the school.

Luke didn't mention to BradLee that the only reason I cared was my infatuation with Maura Heldsman. He wasn't a crappy friend. In fact, right then in the dim classroom, gesturing and using big words in his Lukish way, he was a particularly excellent friend.

BradLee moved to sit on top of his desk.

"They're taking over the school," said Luke. "They're colonizing us as a moneymaking venture. Education is a lost cause, art is a lost cause. All is reality. Nothing is real."

That was Luke's conclusion. He'd obviously written it during French.

BradLee went over to the door and flipped on the lights. When he came back, his eyes were sparkling as if he were about to cry. He shuffled around some papers on his desk. Luke and I exchanged a weirded-out glance.

"You're right," BradLee said finally. "They're taking over. They'll do anything to get more people watching, to raise that Nielsen rating. Selwyn is barely a school anymore."

"It's not *that* bad," I said to cheer him up. I did not want to see BradLee cry. On the grand scale of people it's awful to see cry, where a faraway baby is a 1 and your dad is a 10, BradLee would be up there at 8 or so.

"I didn't expect this," he said. Then he raised his head as if he'd suddenly remembered his audience. "You guys know the story of how I got this job, right?"

Oh man, this again? BradLee was obsessed with this story. "Tell us," said Luke. We'd allow BradLee to soothe himself with his story.

"I was living in New York after college, working in finance. I hated it. One night, my friends and I went out to a bar called Pub of America."

"Right." We'd heard this before.

"Terrible food. But they did have a dartboard of the fifty states. I'm whining about my job, and my buddy goes, 'Throw a dart. Go where it leads you.' Given my darts prowess, it's shocking that it even landed on the board. But it did. Right in the middle. Right here. And I began thinking, Is that a *sign‽*"

"Excellent use of the interrobang," said Luke.

"Thanks," said BradLee. "Remind me to tell you a funny story about interrobangs later. Where was I?"

"The dartboard," I said.

"I figured, maybe I could be the first English major in the history of history to use the degree. I could teach high school in Minneapolis! And it even seemed like a good idea once I sobered up. Er, not that I was very drunk."

It would take quite a lot of alcohol for me to leave New York, move to a flyover state, and teach comma rules to teen-agers.

"And what do you know, I got hired. Five years later, I've fallen in love with this school. Arts, education, my colleagues, you guys."

Thus endeth the most pointless story ever.

"And I guess the point is"—yes?—"the point is, I didn't expect this."

"The censorship?"

"Exactly. What's next? Are they going to censor what we can teach, what we can discuss in class?" He was looking weepy again. "What have we done?"

"We are downtrodden but not dead," pronounced Luke, clearly trying to rouse the troops.

"What have we done?"

"Subjugated but not squished."

We, I thought. Weird.

Luke pulled a dingy legal pad from his backpack. "Can I use that?" He was motioning toward the backup photocopier on the rear shelf.

Good distraction, I thought. When he'd made the copy, Luke handed it to BradLee.

"This is the start of my long poem," said Luke. "You know, revisionary mythopoesis?"

Not that again. The one time I don't pay attention in English. And now I was sentenced to the eternal torment of not understanding revisionary mytho-something-or-other.

"We need to reclaim our society and values and culture. Through art, of course."

BradLee looked impressed.

"Tell me what you think. If you want to read it, I mean. It's not that good."

That sounded as fake as anything you'd hear on *For Art's Sake.*

"Thanks, Luke." BradLee's voice was kind of squeaky. God, I thought, he's really going to cry. Despite his happy little finding-myself story. Despite all our efforts.

"We better get going," I said loudly. "Jackson's got the Appelvan today. He'll be waiting."

"Mr. Lee," said Luke, "you're a villager just like us. You're not in the power structure. You haven't sold out. You're a teacher, but you can still be part of this folk uprising."

I wasn't sure when writing a long poem turned into a folk uprising, but as we walked out to the parking lot, I didn't question it. It was probably true. If Luke Weston wanted a folk uprising, he'd get one.

I was right.

CHAPTER FOUR

Conquistadors, they thundered in,
And dizzy, we succumbed to spin.
They've colonized our native land.
What once was vivid now is bland.
We sing and dance at their command.
                    — THE CONTRACANTOS

This is how our friendship worked: Luke would get into something, and shortly thereafter I would too.

So a week later, I was obsessed with taking action against
kTV, just like Luke. I was embroiled and enraged and ener-
gized. I remember going to Advanced Figure Drawing the
next Monday and thinking that we'd fix this. We *had* to. It all
depended on us.

Dr. Fern was roaming around the class as we settled ourselves in front of the drafting boards. "Get out your manikins,
students," she said.

"Free choice today?" asked Yvonne Waters. I always liked
days when we got to arrange our little wooden manikins

in whatever pose we wanted. I'd done a whole series called "White People Dance Moves."

"No. *Giselle* is opening soon, so we'll focus on ballet poses."

A few girls squealed. Too bad Elizabeth was in a different section of the class; I needed someone to exchange eye-rolls with. Dr. Fern put a slide show of some postures on repeat, and my manikin, whose name is Herbert, reluctantly assumed an arabesque.

"Look at the figure and find a new form," Dr. Fern said in her calm, meditative way. "Find another shape to draw. Not a torso, not a leg. Something outside your symbol set." Her voice was like a yoga teacher's. Art class was one of my favorite times of day. I'm no Bronzino, but I like drawing. The times you don't have to think are when you get in your best thinking.

It had been a crazy week. As soon as I bought into Luke's idea that kTV was ruining the school, I found evidence everywhere. Like, when I eavesdropped on my classmates' conversations? They were all about *For Art's Sake.* You used to overhear people debating the merits of *Aida* versus *Rigoletto.* Or you'd walk down the hall and hear, "Dude, I *know,* Prokofiev is the *shit.*" But now? The subject of every conversation was reality TV.

Dr. Fern gave me a chuck on the back of my neck and I snapped back to attention.

"Pull his knee back," she said, fussing with Herbert. "You need to forget this is a body. Focus only on the angle between back and leg."

I started to sketch again. I was grateful to have an art teacher who actually taught, unlike, say, Ms. Gage, who wafted around the classroom with her long gray hair held up by two paintbrushes, exhorting us to *feel* the lines, to *breathe* the shading. I still wasn't good, but I'd gotten better in Dr. Fern's class.

Part of that was because I drew during every Morning Practice these days, unless I had to cram for a private trumpet lesson. Not that there'd been much Morning Practice lately. It was supposed to be inviolate, ninety minutes of artistic freedom. Yet kTV would need background footage, so they'd barge into the studio just as you had hit that fugue state of cross-hatching, and Trisha Meier would be cussing out her cameramen, never dropping the toothy grin. Or they'd need audience shots, so we'd all be herded into the theater and have to watch Miki Frigging Reagler do a soft-shoe number six times, cheering and laughing on demand.

"They're ruining the school," I murmured to Herbert.

He looked balefully back at me.

"Luke's right. Wait till I tell you about the *Selwyn Cantos*—"

Dr. Fern was walking toward me. "Ethan, I have a question. How are you going to get into a good art college if you can't focus for an hour-long class?"

Dr. Fern, I have an answer. I'm not going to get into a good art college.

"Back leg needs to come out even farther. Now, sketch *quickly*. This is an exercise, not a masterpiece."

Dr. Fern has always been kind enough to pretend I'm good at art. (Either that or she's the most sarcastic person on the face of the earth.) I think Herbert knew the truth. Every time

Dr. Fern corrected his posture, I felt more kinship with him. He was like me, the hapless clunk amidst the graced.

What I'd been about to tell Herbert was that last Friday, an issue of the *Selwyn Cantos* had come out. It had made Luke froth at the mouth. Really. He'd been reading it over lunch, and he'd just taken a big gulp of milk when he hit the unsigned review of *For Art's Sake*. He'd spurted bubbles of rage.

Once he'd controlled the milk situation, Luke read key phrases aloud. "'*For Art's Sake* is well made and gripping, with the allure of teenage stars devoted to making it in the most unmakeable professions of all.'" His face was becoming more dangerous with every sentence. "'Heartthrob Miki Reagler steals the show with his adorable tap-dance routine—'"

"Heartthrob?" I said. I was clutching my fork like a spear.

"Here's something for you, Ethan. 'Foxy ballerina Maura Heldsman grabs attention with her *pas de deux* both on and off the stage.'"

"Foxy?" I sputtered.

"'She's a talented dancer who's also talented at flashing her sass—'"

"Wait," said Elizabeth. "Her *sass,* or her—"

"Because she doesn't really have an—" added Jackson.

"Keep reading," I said quickly.

"'At her male comrades,'" said Luke, "'who are without exception drawn to her and her promise of romance.'"

Jackson took the paper from Luke, who seemed to have

lost all muscular control. "This doesn't read like a review for a school paper," he said. "I don't think a student wrote it."

"The use of the word 'foxy' eliminates that possibility," said Elizabeth.

"'But the theme of the series is the enduring notion that art is worthwhile for the sake of art.' Well, that's just wrong," said Jackson. "*FAS* is about social drama. Which means it's about the artists, not the art. It's art for the sake of life, not the converse."

We looked at Jackson with newfound respect, which happened about every two weeks.

"Also," said Jackson, "the writer of the review is obviously interested in the drama, not the art. But at the end the writer's like, Oh, yeah, this TV show has a *theme*."

Luke was taking notes on a napkin.

"He's assuaging his guilt," said Elizabeth. "This isn't crappy no-brain reality TV. This is *art*. It's practically the History Channel. It's like going to a museum. It's classy."

"We can feel good about hosting a reality TV show," said Jackson. "Because it's not *really* reality TV."

"Brilliant," said Luke. "No actors to hire. No sets to build. This schlock can be filmed with practically no expense to kTV, and then marketed as high culture. And look, everyone's going for it. Willis Wolfe. Coluber. Our parents. The millions watching it every Friday night, including every person in this cafeteria. We've all bought in."

"Coluber," said Jackson.

"He's a snake," said Luke. "Someone had to orchestrate this."

"Someone had to pull Selwyn into it."

"You guys just suspect him because he's so sleazy," I said. "It was probably Willis Wolfe. He knows LA producers from starring on that sitcom."

"Willis Wolfe is a simpleton," said Luke. "He's good at keeping his teeth white and his hair blond. He'd never come up with this."

"We've got to do something," said Jackson.

"*Thank* you, man," said Luke, clapping him on the back. "That's what I've been saying."

"You keep writing your poem," said Elizabeth. "But we have to do something real."

"Poetry is real."

"Yeah, yeah," said Elizabeth. She was wearing jumbo pink feather earrings that made it look like she'd chased down a molting flamingo. "But we need to figure out who's behind it. What they're getting out of it."

"We have to investigate," said Jackson. His eyes glazed over. He pulled out his smartphone and started tapping away.

"Ethan, I have a job for you," said Luke. "We can't take action until we know the facts."

"Whatever you say, sergeant. Command and I shall obey." I figured that "action" meant "the next stanzas."

"The people on the show might know something we don't. Your dream will be realized."

"What?"

"Go talk to Maura Heldsman."

"WHAT?"

"Say something besides what."

"What."

"You're so predictable. Go ask Maura Heldsman what it's like to be a contestant."

"I can't just start a conversation with her. She's a senior."

"And she's pretty, and she's famous, and you're in love with her. I get it. You have to override that, comrade."

"She'd talk to you a lot sooner than she'd talk to me." Luke was good-looking, well liked, and known for his writing skills. Artistic talent gives you street cred at Selwyn. (Unless you play the harp, in which case it destroys any street cred you have, which is probably none, since you play the harp.) I, on the other hand, had the figure of a Q-tip: big head, big feet, nothing in between. My drawings were not chosen for the school calendar, and I wasn't even in the second-highest band. I shouldn't have been the one to talk to Maura Heldsman.

"I think she thinks you're cute," Luke told me.

"Really?"

"Nah, just making that up."

That was not a vote of confidence, but I promised I'd go find her after school. This was Friday. I knew I was doomed to failure, not through my nerdiness or her stratospheric awesomeness but because she had *Giselle* rehearsal till 6 p.m. So I took an easy loop through the dance hallway and then headed to the Appelvan. God, it was a creepy vehicle. If somebody offered you candy to get inside, you'd run away screaming.

I informed Luke and Jackson and Elizabeth that I'd try again Monday. We hung out at the Appelden all evening.

"Weird," I said. Baconnaise was practicing his tightrope walking again. "Did you eat a pebble, Bake?"

When he'd made his glorious leap from the rope to my waiting hands, I'd felt this tiny round lump in his midsection. He looked confused, so I massaged his stomach again to find it.

"Here. Has this always been there?"

He shrugged.

"Jackson, have you ever noticed this pencil-eraser-type thing in Baconnaise's stomach?"

"A growth?" said Elizabeth.

"Gerbils eat anything, right?" I said. "He probably ate something he can't digest."

"Probably," said Jackson, unconcerned. "Either that or he's got terminal cancer."

"Not funny."

"I'm not joking."

I dropped the subject, but I didn't put him back in his cage that evening. During the new episode of *For Art's Sake,* he sat in my lap and comforted me, and I was very careful to avoid touching the lump. It was probably nothing.

CHAPTER FIVE

Selwyn? Sell-outs! That's who we are.
We're orbiting an ersatz star.
We used to spend our time creating
But now we walk the halls awaiting
The latest, greatest Nielsen rating.
                        – THE CONTRACANTOS

They called for votes via text message this time. Brandon, Maura's boyfriend or ex-boyfriend or whatever: he got kicked off. That didn't mean Maura was down to one guy. They kept zooming in on her and Josh DuBois playing footsie. It was foul. And then Kirtse Frumjigger slapped her.

"She knew Josh and I had a thing," explained Kirtse to Adelpha and Miriam.

"A thing or a *thing*-thing?" asked Adelpha.

"A *thing*-thing thing."

I couldn't even keep straight which guy Maura was supposed to be canoodling with. I did not like it. Not in a house, not with a mouse. I spent the rest of the weekend holed up with the triplets. I did not like it in a box. I did not like it with a fox.

But Luke kept texting me. *You need to talk to her.* I still wasn't sure what crucial information he thought I'd glean, but I wasn't exactly opposed to the idea. By Monday morning, I was ready. I'd lifted weights on my dad's bench in the garage on both Saturday and Sunday, and now my delts were sore in a pleasantly macho way. I'd showered that morning and even combed a little gel through my Jewfro. I was wearing my favorite *Catcher in the Rye* T-shirt.

Jackson got us to school early. I headed to the dance hallway.

Bingo. Maura Heldsman was sitting alone on the floor, her back straight as a plumb line. She had a binder open on her lap. Her hair was in its usual bun and she was wearing leggings and a hoodie. My heart throbbed, for real, and I don't know whether it was because I was nervous or because she was just so frigging pretty.

"Hey," I said.

"Hey, Ethan."

She knew my name.

"What's up?"

"Finishing English homework. Did you get number six?"

She knew I was in her English class.

"Which one was that?"

"Sit down and look."

She wanted me to sit by her.

I could not imagine this going any better.

It was a handout on rhetorical devices in Pound's *Cantos*. Number six was obvious.

> *Hast 'ou fashioned so airy a mood*
> *To draw up leaf from the root?*
> *Hast 'ou found a cloud so light*
> *As seemed neither mist nor shade?*

"It has to do with the 'hasts,'" I said.

"That one where you use old words?"

"I guess it could be archaism."

"Is there something better?" She looked right into my eyes. I forgot to respond. I thought about a chunk of the *Cantos* we'd talked about in English:

> *sky's clear*
> *night's sea*
> *green of the mountain pool*

That's what I thought when Maura Heldsman looked into my eyes.

"You don't have to tell me."

"Oh." I looked down at the paper. "Yeah. The repetition of the 'hast.'"

"Oh gosh, what's that called?"

"Anaphora."

"Thanks." She wrote it down. "Done with English. I have like no time now that *Giselle*'s heating up."

"Do you spend a lot of time filming too?" I said. Bad transition, but I had to get to *For Art's Sake* somehow.

"The weekly challenges are a bore. But other than that, it's not bad. They follow me around. It's nothing compared to college auditions and all that crap."

I couldn't believe I was having a conversation with Maura Heldsman. I kept accidentally looking into her eyes, and then I'd have to refocus on the space between them so that I could form words. Otherwise my brain was just overcome by the green green greenity. Which is how articulate I was feeling. *Sky's clear / night's sea.*

"How's that going? College and all."

I hoped she didn't think it was weird, this random guy grilling her about her life. I mean, it *was* weird. But she didn't seem to have noticed. Maybe she was just used to people wanting to talk to her. Like whenever I go to Starbucks with Luke, the female baristas remember his name from the last time. He assumes that they remember everyone's name, which is not the case. Even if you spend your entire summer there.

"College." She flopped her head onto her calves. She could fold in half like a piece of paper. "I got into Juilliard."

"Seriously? Wow." For Selwyn kids, if an arts career is the Holy Grail, Juilliard is a seat at the Round Table.

"And Boston Conservatory and CalArts, but I want to go to Juilliard. Who wouldn't?"

"Are you going?"

"TBD. My parents hate the idea of a dance career. Mostly because they've seen what it's done to my feet. I have the ugliest feet in the world. Bunions, hammertoes, corns, bone spurs, fungal toenails. Sorry, is this grossing you out?"

Maura, you could pick your nose with those fungal toes, and I'd think it was cute. "I'm okay."

"And just in, breaking news, heel bursitis. Feels like being stabbed with a hot poker." She blinked rapidly three or four times. "My parents think I won't be able to walk by the time I'm forty, and not gonna lie, they're probably right. But I don't care if it means I can dance until then."

"So go to Juilliard."

She sat up and rubbed her thumbs against her fingers. "Money money money. They'd let me go if it was cheaper. They'd grumble, but they'd let me. But it's like fifty thousand a year. Not to mention the pointe shoes, another three hundred a month. And I can go to the U for free almost. Where I could minor in dance and have a, I quote, sensible major like communications."

"That's terrible."

"Basically, I have to win."

"Win?"

She looked at me in surprise, as if she'd just remembered she was talking to someone outside her world. "Win *FAS*. Win *For Art's Sake*. If I win that scholarship, I can go."

I felt like an idiot. I'd forgotten my mission.

"I've been freaked out all season they'll cancel the show. That'd be the worst."

"That would suck."

"No kidding."

"Um." I didn't know how to broach the topic, but I didn't want to face Luke if I hadn't tried. "Aren't you kind of mad at them?"

She laughed. "You mean how I'm resident slut?" She was wiggling her feet, pointing and flexing, pointing and flexing.

I wasn't going to be that blunt. I didn't know what to say. "I wasn't going to be that blunt."

"Whatever." She bent in half and then straightened. "I don't have time for that shit."

"For worrying about the show?"

"For guys."

"Oh."

"Everybody who knows me knows that. All I do is dance. And occasionally do homework so I don't fail out. And occasionally poach homework answers off cute juniors."

I could not say a word.

"So I don't really care. All I want is to win this thing. Yes, my life goal is winning a reality TV show. Sad but true. And if they want to make me look like a slut, they can make me look like a slut."

"I can't believe you don't care."

"Ethan Andrezejczak."

She knew my last name. She could *say* my last name. Almost.

"In your universe, people care about stuff like reputations. They care about whether the world is just. I don't. I just don't." She made a gesture that took in her whole body—her bun, her sinewy legs, her big fluffy socks. That gesture said everything.

It meant more than my best drawing could ever mean, more than the most lyrical passage I'd ever played. "I want to be a dancer. A real dancer. I want to go to Juilliard and I want to dance with New York City Ballet. Peter Martins. Lincoln Center. That is all. Period. I don't want anything else."

"Oh."

"So yeah, they're making me look like a slut and I'm not. I don't even *know* those guys. Biblically or otherwise. They edit it in. It's called frankenbiting. I read about it the last time I was on the Internet, which was two weeks ago. Because this. Is all. I do."

"Oh."

She smiled at me. "You're sweet."

"Thanks?"

"The bell's about to ring."

"Don't you have class too?" I looked around. I hadn't even noticed that during our conversation, the dance hallway had begun to fill with other kids.

"I'll be late. It's discrete math." She laughed. "Didn't you listen? I don't care."

"Right."

"You have a great day, Ethan Andrezejczak." I was dismissed. I picked up my backpack, gave her a wave, and walked down the hall.

Herbert's arabesque still wasn't the kind that would get him into Juilliard, but I tried to focus on the light and the lines. My thoughts were swirling, turbid and muddy like a shaken beaker. But about half an hour into class they settled into sediment:

1. Maura's ambition was admirable. I couldn't imagine wanting anything that badly. Even her.
2. Maura's situation, on the other hand, was messed up. She thought she had to let them do whatever *they* wanted so that she could get what *she* wanted. And what was even more messed up? She was right. All that drama was driving up the ratings, increasing the revenues, making the show more likely to keep running, making her more likely to win.
3. We had to do something. But it was complicated. I think Luke had the idea that we'd expose the unethical horrors of *For Art's Sake* to the parents and alumni, and they'd rise up in outrage and force them to cancel the show. But now I knew that Maura's whole life depended on this show. If we got it off the air, she'd go to the University of Minnesota. We'd crush her dreams. She'd never have anything to do with me again.

I put Herbert back on the shelf where he lived. I gave him a nod of farewell and hoped that I hadn't caused him too much embarrassment among his ilk. Dr. Fern patted me on my back. "Nice job concentrating on your drawing, Ethan."

Now it was time for English. That meant I'd see her for the

first time since this morning. Would it be weird? Would she say hi? Should I say hi? I hated major life decisions.

I walked in. From across the room, Elizabeth yelled hello. I gave her a distracted wave and sat down by Luke.

"Well?" he said.

"Done."

"And?"

"Later."

Only after I sat down did I allow myself to find Maura. She was sitting at her desk, straight-backed as usual. I got out my English notebook. I looked at her again. And this was when things were just a little different from usual, just different enough. She gave me a smile. Not a big smile. She didn't even open her lips. Really, it was less a smile and more a brief tension in her cheeks. But it was for me, and nobody else, and it let me know that our conversation had happened, that things had changed. Just when I thought I couldn't fall any further for her, I found a new level. It was like an amusement-park ride, when there's been a bunch of drops that you were expecting and then there's suddenly another one, unanticipated and fresh and sweet. You feel your insides questioning you: what are you doing, and why have you left us behind? That was how fast I fell. That was how deep this went.

"A long poem," said BradLee, "is so long, so all-encompassing and comprehensive, that it can embrace an entire culture's values, history, traditions. It can hold multitudes. And the poet must view himself—or herself, of course—as the one who leads the way through this cultural labyrinth. He can see the things nobody else can see. He can change things, and he can change."

CHAPTER SIX

And whose reptilian plots and schemes
Have slithered round to crush our dreams?
His scales are coins, his tongue a dart.
The Vice's jawbone gapes apart,
Devours whole the Rat of Art.
                    – THE CONTRACANTOS

While we suffer through a week of school, you get to hear about the Selwyn property.

Fifty years ago, the *Minneapolis Sun-Gazette* folded, leaving behind a building that had housed the entire process of creating the paper. Selwyn's founders got it dirt-cheap and did their best to transform it into a school. Despite renovation, some quirks remain. For example, the math hallway, where the papers got folded and packed up, still looks industrial. The metal ceilings are thirty feet high, and there's a lot of exposed pipe.

Also, the printing presses remain in the basement. Why waste good machinery? They use them to print the *Selwyn*

Cantos and the lit mag. They're antiquated by now, but they work.

The following Monday, a bunch of us were hanging out in BradLee's classroom before school, since lately the hallways had been staked out by some territorial janitors. I was on the floor, playing Spit with Luke, Jackson, and Elizabeth. People were stepping over us, some groggily, some making a game out of it, doing jetés or whatever. BradLee was rushing in and out, making last-minute copies and looking flurried. Valerie Menchen had her violin out and was playing klezmer music, and because it's Selwyn there were some improvised dances going on. It was seven-fifteen on a Monday morning but it felt like a party.

Does that make me sound lame?

It was the best I'd felt since Friday night, for sure. The episode had been more of the same. Now that Brandon was out of the picture, Josh Slimeball DuBois and Miki Frigging Reagler had intensified their pursuit of Maura. She'd told me it wasn't real. I trusted her, I swear. And I could see how the frankenbiting worked, how they took different scenes and cut them into a collage of flirtation and intrigue and drama. But the thing was, while I was watching it, I believed it. It was that good. It sucked you in.

When we were chilling in the Appelden before the episode, I'd taught Baconnaise his colors. Or at least, with the help of some treats, I trained him to always go for the green yarn. He was so smart. I didn't even think nocturnal animals could see colors. (Maybe most of them couldn't. I'd always suspected that Baconnaise was a highly evolved genius mutant gerbil.)

Once I'd firmly established the link between "green" and "raisin," I called over my friends.

"Watch," I told them. I lined up the three colors of yarn. "Baconnaise, you ready?" I released him. "Choose green, Baconnaise, you stud!" I snapped my fingers. "Green!"

He ran to the green and looked back at me expectantly. I gave him the raisin.

"Let me try," said Luke. "Choose red, Baconnaise!"

"He only responds to my voice," I said. "We have a special connection."

"Is the snap important?" He snapped. "Red, Baconnaise!"

"I told you," I said grouchily. "My voice and mine alone."

"How's the lump?" Elizabeth asked.

I had done my best to forget it. And I had done my best not to touch Baconnaise anywhere near his midsection. But you could see it now, a gentle swelling on the pale fur of his underbelly.

Elizabeth picked him up. He liked her, which always made me jealous. "It's *huge!*"

"That's what she said. And you're exaggerating."

"Last time Ethan said it was little," said Luke to Elizabeth. "Also what she said. Is it growing?"

She handed me Baconnaise. Reluctantly, I massaged his belly until I found it. "It's about the same size," I said. It was tiny, but he was a tiny guy. "Maybe a little bigger."

"I'll tell my mom," said Jackson.

"Take him to the vet," I said. Jackson nodded. My excitement about his new trick had evaporated. "Choose green,

Baconnaise," I whispered. He paused, uncertain. I snapped. He ran right to the green yarn.

"Benign little lumps happen all the time," said Elizabeth.

During that FAS episode, Jackson deigned to stop playing *Sun Tzu* so that he could WiTSOOTT frankenbiting. He read us information during the commercial breaks, at least until Elizabeth told him to shut up because she wanted to pay attention. The ads were from bigger brands every week, she said. Which meant kTV was making more money. Which meant *For Art's Sake* would stay on the air. Thank you, Maura Heldsman's reputation.

Would you like to know more about this frankenbiting thing?

1. They can run pieces of audio unedited, but out of context. Like, I suspected, when Maura said, "Oh, Miki," over two shadowy figures making out backstage.
2. They can stick together pieces of unrelated sentences. Like, I suspected, this time when Maura told Josh, "Miki is freaking obnoxious. And a terrible kisser."
3. They can edit together whole scenes. Maura and Kirtse are having lunch, and Kirtse says, "Do you even *care* about our friendship?" Then they cut to Maura looking totally unresponsive. "Not

really," she drawls. Here's a Jacksonian theory:
what if that was Maura's response to *another*
question?

The weekend continued to suck. There was a terrible convergence: I had a shit-ton of bio homework, and the triplets got a new Raffi CD. Would *you* like to label cell diagrams while living in a continuous loop of liking to eat, eat, eat, eeples and baneenees?

Plus, I was depressed about the whole Maura Heldsman situation. And I felt silly for getting so worked up about *For Art's Sake*. We were all angry, but we weren't doing anything. Luke was scribbling away at his long poem, but what was the point of that?

BradLee leaned over our Spit game in a break between rounds. We were all breathing heavily from laughter and exertion (look, we go to an arts academy). "You want to stop in and see me after school?" he said, looking at Luke.

Luke froze. "About what we discussed?"

"Ooh, are you going to tell us the interrobang story?" I asked.

Luke shot me an annoyed look. I'd thought that was sort of funny. "Definitely, Mr. Lee," he said. "I'll be there."

Elizabeth was watching them sharply. Jackson was shuffling the cards, but I could tell by the set of his neck that he was listening too.

"All of us, right?" added Luke.

BradLee hesitated.

"We're all involved. We're all having similar thoughts. And we've discussed it at *length*."

I mentally congratulated Luke: what a nice tricolon! Brad-Lee clearly didn't want to deal with the rest of us. Maybe he would have been okay with me, since I was ubiquitously known as the hench to Luke's man. But Luke refused to compromise. Luke wouldn't exclude us.

"Fine," said BradLee.

And another school day passed, another day of long classes that seemed short in retrospect because I couldn't remember what happened in them.

At last the final bell rang and we met in BradLee's room.

"I didn't mean to convene a summit," said BradLee. "I've just been thinking."

"We've been thinking a lot too," said Luke earnestly. "The show just keeps getting worse."

"It does."

I liked how BradLee didn't pretend not to watch it, like some of the other teachers.

"And I read your poem, Luke."

"Oh?" He was pretending nonchalance, but I could hear the tension in that "Oh?"

"It's a call to arms, isn't it? A call to raise consciousness about what's going on here?"

"That's the idea, yeah."

"We don't want the show to be canceled," I stuck in. The

other three had agreed. It'd be too mean. All those kids had given up a lot of normal existence for a shot at that prize. Or at least that's what Elizabeth said. Personally, I couldn't care less about anyone but Maura.

"No," said BradLee. "But it's disturbing, what the show's turning into."

"Exactly," said Luke. "It's not what it purports to be. And it's doing long-term damage to reputations. To the reputations of students too young to control their images, or even to know that those images need to be controlled."

"I am certainly not giving you any ideas," said BradLee. He glanced at the door, which he'd closed when we came in. "But this poem needs to be distributed."

"But it's not finished," said Luke.

"And they won't publish it in the *Selwyn Cantos*," said Elizabeth. "And the lit mag doesn't come out till May."

"And it's not finished," repeated Luke.

"Installments," said BradLee. Again with the look to the door. "Think Scheherazade. Think Dickens."

"But *where?*" said Elizabeth impatiently. "Everything is censored."

"Think alternative publication," said BradLee.

"Like a vanity press?" said Luke, looking disappointed.

"They print the *Selwyn Cantos* right in the basement," said Jackson casually.

"Duh, of course," said Luke, brushing him off. "It saves Selwyn a crapload of money. They'd never let us publish every two weeks if we couldn't print in-house."

"So you know how the presses work?" said Jackson.

"Naturally." Then the light dawned. I think Elizabeth, Luke, and I got it all at once.

"I'm not hearing any of this," said BradLee.

"But——" I said. I had to voice my doubts. "Is a poem really going to change anything?"

Luke and BradLee looked at me. Two true believers. They were glowing. "Art matters, Ethan," said BradLee. "This is art."

BradLee shooed us out. He said he didn't want to know the technicalities. He said that it had already put him in a weird position.

"Problem," said Jackson in the hallway. "Luke, you're the only person in the school who doesn't start groaning at the words 'long poem.' Even the creative writing majors don't read poetry. They just write it."

"Which is why their poems suck," I inserted.

"This is different," said Luke. "This pertains to them."

"It's still a long poem. Nobody's going to see a long poem and go, Oh, hey, it's a tale of my tribe! Look at those carefully selected luminous details! Luke is the bearer of the light!"

"You were paying attention in English?"

"I always pay attention in English."

I broke into a coughing fit and Jackson swiped his leg backward to trip me. I leapt aside just in time.

"We need to present it differently," said Elizabeth. She was so reasonable. We'd never have gotten anything done without her. "We can't just type it and print it and scatter it around school."

"You have another suggestion?" Based on Luke's tone, type-print-scatter was exactly his plan.

"Three things," she said. I looked at her sharply. She had her dreadlocks pulled into a high, massive blob, which was sort of cute even if it did make her look like she had two heads. "Art, layout, branding. Ethan will add illustrations, and I'll do the layout. I want to handwrite the thing. We need to make it seem underground and subversive."

"It *is* underground and subversive," pointed out Jackson. "You call Coluber the Serpent Vice. That would never make it into that crap school newspaper."

Luke didn't even take offense. He was looking agape.

"We could even call it the *Anticantos,*" she said.

"The *Contracantos,*" said Jackson.

"Perfect," said Elizabeth. "Luke, that okay with you?"

"That's okay," said Luke, still surprised. "I mean, yeah. That's perfect."

Elizabeth bared her teeth. I wasn't sure whether she was smiling or getting ready for battle. Maybe both. We were walking quickly now. We had shit to *do.*

CHAPTER SEVEN

The Serpent Vice delights at this,
But Selwynites, let's shout, "Cat-piss!"
Shall we permit this tawdry show
To storm the Muses' high chateau?
Is this okay? It's not! Hello!
                                    – THE CONTRACANTOS

We went to the Appelden, of course. It was our lair, our production center, although Elizabeth made me promise first that I wouldn't get too distracted by Baconnaise. Distraction, Baconnaise? Baconnaise was a muse.

It was a great afternoon, then a great evening, then a great night. We felt like we were the saviors of the school. We were doing something, finally, after weeks of sitting around and moaning and thinking we should do something.

It really was a great time.

Here's what everyone was doing:

I was hunched over the tiny rolltop desk in the den, sketching cartoons to illustrate lines from the *Contracantos*.

Baconnaise was peering at the drawings. Sometimes he'd get bored and climb around on his personal jungle gym, a.k.a. me. The vet had flat-out refused to operate on someone who only weighed 2.6 ounces—in fact, he wouldn't even take a biopsy—but the lump wasn't bringing Baconnaise down. He was his usual sprightly self.

Luke was on the couch, furiously writing.

Elizabeth had commandeered the dining-room table, where she'd laid out four huge sheets of thin vellum paper. She kept making happy comments about how retro this was, how fun it was to do graphic design while not squinting at a computer. She was carefully copying Luke's poem, incorporating my drawings, and every time I walked over there I'd marvel at her talent. She could make stuff, real stuff that people would want. So many kids at school painted scary stuff with scary messages: bloody wombs with their parents and bin Laden inside, or babies suckling at the teats of machine guns. But Elizabeth created elegant, beautiful things, and the *Contra-cantos* was going to be elegant and beautiful.

Then we had our jack(son) of all trades. He helped anyone who needed help. He posed for me when I couldn't figure out how an arm would connect to a shoulder. He composted Baconnaise's poop pellets. He kept a tab open on a rhyming dictionary and he'd give Luke rhymes when he got stuck. He rolled tape into curlicues and spell-checked the poem before Elizabeth copied it onto the vellum.

We were blasting the Beatles on vinyl, since they comprised the intersection in the Venn diagram of the set of acceptable music versus the set of music owned by the Appelmen. Jackson spun their albums chronologically. By the time we finished, in a blaze of glory, you could tell that LSD had become a major part of their artistic process. I didn't dare look at the clock. We collapsed onto the couches and slept like the dead.

The next day, the logistical challenges hit us.

Jackson was the only one who didn't briefly lose faith. Instead, he opened a document. "I need a name for this file," he told us. "What's the name of our plan?"

"What's a plan without a name?" murmured Luke.

"No philosophizing. Hurry up."

"Imagism," Luke said. "That was Ezra Pound's first plan."

"Okay," said Jackson. "But all caps. And I don't like the 'ism.' Too establishment. IMAGE."

"Stop shouting," said Elizabeth.

I interrupted the planning to say, "Why can't we just post it online?"

"That would be far too easy," said Jackson scathingly.

"Plus," said Elizabeth, "I think it's important that we really stick it to the man. As in, the administration."

"The ad-man-istration," I said.

"Ha. Ha. Shut up. We want this in their faces. Under their noses."

Luke was nodding along. "Only cowards post anonymously to the Internet. And then nobody would talk about it at school. We'd never hear reactions."

"And we want equal, universal access," said Elizabeth.

"True," I said. "Maura Heldsman never even gets online."

Elizabeth snorted. "Glad we're on the same page."

"This is what Ezra Pound would have done," said Luke.

But a little while later, I whispered to Jackson, "We could just take it to a copy shop."

"Three hundred copies. Four black-and-white pages. Ten cents a page. That's a hundred and twenty bucks. And that's just for the first issue."

Maybe he thought he could hide it with math, but I could see the fervor on his face. He wanted to sneak down to the presses as much as they did.

So this is what we did. Here's what IMAGE needed, and here's what IMAGE got.

1. Access to Presses.

Jackson wasn't *Sun-Tzu*-ing in between calls for help. He was getting into the Selwyn administration network. He hacked them right from the Appelden. Don't ask me how.

I do know he'd only reached the lowest tier of the network. It gave him access to shared documents, so nothing private or password-protected. But he found one ultra-important file: the master schedule. There must have been a kTV intern whose entire job was to maintain this thing, because it was epic. You could tell where every single administrator, security guard, and kTV employee was supposed to be at any moment.

This was essential information.

Jackson thus knew that on Thursday afternoon, they'd be

filming the next *For Art's Sake* challenge at the Minnesota
Landscape Arboretum. They'd rented the place from noon to
midnight, and all the kTV guys plus all the Selwyn administrators would be there to help manage the filming. Which would
leave the school basically empty.

We had our opportunity.

From there, we—and by "we" I obviously mean "Jackson,
Son of Jack"—just had to figure out how to get down to the
printing presses, which were kept locked. They were dangerous, after all, with lots of machinery and gears and metal crap.
(Or so I discovered. At first, I was imagining really big laser
printers.)

Jackson stole the keys.

He did it during tech theater class. He created a diversion by jamming a color gel into the wrong slot of a seven-
thousand-dollar spotlight, and then he snuck back to the key
closet and snatched—ack, I'm getting all fluttery and adre
nalized just thinking about it. Let's move on.

2. Know-How and Materials.

We descended Thursday afternoon. The school was deserted. We had to go behind the stage, under the stage, across
a furniture-filled pit, down a long hallway, down a staircase,
down another. At every locked door, we'd stand as lookouts
as Jackson tried one key after another. There were six on the
bunch labeled *Presses,* and we ended up needing them all.

Luke had been there many times, of course, and Elizabeth

once for a design project. But we were all creeped out. There were no teachers, no classmates, no gossip or reprimands or dumb jokes to normalize the situation. I was unnerved by the sense that I didn't know my school at all. I'd spent a lot of time there, and I liked the place, and I'd thought I'd understood it. But I hadn't. There were these hidden depths, levels and levels of basements and subbasements, staircases I'd never seen, doors I'd never opened. I almost felt betrayed.

Elizabeth took off her backpack and jacket. "It's warm," she said.

"That's because we're closer to the core of the earth," I said.

"That's because we're closer to the furnace," said Jackson, rolling his eyes.

The room was maybe the size of an elementary school basketball court. A raised sidewalk hugged the walls, and in the middle loomed the machinery, ominously metallic and complicated, taller than any of us. I quickly discovered that if you touched it, it creaked to life. This freaked the hell out of me.

It was Luke's third year on the *Selwyn Cantos* staff, and he knew where their green-tinged newsprint was stashed, how to load the ink, what levers to pull, when to pull them. Jackson felt kinship with anything mechanical, so he was paying close attention, and Elizabeth insisted on being the one to lay out the originals on the laminates. All I did was follow instructions. I loaded up newsprint. I cranked some handle. I got out of the way. We were there a few hours. Then, sweaty and greasy, we filled our backpacks with gorgeous *Contracantos*, flipped off the lights, and traveled upward.

Jackson quoted Vergil. *"The descent to hell is easy. Getting out—that's the work, that's the task."* I was against Latin as a matter of principle, but I had to smile. We'd done it. We'd made it out.

3. Distribution.

Because of the arts academy reputation and all, the *Selwyn Cantos* was a big deal. All over the school were those newspaper distribution baskets, like the ones in coffee shops for free local papers. They wanted the paper's circulation to be the entire student body, or at least whatever percentage of the student body was literate. I had my doubts about some of those dancers.

Jackson got us to school at the putrid hour of six-thirty-one, which was when they unlocked the doors. He'd divided the building into four sectors—there was a color-coded map involved—and we ran around with our stuffed back-packs, dumping *Contracantos* into the *Selwyn Cantos* bins. Then Elizabeth went down to the band hallway to visit her normal friends. Luke and I were feeling the lack of sleep, so we slumped on the floor by our lockers and watched Jackson do some insane math problem that involved forcing two vast matrices to merge. It was very soothing.

First-bell calculus jarred us awake. (That's a sentence I never thought I'd write.) I had my head propped in both hands with my pinkies holding my eyelids up, and I was trying to comprehend what Mrs. Garlop was doing on the whiteboard when Luke poked me.

"Shut up," I said.

"I'm not talking."

"Now you are. Shut up."

"Look around."

Hoping that Mrs. Garlop wouldn't notice my alertness, which surely would have tipped her off that I wasn't thinking about math, I lifted my head. What to my wondering eyes did appear but greenish newspapers. The more diligent students had them underneath their calculus stuff, and they'd glance at them between problems. The ones who couldn't give a shit about conic sections were holding up their textbooks with *Contracantos* stuck inside. Everyone had them, and everyone was reading them.

It was a crazy high. My drawings, everywhere. Elizabeth's cool graphic-designer handwriting. Luke's words. The payoff for the hours of work and the scary trip to the presses, for getting to school before dawn, for breaking the rules. Our plan was going to work. We'd reclaim our culture. Our voice had been denied but now we were bellowing to the high heavens who we were and what we wanted. The mytho-whatever was revised. We'd taken control.

It was one of the best calculus classes of my life.

Okay, that's not saying much.

It was one of the best *days* of my life. There we go.

It was at lunch when the PA system clicked on. I was with Luke and Jackson. We figured it'd be a dead giveaway if we were the only kids who didn't have *Contracantos,* so we were perusing it, chuckling despite ourselves, admiring it while pretending we weren't.

"Mr. Coluber would like to quickly give an announcement," said his smug secretary.

The cafeteria fell silent.

Coluber's voice, sounding testy, crackled out over the intercom.

"It has come to our attention that an unapproved publication has been distributed. According to the Handbook, Section F Point 2, no school-wide publications may be issued without administrator initials. This particular publication is both profane and unauthorized, and is hereby banned. Possession and/or distribution will incur consequences. Destroy your copies immediately. Thank you." He clicked off.

There was a moment of silence before everyone began to talk. Everyone but us. Finally, moving as if he'd just woken up, Luke pushed our *Contracantos* deep into his backpack.

"Profane?" he said.

"Cat-piss," said Jackson.

"Ooh," I said. "I forgot about that part."

"It's not the profanity that's the problem," said Luke. "Nor the lack of authorization. It's that we lambasted him. Coluber's portrayed as a snake."

"Cat-piss and porcupines," I said.

"This is just great," said Jackson. I thought for a moment he was being sarcastic, but here's a fact: Jackson Appelman is never sarcastic. His brain does not traffic in irony.

"Huh?" I said because Luke didn't.

"There was only one thing Coluber could have done to make it *more* popular."

"Ban it," said Luke, following along. His eyes were sparkling again. "Boom."

I got it. Before the announcement, maybe half the lunch tables were browsing the *Contracantos*. Now it was the topic of every conversation. It was illegal and it was alluring.

I thought of Coluber fuming in his office, the *Contracantos* on his desk. He was an idiot, I thought. What ignorance of human nature, to think that a ban would make something less popular. We were contrarians. Now everyone would read the *Contracantos*.

An idiot indeed.

We had English last and BradLee looked at us in a funny way, his mouth tight as if repressing a smile. He was wearing jeans, since it was Friday, and a yellow polo.

"Get out your copies of the *Cantos*," he told the class.

"*Cantos* or *Contracantos*?" said Paul Jones, a funny guy, one of the school's best-slash-only athletes. Some people laughed, but everyone was watching to see BradLee's response.

"Mr. Jones," he said, his mouth noticeably twitching, "I have no idea what you're talking about. And I'd recommend that you allow me to remain in blissful ignorance."

Now everyone was laughing, even Maura Heldsman.

There was a knock. BradLee opened the door to a security guard, the mean one with the Viking beard. His eyes swept our desks.

"Sir?" said BradLee.

"Looking for illicit materials," said the guard. "Mr. C's orders." He walked the rim of our seminar circle, peering into open backpacks with his hands clasped behind his back.

I held perfectly still.

"You let me know if you need a removal."

"Thanks, sir. Will do." BradLee held the door. He's tall, at least six feet, but next to the guard he looked tiny and young. When the door shut, there was silence, a different sort of silence from the one that had hummed in the cafeteria. Still disbelief, but not as much glee.

"*Cantos,* class," BradLee told us again. "Number eighty-one."

We got out our *Cantos* and started to analyze.

> *But to have done instead of not doing*
> *this is not vanity [. . .]*
> *Here error is all in the not done,*
> *all in the diffidence that faltered. . . .*

He was talking to us. I knew it.

I had to catch the bus alone that day: Jackson had *Giselle* tech rehearsal, Elizabeth had a portfolio review with her graphic-design teacher, and Luke had an editorial meeting for the *Selwyn Cantos.* I was by myself when I left, my thoughts spinning after that English class. And I saw the weirdest thing I'd seen all day.

There's a spot up the hill from the buses where the kTV

guys gather on breaks to smoke, hang out, and escape the tanned demon that is Trisha Meier. One cameraman was sort of my pal. This fall it had seemed that I was always running into him, so we'd started to exchange casual hellos, just nodding, maybe smiling on Fridays. Then one day when I was waiting for my mom, he was the only guy out there. We talked. His name was Thomas. He didn't much like reality TV—he wanted to work in movies—but he figured he had to work his way up. He was from Omaha and he liked Minneapolis better than LA. He didn't mind the cold. He did mind Trisha Meier. (I asked.)

As always, I looked for him in the group of smoking kTV guys. There he was. He didn't see me. He was very absorbed in something. Something green. Some green-tinged newspaper.

Now that I knew to look, I saw that all the other cameramen were holding them too.

Call me clueless, but I had no idea what that meant. I felt triumphant for infiltrating kTV. I wondered what Coluber would think if he saw them reading it. Then I started thinking about whether the triplets had found my Cheez-It cache, how much homework I'd have to do that weekend, how much homework I could postpone till Monday morning before school.

I didn't remember to tell anyone that the *Contracantos* had infiltrated the coterie of cameramen. I didn't call Jackson, or Elizabeth, or Luke.

Instead, I played Candy Land with my sisters on the kitchen floor. My mom was cooking dinner. We were driving her crazy. She hates Candy Land with the fire of a thousand suns, so we play in her vicinity whenever possible.

"I am Queen Frostine," said Lila, holding the card to her forehead.

"Just because you get it doesn't mean you are it," chanted Tabitha.

"Yeah," said Olivia. She snatched the card. "Now *I'm* Queen Frostine." Lila snatched it back. That card looked like it'd been chewed by Baconnaise.

"Guys," I said. "I mean, girls. How about you all are Queen Frostine?"

They looked at me with the pity one generally reserves for lobotomy victims. "No," said Tabitha. "There's only one Queen Frostine."

"Duh," said Lila.

"Duh," said Olivia.

"Fine. But what about me? Maybe I should get to be Queen Frostine."

"You're too ugly."

"Plus, you're a boy."

"You can be Plumpy."

"I am not Plumpy!"

"Actually," said Olivia, "Ethan looks like Gramma Nutt." Lila and Tabitha cackled.

"Mom!" I said. "They're calling me Gramma Nutt!"

They found this hilarious.

I sprawled onto my stomach and began to flail. "Don't wanna be Gramma Nutt!"

My mom stepped over me as she carried a pot of noodles

from the range to the sink. "Ethan, if I spill boiling water on you, it's your own fault."

"Cooked Gramma Nutt," said Lila. More hilarity. Sometimes I envy those girls. It must be fun to be part of a living, breathing tricolon.

CHAPTER EIGHT

O Serpent Vice, what hast thou done?
Thou's gone and ruined all our fun!
What fault inspired such a deed?
Stupidity, or too much weed?
No: serpents have one vice. It's greed.
                    — THE CONTRACANTOS

I'd barely noticed that Josh DuBois, Maura's new love interest
on *For Art's Sake,* was in our Latin class. Not until the Monday
after the next episode.

"Children," said Ms. Pederson, "please give me an example
of the dative of possession."

I could give her an example of possession. Because I was
possessed, obsessed, by the sprawled figure of Josh DuBois. He
was tall, but not so tall that it was necessary for him to spread
his legs wide and stretch them into the aisle. That was totally
a pose. It was the pose—pardon me; it must be said—it was
the pose of someone who thought he was so well hung he
couldn't make his thighs touch.

"Ethan," whispered Jackson, "you're acting creepy. Stop glancing back."

"He's the creepy one! Did you *see*—"

"We all saw," said Jackson wearily.

Ms. Pederson fixed us with her strict Swedish gaze and we shut up, fast, before she asked us to translate.

Friday's episode had been at the Landscape Arboretum, and everyone had gradually developed a faint blue tinge from the cold. When Trisha wasn't reminding everyone that it had been Damien's idea to film outside in February, she kept flogging the upcoming live finale. It'd been so boring that I'd paid way more attention to Baconnaise, who was now a boss funambulist, than I'd paid to the show.

Until Elizabeth said, "Yuck."

All I could see on-screen was a large shrub. But you could hear Miki F.R.'s voice, and it was going, "Mmm."

The bush shook. I squeezed Baconnaise. "Who's back there with him?" I demanded.

"Um," said Jackson delicately, "it may be Maura."

"Frankenbiting!" said Elizabeth. "Remember frankenbiting!" That was probably to keep me from squeezing poor Baconnaise to death. I was a little tense.

"That had to be frankenbited. Frankenbit? Frankenbought?" she said during the next commercials.

"Yeah, that wasn't even a good one," said Luke lazily.

But the next scene opened on Maura, rehearsing a dance in yoga pants, tennis shoes, and a puffy coat. (Not a good look for most people. A good look for Maura.)

"Hey, girl," said Josh. "Let's get outta here."

"To where?" said Maura.

"Isn't there somewhere we can—be alone?" He performed a suggestive eyebrow-raise. I didn't even know the suggestive eyebrow-raise existed in the wild.

"Let's see," Maura said. "Maybe behind a bush?"

"WHY CAN'T THEY FILM BEHIND THE BUSH?" I'd shouted in the Appelden.

"Well, according to FCC regulations—" began Jackson, but Elizabeth cut him off.

"Use your imagination, Ethan."

Now, in Latin, I shot another furtive look back at Josh. His pants were way too tight to sit with his legs so far apart. I hope the seams split, I thought bitterly. That bulge. That bulge was like roadkill. I couldn't look away. Frankenbiting. It was all frankenbiting, right? I had to believe that. I was pretty sure I *did* believe that. But I still wouldn't mind taking my newly sharpened pencil and aiming it over my shoulder and with the precision and force of a professional backward dart-thrower hurling it right toward that bulge, which would emit a sad little *pop!* and then deflate, the air whistling out

"Ethan, please translate line forty-nine," said Ms. Pederson.

"Like a punctured tire," I said dreamily.

"Excuse me?"

Jackson's pointy elbow found the gap between my ribs.

"Ouch! Um, sorry. I, uh, misheard. Line forty-nine? *If you complain about the timber of a long love*"—

Timber of love? What? The stuff that comes out of my mouth in Latin class makes it sound as if I've just woken up from a coma.

Which, come to think of it, is not completely erroneous.

"Your vocabulary is abysmal," said Ms. Pederson. "Will someone help Ethan, please?"

"Please," I echoed.

At least the universe wasn't so ironic that she called on Josh. Jackson ended up jumping in. Our Latin suckage is at about the same level. He can't do literary analysis for shit, but his vocabulary is immense. He also wrote an app for his phone that can parse any verb. I'll spend forever staring at a god-awful form like *proficisceremini* that may bear all responsibility for the fall of the Roman Empire, and his phone will be like, duh, it's second-person plural imperfect subjunctive.

Josh probably couldn't have provided much help anyway. The one consolation of Friday's episode had been how dumb his performance was. The challenge had been to integrate art and nature. They'd even brought in two locals from the North Star Sierra Club to help judge. Josh had run out of time to prep a monologue—no comment on why—and he did an improv scene about spring, in which he impersonated a flower, the sun, and a bear cub coming out of hibernation. It was dreadful.

But he hadn't even been kicked off. Kirtse was so mad about him and Maura that she'd outright refused to perform.

"The show must go on!" Trisha screamed.

"Not here, not now," said Kirtse. It was the first time I'd ever felt any respect for her. Then she ruined it by breaking into "Do You Hear the People Sing?" from *Les Mis* as she marched offstage. Quitting a reality TV show, leading a revolt in Paris: am I the only one who sees a difference?

*   *   *

Over the weekend, Jackson had spent some quality time with
the Selwyn shared drive. He told us that the next opportunity
to hit the printing presses would be the following Thursday,
when they'd be filming a challenge downtown. We spent that
whole week putting together another issue, and I thought
about little else. It was still big news. I'd overheard four or five
groups a day wondering who'd had the balls to publish it.

On Thursday, English was the penultimate class of the day.
I had something important to tell Luke and Jackson. But Luke
was too interested in BradLee, and Jackson was totally absorbed
with his take-notes-in-binary-code thing. Effing Thursdays.

"How were the *Cantos* received?" said BradLee. "Here's one
example."

Luke was rapt, and I was annoyed. I'd spent bio preparing
a summary of the incident. It would have taken him thirty
seconds to read it.

BradLee switched on the projector. "This is a poem by Basil
Bunting." Note to self: do not name children after alliterative
herbs. "It's entitled 'On the Fly-Leaf of Pound's *Cantos.*'" I was
annoyed at BradLee too, for hogging all of Luke's attention,
but I read the poem anyway.

> *There are the Alps [. . .]*
> *There they are, you will have to go a long way round*
> *if you want to avoid them.*
> *It takes some getting used to. There are the Alps,*
> *fools! Sit down and wait for them to crumble!*

"Interpretation?" said BradLee.

Luke raised his hand and BradLee, unsurprised, nodded at him. "He's saying the *Cantos* are immovable," said Luke. "They're eternal, at least as far as humans are concerned. They're not going anywhere, so we'd better deal with them, rearrange our worldviews to admit them."

No wonder teachers liked Luke.

I liked his explanation myself, because understanding this poem made me like the *Cantos* more. The lines I've taken out of context may have deluded you into thinking that this is a normal poem. False. It's impenetrable. Here, I'll turn to a random page—okay, on *one page* of my 824-page edition, the proper names include Manes, la Clara, Dioce, Kiang, Han, Herakles, Lucifer, North Carolina, Odysseus, Sigismundo, Duccio, Zuan Bellin, and La Sposa. And—on *one page*—the languages include English, Italian, transliterated Greek, actual Greek, and Chinese. Totally impenetrable.

Much like the Alps.

Hmm.

I raised my hand and said so.

For the first time all class, I had Luke's attention. But I couldn't hold it. He snapped back to BradLee and my summary remained unread on my desk. But allow me to tell *you,* dear Reader, of the latest conversation I'd had with Maura Heldsman.

I'd walked right up to her. Where did I get the gumption? From the *Contracantos.* No one would have ever suspected I was a part of it. But I felt this delightful buoyancy every time someone said, "But who would have the *balls?*" Because I got to think: *ME!*

That morning, I'd been at Selwyn alone and early. Jackson was off failing an eye exam. (He does it on purpose, so his glasses correct him to 20/10. He says raptor vision is worth the occasional headache.) My mom had wanted to take me to school before the triplets woke up. So I'd thought, Why not stroll through the dance hallway? Then—thank you, *Contracantos*—I'd actually strolled through the dance hallway.

Sure enough, there was Maura Heldsman, sitting cross-legged, a binder on her lap that I sure hoped was English. I ambled over. So frigging suave.

"It's Ethan Andrezejczak," she said.

"Maura Heldsman."

"I get more points for knowing your last name than you do for knowing mine. Are you going to live your life with that thing?"

"Do I have a choice?"

"Sure. You could take your wife's name." Ethan Heldsman. "Andrezejczak is sort of adorable, though."

I felt myself go beet-red. Suddenly, I loved my name. Thank you, I thought fervently. Thank you, Slavic forebears, ye heavily into consonants. Ye fans of high-scoring Scrabble tiles. Ye who boldly dropped *z*'s where no *z*'s had been dropped before. I appreciate it.

"So," she said.

"So, how's life?" Desperate grasp for the conversation to continue.

"If you want to know how life is, you're going to have to sit down."

Gladly.

"On second thought, you might have sat down for nothing." Never. "I don't even know what to say. Life is dance. Dance is life. I'm always rehearsing and filming and practicing. If not, I'm eating. Occasionally sleeping. Never doing English homework. Want to help?"

We'd had to write a short analysis of a few lines from canto 81. I'd done the assignment fast the night before, but reading the lines now, the paper held in her hands, her wrists knobbly, her thumbnails short and square and human and unbeautiful—well, those lines got a whole new significance. The fabric of her sweatshirt touched the fabric of mine. I would have wanted to be the sweatshirt, except I was so happy being me. I'd never liked Pound so much.

> *What thou lovest well remains,*
> *the rest is dross*
> *What thou lov'st well shall not be reft from thee*
> *What thou lov'st well is thy true heritage*
> *Whose world, or mine or theirs*
> *or is it of none?*

I talked her through it. I told her that "dross" meant "rubbish," like the girl spinning dross into gold in "Rumpelstiltskin." I told her about the tricolon and the rhythm. I didn't tell her much about the last line since I didn't get it myself.

Mostly, I kept looking at her and then looking away, because I'd be thinking: *What thou lovest well remains.* Nothing else matters. *What thou lov'st well shall not be reft from thee.*

"Done," she said, closing the binder with a thwack. "Could it be? I have nothing to do. Eight free minutes."

"Amazing," I said.

"Seriously. Thanks to you."

"How's the show?" I asked. Yes, I was pumping her for information. I'd already imagined telling Luke about this conversation, new material for the *Contracantos.* I wanted it all: the approbation of Maura *and* Luke. *What thou lov'st well is thy true heritage.*

"The usual stinking pile of shit," she said brightly. "I'm perfecting my slut act. Should be useful if I ever get to dance the part of Manon Lescaut."

"But you *aren't* a slut!"

"No?" She raised an eyebrow at me.

"You said! You said—"

"Calm down. You're right. I'm not. I have my limits." She shrugged. "Theoretically."

"Okay, okay—"

"Though I wonder. I say what I'm supposed to say, do what they tell me to do—"

I didn't want to go down this route. "Aren't you kind of mad at them?"

"Andrezejczak, didn't we have this conversation last week?"

"Sort of."

"Not sort of. All of. You literally repeated yourself."

"Sorry."

"Don't be sorry. I like that someone is concerned for the

welfare of my reputation." She raised a leg and, as casually as we normal people cross our arms, put it behind her head. "Nobody asks me that but you."

"No way."

"It's true." Her other leg went up. She addressed me, pretzel-style. "And I don't say these things to anyone else. My parents don't watch. They think it's *dross*, which it is. My dance friends aren't speaking to me."

"What? Why not?"

She shrugged. "I don't know. I don't care. Jealousy, probably."

"But they were your friends! Friends aren't jealous. Friends wouldn't abandon you."

"I abandoned *them* when I went on *FAS*," she pointed out. "And I didn't think twice about it. Dance is about yourself, Andrezejczak. You're always watching yourself in the mirror. Even when you're dancing with the corps, you're trying to stand out as superior so that you don't *have* to dance with the corps."

"Oh."

"Until you're the prima, you can't afford to actually like people."

"Sheesh."

"Awful, right?" Like a spider, she unfurled each leg in turn and placed them straight on the floor. "My children won't be dancers."

"Or reality TV stars?"

"God, I hope not." She pointed her feet and tapped them against the floor, beating out the meter of her words. "It's the same thing there. Fake friends, Miki and Josh and all those guys. Everyone's jealous of everyone else. We're like marionettes."

That comment stuck with me all day, growing gritty and solid just like the spit residue on the mouthpiece of my trumpet. Speaking of neglecting my instrument, I spent Morning Practice in art. Now that I was Chief Illustrator for a school-wide publication, I figured it was my duty.

Plus, I wanted to talk to Herbert.

I had a long conversation with him about Maura. In my head, of course. At first he was a little teed off because I made him squat as if he were taking a dump. (I was planning a series of drawings called "The Art of Excretion." It'd be very avant-garde.) But he eventually stopped being so anal—heh heh—and told me that the marionette line was important.

I tried to tell Luke and Jackson in English, but no, BradLee and binary were clearly more fascinating than I could ever hope to be. So I gave up and suffered through Latin. Jackson and I stumbled from the classroom, hamstrung. You wouldn't think translating a poem called *The Art of Love* could bring you so close to death.

But at last the day was over. When the kTV crew headed downtown at four, we'd be able to print the next *Contra-cantos*.

We met in BradLee's room. "She definitely said 'marionettes,'" I said. "That means they're puppets on strings. That means somebody's pulling the strings. But it's reality!"

"Maybe she doesn't know what 'marionette' means," said Elizabeth.

"Maura Heldsman has a better vocabulary than you do," I retorted.

Luke and Jackson erupted into twin coughing fits.

"I hate you guys."

"Where's BradLee?" said Jackson.

"At a meeting," said Elizabeth. "He'll be gone until three-thirty."

Jackson moved behind BradLee's desk and started clicking around on his computer.

Luke's eyes flicked over to him, but he didn't ask. "We know they frankenbite after the filming," he said. "Maybe they direct them beforehand too. Didn't you say that Trisha told Maura and Brandon what to do with that padlock conversation?"

"She just wanted a good visual," I explained. "They'd already had the conversation somewhere else." Then I realized that was a big fat assumption. What if—but Luke was off and running.

"Coluber has an incentive to keep the show on the air. Selwyn's got a lot hanging on it."

"The Serpent Vice doesn't care about Selwyn," said Elizabeth. "He's out for number one."

I got out Latin homework. I wasn't really in the mood to dissect the marionette thing. I'd just wanted to talk about Maura. I hadn't even told them how she'd said I was adorable. Or my last name was. Same thing.

"Maybe it's a personal incentive," said Luke. "Maybe kTV's paying him."

"That's *so* underhanded."

"But we don't have any evidence."

They kept arguing. I was half listening. Another quarter of my brain was reliving my conversation with Maura, and the last quarter was attempting to translate while keeping one finger on the lines, one in the glossary, and one in the appendix. Basic ratios should tell you that my translation was about a fourth as good as usual. This did not bode well.

"I've found some stuff on Coluber," said Jackson.

"Hold up," said Luke. "How are you going to explain when BradLee sees that somebody Googled Coluber on his computer?"

"I'll say it's for homework," said Jackson dismissively. "Listen to me."

"You're stalking the vice principal for homework? Airtight, dude."

"I'll expunge my traces. Listen. You know how Coluber used to be a TV producer?"

"How did he ever get into secondary education?" muttered Elizabeth. I think she was joking, but Jackson looked at her seriously.

"We should investigate that. But look." We crowded around. Pictures of Coluber with bronzed, blond people. He was holding a drink. His top two buttons were undone.

"He's with kTV producers."

"So?" I said. "He must know them. That's how they got interested in Selwyn."

"We've been told it was Willis Wolfe's connections," said Luke. "Interesting, Son o' Jack."

I was lagging behind. When had we been told this? Probably while I was daydreaming. I looked at my friends. Luke was as focused as when BradLee talked about Ezra Pound. I felt shut out.

"Now," said Jackson, "the true revelation." He typed in something URL-esque, except he wasn't online. He was accessing the mysterious innards of the computer. Don't expect any more details than that.

A PDF appeared on the screen. It looked like a receipt.

"The budget," whispered Luke.

"Yep," said Jackson. "Selwyn Academy, Comprehensive Budget." He scrolled. "Let me move past the debits."

I could see teachers' names whizzing past next to five-digit numbers. "Salaries!" I yelped. "Slow down."

"Irrelevant," said Jackson. "Behold. Credits."

Tuition, separated into the four classes, was the big one. But next was a line item called "Kelvin Television." This was kTV. The number next to it: $180,000.

"That's ten thousand per episode," said Jackson.

"This is crazy," I said. "This is just sitting on the Internet for anyone to find?"

"Well, I——" Jackson tilted his head to the side and played air-piano. The universal gesture for "illegally infiltrated a few secure networks."

"Shit, Jackson," said Elizabeth.

"It was nothing. I was on the school network already. It's a lot easier to get into protected files that way. Anyway, this is what I'd like to do now."

Jackson doesn't get animated. A translation of "I'd like

122

to" from Appelese to Standard American English would be something like, "I have to or else my curiosity will never be sated."

"Uh-oh," said Elizabeth.

"Coluber has put a two-factor authentication block on his personal network files. He's also blocked the use of VPN protocol to infiltrate his account. It's quite sophisticated, really."

"Translate."

"I can't get in."

"Oh."

"But I think under the right—it's possible if—" He paused. "He knows kTV people. He knows them well. And the school's getting paid 10K per episode. That's diddly-squat. I mean, connect the dots."

I wasn't sure where the dots were. But Luke stood and raked his hair back. "That's *awesome*. I see where you're going." He began to pace.

"It'd be child's play for him," said Jackson.

"It'd be simple. Simple and tempting," said Luke.

"I don't get it," I said. "Explain for those of us without dirty, suspicious minds."

"Jackson thinks that Coluber's getting paid for each episode," said Elizabeth.

"That's one hypothesis. I wouldn't be surprised."

"Or he's skimming off the top of what the school's getting." That was Luke.

"Let's hope so," said Jackson. "If kTV is paying him directly, it'd be going right into some clandestine, offshore bank account. It'd be far beyond our powers of investigation."

Our, he said. Very diplomatic.

"Speaking of investigation . . . ," said Luke.

"Yeah," said Jackson, deflating. "I need his personal files. I'd definitely need to get into his office."

"So we'll get into his office."

CHAPTER NINE

Behold this darkness, Selwynites!
Our school approaches its last rites.
The Serpent Vice has stripped us bare
Of all that gleamed as just and fair.
And what's left for us now? Despair.
— THE CONTRACANTOS

The idea hung, suspended, while we printed the *Contracantos*. But it had been spoken. For me? Printing the *Contracantos* was illegal activity enough.

We knew our distribution had to be surreptitious this time. Coluber was out for us. Jackson bought a couple reams of this blue-gray newsprint from an online wholesaler, just so this issue was a different color than the last, and after the ink dried we folded them into brochures.

"Let's make six hundred," said Luke.

"The student body only numbers five hundred," said Jackson.

"Then there'll be lots of extras floating around. For the

teachers, and the administrators, and everyone associated with kTV."

"You really like the idea of them reading your stuff, don't you?" said Elizabeth.

He liked it in an innocent way. In a sort of wonder that something once in his head was now in their hands. In a sort of wonder that they cared.

I knew all that because I felt the same way. Do you know what life was like before the *Contracantos*? Take the annual Selwyn Art Show. "Can you believe a high schooler did that?" my dad would say.

"Is that a photograph?" my mom would reply. "Oh my goodness, honey, it's a painting."

"Whoa. Ethan drew that." That'd be a triplet.

"Uh, no, that wasn't me. I drew the stuff over there. In that corner. No, lower down."

But now? Everyone was inspecting my little inked cartoons. Everyone was trying to guess who'd done them. Everyone was looking at my work. It was an addictive feeling.

And then, everything fell apart.

We didn't finish until almost seven, and we didn't want to pop up all at once from the subbasement. According to the spreadsheet, the kTV people and most of the administrators were downtown at the challenge, but we had to be careful. Four kids emerging all at once, hauling stuffed backpacks: even the thickest of security guards might suspect something. Jackson had checked, and they were legally permitted to seize and search our bags. Not good.

So we sent Luke ahead as a scout. He'd text us when the coast was clear.

We waited. We sat on the floor by the presses for over half an hour, getting twitchier and twitchier. I got out my Latin just to calm down. Elizabeth was pacing the catwalk around the machinery, giving Jackson and her watch alternating looks of impatience.

"Let's go," she said.

"We can't," I said.

"It's been forever."

"He'd have texted us."

"So he forgot."

"He wouldn't have forgotten."

Jackson spoke. "We'll go up to the last doorway, the one behind the stage. *Giselle* rehearsal lets out about now. When the orchestra leaves, we'll go with them. We'll blend in."

"Fine," said Elizabeth.

I didn't move. I wanted to wait for that text. It felt treacherous not to wait.

Elizabeth flicked the lights off and then on again. "Fee. Thin. Stand. Up."

One moment in the complete blackness was enough. I stood and followed them.

Jackson's plan worked. With no instrument cases, we felt like glaring misfits among the orchestra kids. But to the guard we passed on our way to the atrium, we were just a pack of students. The orch dorks scattered to go find their rides. We headed for the front door.

Then we saw Luke.

He was talking to Trisha Meier.

She had him pinned against the wall. She was gesturing dramatically. Granted, she gestured dramatically all the time.

I stared at him. Jackson and Elizabeth saw him too. The force of our collective gaze was enough to make him notice us. His eyes lit up. He refocused on Trisha Meier, but I knew that he'd seen us and I knew to watch his expressions. His eyes flicked back and he gave me an almost imperceptible nod, an eyebrow twist, a light lift of his right shoulder. *Go ahead,* he meant. *Pretend not to know me. I'll catch up as soon as I can.*

I nodded at him. We walked onward. We didn't dare speak until we'd dumped the contraband *Contracantos* into the back of the Appelvan and sunk into the familiar, stained seats. I heaved the sliding door closed.

"Do we leave?" said Elizabeth.

"I think we leave." Jackson turned the key in the ignition. Rattle, cough, silence.

"It's faster for him to walk anyway," said Elizabeth.

Jackson turned it again and the engine caught. "Not quite," he said. "But a difference of ninety seconds. One-twenty, max." The Appelvan had issues navigating Luke's street, which is on a Himalayan hill. Once we had to get out and push while Jackson floored it.

"I'll text him." I felt better now that we'd seen him. I got out my phone. *We're out. Wtf going on with you and Trisha?!*

"Tell him that if he wants a ride, his pickup time tomorrow is six-forty-seven," said Jackson. "Six-forty-one for you, Ethan. Elizabeth, you're six-thirty-five."

"That's the asscrack of dawn," she said.

"Actually, it's thirty-five minutes before sunrise."

"So it's up dawn's ass."

"We need to get these things distributed. I don't want them in the van over the weekend."

"Yeah, much safer if they're out to all Selwyn."

I conducted a wrestling tournament with the triplets (I lost) and played some *Sun Tzu* (I lost) and argued with my mother about whether her prohibition against microwaving aluminum foil was based in fact or myth (I lost). I finished my Latin, started my bio, and blew off my calc. I read some *Cantos*. I brushed my teeth. I got into bed. I did some thinking.

I was weirded out.

Luke was still incommunicado. I'd texted him again once I got home, asking whether he wanted to walk or catch a ride. No response. The whole thing was so weird. He'd been stuck there with Trisha for thirty minutes. That was at least twenty-eight minutes too long to spend with her. And Luke despised Trisha Meier. He was real, and she was fake. He never would have chatted with her for half an hour.

But he had. Laughing and joking and gesturing right back at her. I saw it.

And he'd known that we were stuck in the subbasement, waiting for the all clear.

And anyway, why was Trisha at Selwyn? Even if the filming downtown was finished, why return to the building and chitchat with a high schooler? Didn't she have a life? She could have watched kTV in her hotel room, or explored wintry Minneapolis's cultural offerings, or gone on a hate-date with Damien Hastings. I'll say it again: it was weird.

It took me forever to get to sleep.

6:32. Phone alarm plays maddeningly cheerful tune. I fall out of bed and spend thirty seconds rubbing my eyes on the floor. No texts.

6:33. Shower.

6:35. Drape wet towel over toilet. Reconsider given mother's recent ragefest re wet towels on toilet. Drape towel on rack.

6:36. Pull on jeans, a Twins shirt, and over that, a T-shirt that has been Sharpie-emblazoned with THE IMAGISM CLUB.

6:37. Brush teeth while simultaneously stuffing books in backpack. Drip white froth all over Latin homework. Hope Ms. Pederson knows it's toothpaste.

6:40. Stumble to kitchen. Accept granola bar from mother. Triplets are chatting perkily; give them the stink-eye. Ignore mother's admonitions to wear coat.

6:41. See headlights. Forget lunch. Leave. Return for lunch. Leave.

Jackson and Elizabeth were slumped in the car. Every morning, Jackson adjusted his seat so he could drive while basically lying down. It was probably harrowing to be driven by a teenager who'd been awake for less than fifteen minutes, but I was always too groggy to care.

"I guess Luke is walking," I said. "He never texted me back."

"Odd," said Elizabeth. "Jackson? You awake? Drive by his house to check."

"Murmph," grunted Jackson. That means yes. No is more like "nurmph."

But Luke wasn't waiting on his porch, and he didn't spring into the car, and he didn't roll down the windows to blast us with cold air, and he didn't serenade us with one of his obnoxious morning songs.

"We can't linger," said Elizabeth. "We've got to get into our positions."

"I was really hoping for some 'Rise and Shine' today," I said mournfully.

"Ethan, you always claim 'Rise and Shine' makes you carsick."

"I'd even go for 'It's a Beautiful Day in the Neighborhood.'"

"He'll meet us at school. He knows the plan." But Elizabeth sounded anxious too.

Once we got our schoolbooks in our lockers, the covert operation began. I should mention that at Selwyn, everyone wants to start clubs for college applications. The problem is that nobody has time to join clubs, so you really have to grovel for members. That's the impetus behind the Selwyn tradition of students standing at the front doors, wearing club T-shirts, and passing out informational brochures, which everyone takes since they often include a coupon for an upcoming bake sale. (Then the bake sale doesn't make any money due to the coupon glut, and the club has to hand out more coupons so that people will patronize their next bake sale. It's a self-perpetuating cycle. I've enjoyed many a free muffin in my day.)

We'd invented a Pound-inspired club, and we'd brought in full-head balaclavas. We stood at the door handing out brochures, which—in case you need it spelled out—were *Contracantos*.

"Where's Luke?" hissed Jackson, who was at last fully conscious.

He hadn't been by our lockers. Now he wasn't at the doors.

"Forget it," said Elizabeth. "And shut up, someone'll recognize your voice."

"He probably overslept," I said, but shut up myself when I noticed that her eyes, through the balaclava, were slits.

Once I'd convinced myself that Luke was asleep, I started to have fun. I liked the mask part. It was a lot easier to shove leaflets into people's hands when they didn't know who I was. Some people just flat-out rejected them, but they circled back once they realized what they were. It's strange how much people will ignore you if you're (1) masked and (2) giving them something illegal that (3) they desperately want. I felt like a drug dealer.

Jackson gave the call of the cerulean warbler, the pre-arranged two-minutes-to-the-bell signal. We dumped the few we had left by the doors, rushed to the bathrooms to pull off the disguises, rushed to our lockers for our books, and rushed to our first-bell classes.

I slammed into my seat ten seconds after the bell rang. Mrs. Garlop gave me a pursed-lip glare. "Missed the bus," I said. I tried to pretend that my heavy breathing was because I was stressed out about parametric equations, not because I'd sprinted from the front doors under a heavy load of breaking-

the-rules adrenaline. I remembered I hadn't done my homework, so I found an old assignment, wrote "PARAMETRIC
STUFF" really big on the top, and hoped it would pass. I finally relaxed. My heart rate subsided enough for me to look
around.

I saw the telltale margins of blue-gray newsprint underneath papers, inside books, protruding from backpacks. I
smiled. I wished Luke and I could smirk at each other, but his
desk, next to mine, was empty. He must really be oversleeping,
I thought. I was surprised that his super-intense mom was allowing it. Maybe his whole family was asleep. Struck down
by sleeping sickness. Except wasn't that a tropical disease?
Our November snowstorm still hadn't melted. But perhaps
he had some other illness. He definitely wasn't at school; you
had to come in the front doors unless you were "requested
elsewhere," either by the administration or kTV.

He *must* be sick, I thought. He was already feverish last
night, which was why he hadn't been able to squirm out of
Trisha Meier's clutches. And that explained why he hadn't
texted me; he didn't want to contaminate his phone with barf
particles. He was probably really upset that he was missing the
big distribution day for Issue II.

Yep. I bought it. I bought my own spiel.

I started to text him an update under my desk, but the
Garlopian harpy radar started bleeping and she swooped
down upon me. So I wrote down some nonsense about dx
and dy and dt, hoping that wouldn't inspire her to give me a
real DT.

Morning Practice: trumpet, because I wanted to be alone

in a cubicle. Bio: notes on electrophoresis. Latin: Ovid encourages lovers to be pale and skinny (like me!). And all throughout, rumors whistling through the air, winging from one classmate to another:

1. Luke Weston masterminded the writing, publication, and distribution of the *Contracantos.*
2. Mr. Coluber and kTV have both figured that out.
3. Luke has been saved from the iron fist of Coluberian justice because kTV loves the *Contracantos:* kTV thinks it's just so original and rebellious and deep; kTV can't believe such artistic talent wasn't featured on *For Art's Sake* from the beginning; kTV has picked up Luke for the final six episodes; kTV has anointed him their next star; kTV has swept him out of classes today to film an introductory sequence; kTV is snatching away Luke, my main man, my best friend.

CHAPTER TEN

The Serpent Vice betrays our cause.
He trades appraisal for applause.
True art is beauty; beauty, truth.
But <u>For Art's Sake</u> *is low, uncouth.*
It sells our talent, vends our youth.
              – THE CONTRACANTOS

It was finally lunchtime. Elizabeth and Jackson and I staked out a corner table, surrounding ourselves with a menacing siege-wall of books so that nobody would be tempted to join us. They had also heard. I don't know what stage they'd reached, but I was firmly ensconced in denial. Jackson was the closest to realizing what had happened. He was a math genius for that reason: he could put together the known information in a way that led him to the truth.

"He's absent because he's sick," I said. I was already wishing I could go back to calculus, when I'd actually believed myself. "These are just rumors."

"I don't think we can write them off as 'just rumors,'" said Elizabeth. "There's a surprising amount of truth in them."

"There is not."

"But there is. As of this morning, nobody knew he was involved with the *Contracantos*. Now everybody knows it."

I began to maim my corn dog. "He must be furious. If he's missing class because of kTV, I mean. We've got English. And he was going to spend Morning Practice and creative writing on Issue III. He must be so angry. He hates them."

"They can't force him to be on the show," said Elizabeth.

"They must have," I said. I remembered how sparkly he'd looked while talking to Trisha Meier. I remembered my phone's empty in-box. "He was definitely forced."

"If it's true," said Elizabeth, "he chose."

"She's right," said Jackson.

"Luke wouldn't choose kTV!" I cried. "He *always* chooses right. He hates kTV more than anyone."

Every time, I was the one who didn't get it, the one who believed too hard.

"There he is," said Jackson, sounding resigned.

Already Luke seemed like a mythical figure. I'd spent the past four hours obsessing over him, wondering about his motivations, wondering where he was, and I'd almost forgotten that he existed, that I could just ask him. I jerked around to see the cafeteria door.

There he was, the real Luke, looking so comfortingly normal, so familiar and nonchalant in his jeans and flannel button-down, that I jumped up and began waving my arms as if I were directing a jet's landing. I was practically wearing an orange vest. "Luke!"

He saw me and gave a compact wave, a flip of the hand. He turned to the girl behind him and said something. It was Maura Heldsman. She laughed. They dumped their bags on a table and headed for the food lines.

I sat down.

Jackson and Elizabeth were staring at each other, doing their cousin-telepathy thing.

My corn dog was in crumbles on my plate.

I lifted my head again.

Jackson and Elizabeth were still looking at each other. I felt like I'd slipped into a state of being in which I no longer existed on the same plane as the rest of the world. I could see them, but they couldn't see me.

"He chose," said Elizabeth again. Her face shone fiercely from behind her dreadlocks.

Jackson nodded.

That was the first time I remembered that he was their friend too.

English class, last period. Luke and Maura weren't there. I'd heard from Cynthia Soso that there'd been an announcement on the kTV website: tonight's scheduled episode was pushed back to next week, and they'd have a rerun instead.

"So that's why Trisha was here," said Jackson. "They needed more time downtown."

"Or else they wanted to work in Luke," I said.

"Maybe both."

Elizabeth was watching us from across the room. I almost gestured for her to come sit in Luke's empty seat. I don't know why I didn't. Instead, with no Maura to gaze at, with no Luke to talk to, with Jackson mired in his "Guess the Square Root" calculator game, I actually paid attention. And I was in that zone where all emotions are heightened. You know? One of your miniature sisters starts chanting, and you want to stuff her PB&J into her face. When you can translate a line of Ovid, you feel utter joy. Then you can't define any word in the next line and you're crushed by despair. You tear up at a sappy TV commercial. (Then you realize it's an ad for tampons and you feel like crying again, though for a different reason.)

"Today, we're talking about the general topic of long poems," said BradLee. He was dressed for casual Friday in jeans and an interrobang T-shirt. Where did one find punctuation-themed clothing? "We'll start with the work of a literary theorist named Smaro Kamboureli."

Usually hearing the words "literary theorist" was like pressing Ctrl+Alt+Delete on my body: instant power down. But I thought that if I focused on BradLee, I might forget about Luke.

"She describes the long poem as *mise en abyme*. Anyone here take French?" Luke took French. "Yes, Vivian?"

"Like. Placed in, um—I don't know that word."

"Abyss," said BradLee.

"Placed into an abyss," said Vivian triumphantly.

"Exactly. Now, all of you. Imagine standing between two mirrors."

"Like at the mall?" Once Vivian gets the floor, she never wants to relinquish it.

"Sure. You'd see an infinite series of yourself, right?"

"Actually, it depends on the angle."

"Let's say the angle's correct. Got it? Now, how does that apply to a long poem?"

He'd stumped us. Not even Vivian had anything vapid to say.

"Here's a hint. Kamboureli describes the long poem as 'a genre without a genre.' It's a poem, it's an epic, it's a novel. It's everything." He turned on the projector. The text swam into focus.

> [The long poem] is . . . not a fixed object but a
> mobile event, the act of knowing its limits, its
> demarcated margins, its integrated literary kinds.
> The long poem ceases to be a kind of a kind by
> becoming the kind of its other.

I was lost. I knew what the words meant when they were by themselves, with the possible exception of "demarcated." But putting them together was a problem. Maybe this Kamboureli dame was bullshitting us all. Making clothes for the emperor.

"What's she saying here?" said BradLee.

I considered sharing my hypothesis that literary theory is akin to the square root of negative one: we're just pretending it exists. Nobody spoke. Vivian pulled out a hand mirror to check her hair. BradLee cast a longing glance at Luke's empty desk.

I raised my hand.

"Ethan!" He sounded pathetically happy.

"Okay." My stomach gave a lame little churn, and Maura wasn't even there. "She's saying the long poem isn't one genre. It's always between genres. It wiggles around on you."

"My favorite part about Ethan's answer is the word 'between,'" said BradLee. "Kamboureli writes that the long poem is 'a textual process of betweenness.' Tell me why she included the word 'process.'"

I raised my hand again. "Without the 'process' part," I said, "it's just another genre, a genre that's a mix of genres. But long poems aren't stuck. They shift." I had a stroke of genius, if I do say so myself. "Like the mirrors! The genre moves! It changes!" I could see that infinite series, all those images reflecting the slightest motion, quivering like water under sunlight.

"Yes!" said BradLee.

It was rare that I exacted an exclamation point from a teacher. They used a lot of ellipses when talking to me: *yeah, but . . .* or *okay. . . .* Elizabeth gave me an air-five from across the room.

"The long poem is an enactment of betweenness," said BradLee.

I loved the word "betweenness." I wrote it down. Several times.

"Generic betweenness, and other types too. One critic called it 'the tremulous fusion between self-trust and self-doubt.'"

If you have ever wondered what it's like to be me, or a teenager, or a human, that does a pretty nice job of explaining it. The tremulous fusion between self-trust and self-doubt.

The lecture ended. We were supposed to be doing a close-reading worksheet on Pound, but I was reeling with all these ideas.

Reality TV. It was also *mise en abyme,* a genre without a genre. But a long poem flaunted its betweenness, and reality TV tried to hide it. It tried to claim that reality and TV could coexist, no problem. But even its name betrayed the problem. Reality, TV: two antonyms right next to each other. It was as bad as "jumbo shrimp" or "fun run."

Reality TV couldn't be both art and life. It could be between, but it couldn't be both.

I think I was so into *betweenness* that day because it described everything I was feeling. Talk about the tremulous fusion between trust and doubt. I doubted Luke, but I couldn't stop trusting him. I was angry at him. I was worried for him. I knew the truth and didn't believe it.

How could so many emotions exist within one person at one time? I was sitting in a plastic desk-chair contraption in an English classroom in Minnesota, tapping out the meter of lines from Pound's *Cantos,* wearing a baseball shirt with a small hole in the armpit. But I was also roiling with feelings and thoughts and doubts and conjectures and worries and layers of complication. I looked around the classroom. Elizabeth was playing Hangman with her normal friends. Jackson was approximating square roots in his head. Vivian was fixing her eyeliner. Cynthia was texting under the desk. BradLee was trying to explain metonymy to Paul Jones, who was trying to make BradLee laugh. But that was only what I could see. If so much happened in my head, didn't I have to conclude that it was the same way with everyone else? I had to look down again. The world was too big.

Twenty minutes later, I had the following conversation with BradLee.

"Hey, Mr. Lee, can I talk to you for a minute? I'm worried."

"You're doing very well in class, Ethan. I loved your comments today."

"No, I'm worried about the *Contracantos*."

"Why's that? By the way—not that I know anything of its provenance—the issue today was excellent. Sophisticated and cutting."

"That was Luke. Mostly Luke. He's what I'm worried about."

"Why's that?"

"People are saying that he—no, forget it. It sounds dumb when you say it out loud. See you tomorrow."

"Say it."

"I'm sure it's not true. It *couldn't* be true. People are saying—"

BradLee took over. "That he's behind the *Contracantos*. That somebody told Coluber, and Coluber told kTV." He was speaking flatly. "That they've offered him a contract for the remaining six episodes, and that he's very gratified and has accepted with pleasure."

I was gaping. "You heard too?"

"Ethan," he said. He glanced at the closed door. "It's all true."

"All of it? I don't believe you."

"You should believe me."

"But how would you know? No offense."

"Trust me. I know. And Ethan, think of the greater good. *For Art's Sake* is doing excellent things for Selwyn."

"Luke's our *friend*!"

"It's just not that big of a deal—"

But I was gone.

"At last," said Elizabeth crankily as I climbed into the Appelvan.

Jackson turned the key. The car didn't start, and I didn't respond to Elizabeth.

"An apology would be nice. We've been sitting here fifteen minutes."

Another turn of the key. The van shuddered and fell still.

"Ethan? Hello?"

I'd been staring out the window. "It's all true," I said.

There was a nasty sound like gears grinding together, but even that didn't last.

"BradLee told me it was all true. He said they offered a contract, and Luke accepted."

"How would BradLee know?" said Jackson, turning toward me.

"You get your car started," said Elizabeth. "I will interrogate Ethan. But yeah, how *would* he know?"

"There he is," said Jackson, staring at the rearview mirror. I swiveled. BradLee was walking across the parking lot, deep in conversation with—

Weird.

My view was obstructed by flying leggings of the traffic-cone-orange variety. Elizabeth dove over the front seat, and then past me into the back. She knelt on the rear seat and stared.

"Shit," she said. "Shitacular. Shitaculacious."

BradLee was walking with someone. That someone was Coluber.

The Appelvan rumbled to life. "Victory!" cried Jackson.

"Don't move," said Elizabeth.

"They're going to see you!" I said, worried.

"Tinted windows, dumbass," she said, without looking back. "And they are *into* this conversation."

I couldn't see clearly. I was tempted to dive over the seat, but I was likely to kick her in the head if I tried, and if I kicked her in the head she'd probably shiv me.

"The Appelvan won't idle for long," said Jackson.

"Take a slow loop around the lot," Elizabeth commanded.

After Jackson backed out, I could see better. Coluber was gesturing expansively. He was smiling. As we passed them—"*Slow*, Jackson!"—I could see that BradLee was smiling too.

"Tell me everything BradLee said," said Jackson.

"He said it wasn't a big deal. He told me to think of the greater good."

"Did he say that in a soothing way? Or in a self-justifying way?"

"I don't know. Both?"

"They're getting into a car. Go! Go!" That was Elizabeth.

BradLee got into the driver's seat of a prehistoric two-door Volkswagen. Coluber slid into the other side.

"BradLee!" I couldn't believe it. "He drives Coluber around? That shithead!"

"Follow them, Jackson," said Elizabeth as the Volkswagen backed out.

"I refuse. We know everything we need to know."

The Volkswagen had no front license plate and lots of bird poop on the hood. "You'd think BradLee could have afforded a nicer car with all that banking money," I said.

"Follow him."

"No."

"Then I will." Elizabeth plunged feetfirst into the middle seat and headfirst into the front. She grabbed the wheel while still horizontal. The Appelvan made a crazy swerve.

"What the hell, Elizabeth ___"

"Move over."

"No!" Another swerve. The right mirror came within inches of the Students Xing sign.

"Brake, goddammit."

We accelerated and went over a speed bump diagonally. I grabbed my tailbone in agony.

"That was not the brake!"

"Yeah, because you're shoving me and my feet were displaced from their typical—"

"Then move over."

Jackson hit the brakes, heaved a great sigh of resignation, and squirmed under Elizabeth to the passenger seat.

"Let's hope your lollygagging didn't lose us our only chance," she muttered. "Where are they?"

They had bypassed the lot's exit. "Heading toward the front circle," I said.

"Crap," said Elizabeth. "Much easier to tail someone on the open road." She reached down to slide the seat forward. It zoomed up so far that her nose almost hit the windshield.

"Only two settings," Jackson told her, sounding satisfied. "It's broken. You're either way back or way forward."

"This car is two percent metal, ninety-eight percent shit. My nose is three inches from the glass. I feel like an old lady. Nonetheless, are you familiar with the acronym 'FIDO'?"

"I don't think so," said Jackson cautiously.

"'Eff It, Drive On.' That's my motto." She hit the gas, and the Appelvan lurched forward like a bumper car. I'd never appreciated the finesse Jackson brings to our daily carpool. She drove to the front circle.

"There is no rhyme or reason to this mission," said Jackson. "So a teacher and a vice principal are driving around their school. Big freaking whoop-di—*oh.*"

Trisha Meier was standing on the school steps. When Brad-Lee's car pulled up, she hung up her phone with a flounce. Coluber lounged inside and BradLee hopped out of the car. He hugged her. He actually hugged her.

"Foul," muttered Elizabeth.

"This mission is impulsive and rash," said Jackson. "They're going to guess what we're doing. Pretend you have to go get something from your locker, Ethan."

"I'm not missing this. You go get something."

"You."

"You."

He lobbed an aggressive sigh. "Fine. I'll pretend to check the tires."

"Wait wait wait," said Elizabeth. "He's pulling back the seat for her! She's climbing into the back. Trisha, honey, your skirt is way too short to—ugh! My eyes! They burn!"

"Missed it," said Jackson, squinting out the windshield with interest.

"So BradLee is dating Trisha Meier," said Elizabeth.

"That's not true," I said automatically.

"It's likely," said Elizabeth. "Did you *see* that hug? She totally did a boob-thrust."

"Confirmed," said Jackson.

Elizabeth swiveled around to give me a triple eyebrow-raise and a leer. It wasn't the most attractive facial expression, which I was about to point out, but Jackson interrupted.

"They're leaving."

"Ooh, almost distracted myself." She followed the Volkswagen to the exit, where a line of cars was waiting to turn out onto the busy street. BradLee's left-turn signal went on.

"Not good," said Jackson. "A left turn here can be dicey. There's not often space for two cars to pull out at once."

"Our bumpers shall be as one," pronounced Elizabeth. She crept toward BradLee's car.

"That will do," said Jackson. We were so close that I could read the papers strewn on his rear window ledge.

"Hey, that's my *Mansfield Park* essay," I said. "I forgot that even existed."

"Watch his brake lights," Jackson ordered me. "I'll take the traffic. You go when we say, Elizabeth."

She was perched over the wheel like a bird of prey.

"Gap in traffic imminent," said Jackson. "Three seconds."

"Brake lights off," I said.

"GO!" we yelled. BradLee neatly inserted the Volkswagen into the gap. With a screech and a roar, the Appelvan was on its tail.

Jackson turned and high-fove me.

"I'm the one who deserves congratulation," said Elizabeth.

"Every time you talk, you look back," Jackson said. "That worries me."

"Every time you talk, your breath fogs up the windshield," I added. "Which worries *me.*"

We followed them down the street. "You know what?" said Jackson. "We're tailing the wrong people."

"How is it even possible that we have this wrong?" I said. "We have a teacher, an administrator, *and* a Trisha Meier."

"So they're all in collusion. What more do we need to know?"

"Duh. Where they're going? What they're talking about?"

"Yeah, like we're going to crash some ritzy bar and eavesdrop on them?"

"We could try."

"That's ridiculous. And besides, they don't matter. We should be talking to Luke."

"There's no need to—ACK!"

That was my head hitting the front seat. Elizabeth had

slammed on the brakes. Once I got my face to function again, I saw that the Volkswagen again had on its left-turn signal.

"They're turning *there*? That's an entrance ramp," said Jackson. "You are not taking my Appelvan onto the highway."

"Watch me."

"This car does not do well with high speeds."

"Like I give a flying—"

"And it's practically rush hour!" The Volkswagen turned.

"Onward! FIDO!" shouted Elizabeth.

"NO!" shouted Jackson. "NO FIDO! BAD FIDO!"

To my surprise, she didn't follow them into the turn. "You're right," she told him.

"Of course I'm right! In dog years, the Appelvan's a hundred and nineteen—"

"No. About Luke. Who cares about BradLee? Who cares about Coluber and Trisha? We need to figure out what's going on with Luke."

CHAPTER ELEVEN

And so, to arms! All good men, fight!
For what is real and good and right!
Don't settle for this sham, this fake.
Take up the standard! Kill the Snake!
We fight for one true cause: art's sake.
                    — THE CONTRACANTOS

Same day, 8 p.m.

I was looking around my room appraisingly. It was nowhere near as cool as the Appelden. For one, there was no Baconnaise. I'd thought about asking Jackson to bring him over, but I didn't want them to think that Baconnaise was my security blanket or something. I didn't need solace from a gerbil. Not at all.

Anyway, even Baconnaise wouldn't be enough to make my room cool. My mom had once been the type to decorate a bedroom, but this was before she decided she wanted more children, preferably girls. (I'd tried not to feel insulted.) Therefore, my room looked like an eleven-year-old boy lived there. There were Star Wars action figures. Bins of Legos were stacked at the foot of the bed. On the walls were posters for old Pixar films, which I briefly considered taking down before Elizabeth came over.

But it'd be fine for our emergency meeting. The Appelden was unavailable, since it was Jackson's parents' turn to host their friends for their monthly Settlers of Catan party.

Jackson drove over with Elizabeth after dinner. He sprawled onto my bed and started scrolling through his phone. Elizabeth stood, looking curiously at the decor.

"*Ratatouille,* huh?" She was grinning.

I knew I should have taken that poster down.

"Let's get down to business," I said. I sat at my desk chair.

"Sit up, Jackson," Elizabeth commanded. "Move over." Jackson was still poking at his phone—you can never tell whether he's doing vital research or playing *Tetris*—but he swung his legs over the side of the bed so there'd be room for her. "Let's debrief."

I reported everything BradLee had said. "He thinks that Luke's, quote, very gratified."

"Who believes that?" demanded Elizabeth. She seemed to expect us to raise our hands for aye or nay.

"He was gratified at lunch today," I said. "Sitting with Maura Heldsman."

"True."

"Maybe it was all a plot," I said bitterly. "Maybe he engineered the *Contracantos* to get on the show."

I'd been wondering that all afternoon. I'd been lying on my bed, hands behind my neck, stewing. Stewing in the Crock-Pot of betrayal. And because it felt horribly good, like prodding a pimple, to believe the worst, I'd basically concluded that yes, he'd masterminded it all. His two censored reviews, his long poem, the publication of the *Contracantos:* all an elaborate ploy.

But they couldn't be.

"No," I said. "He's good. But he's not that good."

"We don't want to underestimate him," said Elizabeth.

"He couldn't have faked all that outrage."

"He could have," said Jackson. "But he didn't. Think about the sequence of events. If he'd wanted to be on the show, he would have made the *Contracantos* by himself. It would have been stupid to involve us."

"Proof enough for me," said Elizabeth. "Luke's not an idiot."

"He's an idiot," I muttered.

"He's not a tactical idiot. Even if he *has* been taken in by *For Art's Sake.*"

"BradLee, on the other hand, is an idiot," said Jackson. "He clearly reports to Coluber."

"Yeah," I said. "This is all BradLee's fault, not Luke's."

"Luke's the one who agreed to be on the show," said Jackson. "Don't let him off so fast." He picked up his phone again and zoned out.

"We need to talk to him," said Elizabeth.

There was a knock on the door.

"Oh no," I said. I dove to block it, but I forgot that my desk chair had wheels and ended up on the floor. They processed in like pallbearers with the Candy Land box.

"Time to play!" said Olivia.

"Ethan, why are you lying down?" said Tabitha.

"I love Candy Land," said Elizabeth.

"No, you don't," I said, heaving myself up. "Trippers, go away."

"Trippers? Are they on drugs?"

"Sometimes I wonder."

"If you say you have a headache, Mom gives you candy," said Lila.

"It's called Tylenol," said Tabitha. "I like it."

"EEEEEETHAN," said Olivia. "You said you'd play."

"You promised."

"I promised nothing of the sort."

"You did too!" Lila screwed up her face and opened her mouth for a wail.

"Don't you fake cry."

She shut her mouth and opened her eyes. "I never fake."

"Yeah!" said Olivia. "Lila never fakes."

"Lila never fakes," said Tabitha.

"I never fake."

"Lila never fakes."

They get stuck in these continuous-feedback loops.

"Girls," I said, trying to sound like my mom, "I'll play tomorrow. As soon as I wake up."

"But you promised!" said Lila, her chin trembling.

I glanced at Elizabeth, who was watching the proceedings with interest.

"You're a bad brother," said Tabby. "You're going to make Lila cry."

"Bad brother."

"Bad bad bad bad brother."

"Like an ogre."

"Fee, fie, foh, fum—"

"Ethan won't play Candy Land because he is dumb!" That was Olivia. Elizabeth cracked up, but not as hard as those three did. They hit the floor, laughing so hard they were wheezing. Olivia would repeat the line every time anyone was in danger of catching her breath.

"You're not supposed to laugh at your own jokes," I told Olivia grouchily. "Fine. Set it up." I gave Elizabeth and Jackson a despairing look. "Sorry, guys."

"I really do like Candy Land," said Elizabeth, hopping off the bed.

"Then you really are an imbecile."

She kicked me as she dropped down to the floor.

"We like you," said Olivia.

"Can I be the green one?"

Tabitha appraised Elizabeth's request. "I'm always green, but you're nice, and you kicked Ethan. So you can be yellow."

"Like the sun," said Elizabeth.

"And pee," said Lila.

"And bananas," said Elizabeth.

"And pee," said Lila.

I did some stealth deck-arranging so the girls would get all the good cards. We commenced.

"We should call him," said Elizabeth. "Now."

My stomach dropped.

"Don't get all excited. But maybe he's still on our side."

"Yeah! He's infiltrating kTV! With his insider knowledge, we'll bring them down—"

"I just told you not to get all excited," said Elizabeth.

"Go, Ethan," whined Lila.

"I'll call him," said Jackson from the bed. "Since you two are otherwise engaged."

I wouldn't have expected it, but Elizabeth looked relieved too.

Olivia pulled the Queen Frostine card. They broke into their Queen Frostine song. I won't sully these pages with the full lyrics. An excerpt: *Queen Frostine / never mean / Queen Frostine / as sweet as frosting.*

Jackson went into my closet to escape the noise.

"I wish I knew that song," said Elizabeth longingly.

They were happy to oblige. By this point, Tabitha was in Elizabeth's lap, playing with her dreadlocks. I was sort of envious. I'd always wondered what those dreadlocks felt like.

"I wonder why BradLee spilled the beans to Coluber," said Elizabeth.

"I wonder *when,*" said Jackson ominously as he emerged from the closet.

"Maybe he didn't," I said. "Maybe he's just, like, casual acquaintances with Coluber and Trisha."

"'Think of the greater good'?" Jackson quoted.

"That was a throwaway line!"

"Nothing is a throwaway line," intoned Jackson.

"Oh, Ethan," said Elizabeth. "Now that I know you spend your free time playing Candy Land, it's much easier for me to understand how you're such an innocent."

Jackson chortled.

"What happened on the phone?" I asked him.

"I talked to him. All rumors are confirmed."

I was so agitated I moved my piece backward.

"One question," he said. "How long ago did BradLee blab about the *Contracantos*?"

The triplets broke into their new *Fee, fie, foh, fum / Ethan is really dumb* song.

Elizabeth was nodding. "Way back. I bet it was *way* back."

"So Coluber's ban must have been purposeful."

I couldn't both follow their conversation and escape the gluey grasp of the swamp monster Gloppy. I was back at the beginning of the board. "I can't concentrate!" I wailed.

"That's because you're dumb. That's okay. I just won," said Olivia.

"You always win," said Lila.

Tabitha is hyper-competitive, and I eyed her worriedly. She's been known to throw pieces. "That's just because you got the Queen Frostine card," she said meanly.

"*Queen Frostine, not a human bean*," sang Elizabeth as she helped them pick up.

They were finally gone.

"Wow," said Elizabeth. "You're so nice to them."

I looked around. I thought she might be talking to someone else.

"They love you. It's obvious."

"Um, if you didn't notice, they think I'm dumb."

"But so do all your friends."

I laughed despite myself. "What were you guys talking about? Summarize."

Jackson hopped to. He likes the word "summarize." I like the word "tricolon."

1. BradLee most likely blabbed to Coluber sooner rather than later. That idiotic ban on the *Contracantos*? I'd underestimated Coluber. He did it on purpose, so everyone would read it. So that when it was on *For Art's Sake,* it'd already be famous.
2. Luke hadn't plotted this, but he'd sure as hell sold out. Here's what he said to Jackson on the phone: "Hey, can't really talk, super busy with *FAS* stuff. I'm on set right now. Hold on, Maura, I need like twenty seconds. Yeah, they like the poem. I'm going to be on the episode next week. Totally unexpected, right? What? Look, let's talk later."
3. Why had BradLee told Coluber? Why had Luke agreed to be on the show? I, at any rate, had no freaking clue.

"He's hanging out with Maura," I moaned. I was lying on the floor again.

"Your infatuation is inane," snapped Elizabeth. "Can we focus on what's important? Luke changed sides. Why?"

"He was probably on their side all along."

"Oh, come *on,* Ethan. He believed in the *Contracantos.* You know he did. He was leading the revolt! The revolt was his *idea!*"

Jackson snorted. "Money."

"You really think that would be enough?" said Elizabeth.

"An agent. National exposure. Cool friends."

"We were his cool friends!" I wailed.

"He chose lo these many years ago," said Jackson. I knew he was talking about MinneMATHolis. "Now he chose again."

"Don't forget he had friends back then too," said Elizabeth. "Friends he abandoned."

"But they were people like Miki Frigging Reagler! People who don't even count as people!"

"Money, an agent, fame, cool friends," repeated Jackson. He took off his glasses and stared at me in a creepy, probing, unfocused way. "Hanging out with Maura Heldsman, all the time. Think about it. You don't have to answer, but think about it. What would you have done, Ethan? What would you have done?"

I wasn't stewing any longer. The Crock-Pot had been turned off and the meat was congealing into a sad, sorry mess.

On Monday, I went to lunch with Elizabeth. "There he is! There he is!"

"Ethan, just ignore him."

"For the ever-loving love of—look who he's sitting next to."

"Kyle's not that bad."

"Not Kyle."

"Who then? I'm not looking."

"MIKI F.R.! MIKI F.R. IS THAT BAD!"

"Eat your taco salad."

"MIKI FRIGGING REAGLER! The guy whose name needs an inserted expletive just to jive with natural law! MIKI FRIGGING REAGLER!"

It was true. Miki F.R.'s swoopy-haired self was back at Luke's side with the aplomb of someone who always knew this would happen. I stood up. "Let's go. Let's go ask him why."

"Jackson already did."

"You know Jackson's incompetent on the phone. That man orders pizza online. We'll go talk to him face to face."

"But my taco meat will get all cold, and the lettuce'll get warm, and you're perfectly aware the only thing that makes cafeteria taco salad edible is the temperature divergence . . ."

Was she nervous? "Elizabeth!" I grabbed her hand and pulled her up. "I'll buy you a new taco salad."

"You borrowed my money to buy *yourself* a taco salad." But she stood up. I was about to drop her hand, I swear, but as we headed toward Luke, she laced her fingers through mine.

I was very glad Jackson had a different lunch period that day.

We were standing right behind Luke. Elizabeth dropped my hand to tap him on the shoulder, and I covertly wiped my sweaty palm on my jeans.

"Yo," she said.

"Hey!" said Luke, nonplussed. "It's you!"

"Can we talk to you in private?" I said.

Luke looked pained. "I'd say yes, but"—he gestured to his taco salad—"you know the Divergent Temperature Principle."

"What's *that*, Luke?" said Miki F.R. "That sounds *hysterical*!" He started laughing.

"Can't we just talk here?" His eyes weren't meeting ours.

"Why are you on the show?" I blurted out.

Miki F.R. started laughing again, but I ignored him. Or tried to. I've never heard a screech monkey die a slow and painful death, but I can't imagine the sound is dissimilar.

"They asked me," said Luke.

"But we thought you hated it!"

"Yeah," said Elizabeth. "What about the indigenous society protesting the colonizing overlords of the schlocky lowbrow sell-out consumerist culture?" She was leaning forward, getting into Luke's space. I'd have been terrified.

He looked nervously at his tablemates. Kyle was talking to Josh and Kirtse, but Miki F.R. was following the conversation with interest. "You were right!" he cried. "You called it! You *know* human nature, Luke. You totally predicted they wouldn't get it."

Now Luke looked embarrassed. His skin was pretty brown, but he was blushing. "The publicity . . . the scholarship . . . the chance to network—"

The old Luke always thought it was vile to use "network" as a verb.

"It's a really good opportunity."

I tried to look straight into his eyes. Surely he'd be telegraphing something like, "I have to say this in front of them, but really, I have an excellent way to explain all of this! I still like you the best! I'll be back, Ethan! I'll be back!"

But he looked down and took a bite of taco salad.

"Come on, Ethan," said Elizabeth. I followed her across the cafeteria.

"I hope his meat and his lettuce are both room temperature," I said.

Any fool could have hit a solid "lukewarm" joke with that
setup, but she didn't even take a whack. That's when I knew
she was as upset as I was. "Me too," she said.

"James Joyce, T. S. Eliot, H.D., William Carlos Williams," said
BradLee. "All writers who were strongly influenced by Pound.
All modernists. What are the hallmarks of modernism? Frag-
mentation. Collage. An unreliable narrator."

An unreliable narrator. That was me! "Everyone has a filter," Luke had told me in calculus, back in the good old days.
And my filter was wrong. I'd been choosing the wrong luminous details, frankenbiting reality, and I hadn't ended up with
anything close to the true story. I didn't know Luke at all.

That Thursday, there was a new issue of the *Contracantos*.

CHAPTER TWELVE

An age of creativity
Was heralded by kTV.
We strive for peaks, first high, then higher,
For we'll be judged by Muse-like choir:
Damien, Wolfe, and Trisha Meier!
      — THE CONTRACANTOS

"What the eff, Herbert," I whispered during Morning Practice. There were a few other people in Dr. Fern's studio, but they had on their iPods and were actually concentrating on art. I figured it was safe to have a brief conversation with my manikin.

I had picked up Issue III of the *Contracantos* from a newspaper distribution bin before school. I'd wanted to boycott it, but I'd been too curious to resist. Then I'd had to wait all through first-bell Latin. There was no way I was going to read it under Ms. Pederson, she of the invisible eyebrows and Scandinavian discipline.

Now I put it on my lap, angling Herbert so he could peer down too.

The paper was glossy. The words were typed. There were still drawings, but they'd gotten some real artist to do the sketches. I steeled my nerves and started to read.

"Vintage Luke," I told Herbert as I flipped to page two.

"Same style, but . . . ," I told him as I flipped to page three.

"This is disgusting," I told him as I flipped to page four.

I closed it and stuffed it in my backpack.

I felt sick. It was Luke's style, Luke all the way through. But now the show was hailed as the school's savior. A new era had dawned for Selwyn, and it was ushered in by reality TV.

"Damn it, Herb," I said. He scowled at me and I realized that he wanted me to draw him. I was still working on "The Art of Excretion," so I moved him into a squat.

"Better?" I asked.

He still looked angry, but at least that fit with his constipation pose.

"Listen up, man." I started to sketch him, trying to see him as lines, not a person. (My habit of chatting with him admittedly made that more difficult.) "He's made a philosophical about-face. He's claiming *For Art's Sake* is the best thing that's ever happened to Selwyn."

Herbert nodded. Maybe it was a draft of air.

"So everyone's going to notice. They'll rebel. They'll call him out on his hypocrisy."

Dr. Fern came into the room and walked around. I shut up.

"A pose of despair, Ethan?" she asked me.

"Oh, uh, yeah," I said. Now that I looked at Herbert, crouching with his face in his hands, his shoulders hunched with tension and anxiety, I could see where she was getting it.

"A little disproportionate," she said, squinting at my sketch. "The torso's too stumpy for the length of the legs."

"That's why he looked weird. Thanks."

"But Ethan? Your drawing has greatly improved of late."

Dr. Fern sounded so sincere that I had no choice but to conclude that every word she'd previously spoken to me had been sarcastic.

"Your skills are increasing, but there's something else. You've been inspired, I think. I don't know if it's the poses you're working on"—she raised an eyebrow; Dr. Fern is no dummy—"or something else in your life. But you're bringing a new focus to art."

The reception of Issue III was nauseating. Really. I had to go home because I threw up. I spent the rest of the day in bed pretending to my mom and very revolted sisters that I had a stomach virus, when in truth I was sickened by betrayal.

Nobody had commented that the issue was different. They were all like, "Oh em gee, it *was* Luke Weston!" And, "Luke and I have always been close." And, "Yeah, he's super cool."

He didn't show up to English class, which disappointed a bunch of my classmates who were wondering before the bell whether it'd be weird to ask him for an autograph. BradLee lectured. I was feeling bad by this point. I kept plucking at the collar of my shirt, imagining that its friction against my neck was the cause of my burgeoning nausea.

"It's interesting to consider certain elements of Ezra Pound's life as you read the *Cantos*," said BradLee. "He was an anti-Semite. He supported the Nazis in World War II. He was shut up in a mental asylum for thirteen years."

I wiped sweat off my forehead—why did no one else seem warm?—and tried to listen.

"By the time Germany surrendered in 1945, he'd been indicted for treason and imprisoned in an American military compound in Italy. He told a reporter that Mussolini was an 'imperfect character who lost his head.' And that Hitler was like Joan of Arc, 'a saint.' He thought Hitler was the savior of his people."

It was easy to tell who was paying attention, because they were all gasping.

Cynthia Soso raised her hand. "So why are we reading him?"

Miles Quince jumped in. "Ezra Pound called Hitler a *saint*?"

"We've read the *Cantos*. It's obvious the guy is crazy," said Vivian Hill. She got a laugh, which irritated me. "We already *know* that." She was milking her dumb joke, and it worked. The class sniggered again. "But I didn't know he was some *fascist*."

Everyone was nodding. I felt like defending Pound, but I didn't know why.

"He's controversial," said BradLee. "Lots of people would say I shouldn't be teaching him in a high school English class."

"But that doesn't have anything to do with his poetry," I said. I could hear the tremor in my voice. Dang, I hated when that happened. There was no non-lame explanation: either I was nervous, or I cared too much about what I saying.

But maybe it was the nausea, I thought. Because I didn't feel nervous. And I didn't even *know* what I was saying.

"Could be true, Ethan. Class, what's the big question we're dealing with here?"

A few people tried, but they were off the mark. They didn't get big enough. They were like, "Should we read fascist poetry?"

I propped my right elbow on the palm of my left hand and flopped my arm into the air. "How much an artist's life should affect our interpretation of his work," I said flatly.

"Perfect. Life versus art."

While BradLee scribbled that on the board, Elizabeth caught my eye. "Are you okay?" she mouthed. I shook my head.

"Should it matter that Pound was treasonous?" continued BradLee. "Should it matter that he betrayed his country for a cause that was categorically wrong? Is it possible to read his work without our knowledge of his beliefs coloring our reading? Should we even try?"

The room was spinning around me. I put my head down on my desk.

"Mr. Lee?" I heard Jackson say. "You know Ethan?"

"I do," said BradLee. The words sounded as if they were coming from very far away.

"I've deduced he's sick."

Then I just had to keep my mouth shut and hold very still.

I was done thinking about Pound. All I could think was *please please please don't hurl not now not in front of Maura stop stop stop stop.* . . . Then I sprinted.

I made it to the trash can in the hallway. It was the best thing that happened all day.

CHAPTER THIRTEEN

Perhaps this show's misunderstood.
Folks, contemplate the Greater Good.
The national publicity
That's earned by FAS and kTV
Will foster art for all to see.
                    — THE CONTRACANTOS

I kept barfing, so I skipped school the next day. The most productive thing I did was watch the latest episode of *For Art's Sake*. Probably not the best remedy for nausea.

"Is that Luke?" said my mom, coming into the living room with a hot-water bottle. "Put this on your stomach, honey. Why, it *is* Luke." She sat down by my feet. "Jonathan! Girls! Luke's on kTV!"

"I'd rather finish the crossword," my dad, a smart man, called from the kitchen. The triplets tumbled in wearing their footie pajamas.

"LUKE!" they screamed when they saw him on the screen. He was wearing dark jeans and a black T-shirt, and he looked

168

solemn and artsy until he grinned at the applause from the studio audience. Then he looked like my friend.

"Why is Luke on TV?" said Olivia.

"Why *is* he on TV?" my mom asked me.

"Shh," I said. "She'll explain."

The image had returned to Trisha, who was beaming at Luke as if he were the fruit of her loins. "It's always a great joy to discover a new talent. It's like finding a violet that has blossomed in a landfill."

"She's pretty," said Lila.

"She's evil," I said.

"Like the wild things?" said Tabby. Tabby is a big fan of *Where the Wild Things Are*. She was Max in his wolf suit for Halloween last year, at least until she got sent home from nursery school for starting a wild rumpus.

"I am so pleased to present *For Art's Sake*'s newest contestant: Luke Weston!"

Luke waved.

"Tell us a little about yourself," said Damien.

"I've always loved writing. I think it's amazing that mere scratches on a page can signify emotions, characters, ideas. That's why I decided to write and publish a poem about Selwyn. Just for fun, of course: I had no idea that it would land me on *For Art's Sake!*"

"And we'll be hearing new installments of this poem every week," said Trisha. "We've got only a few episodes left before the live finale, when we'll crown America's Best Teen Artist."

The scene moved to other contestants, bitching about how Luke got to jump in two-thirds of the way through the season.

169

"I wanna see Luke," whined Lila.

"He'll be back," said my mom, mesmerized. "Oh! Goodness! Girls! Close your eyes!"

I closed my eyes too. Maura and Josh were making out. You don't want kisses to be that up-close and personal unless you're on the receiving end.

But I had to squint my eyes open when I heard her voice, somewhat muffled. "Hey. We have to talk, Josh."

"Uh-huh," said Josh. Was he biting her neck? Holy bejeezus, he was nibbling at her neck as if it were a giant pale hot dog. I couldn't watch this in the same room as my mother.

"Now," said Maura.

"Yeah, yeah. Mmm."

"We're over, Josh."

"*Over?*" said Josh, pulling away with a squelch. "What are you talking about?"

"I can't do this anymore."

"Maura—"

"I'm too stressed for a relationship right now."

The image suddenly cut away. "Lukie!" cried the girls. Maura was sitting on his desk in a library writing pod. They were smiling at each other.

"She's pretty too," Olivia said.

"Is she evil?" asked Tabitha.

Back to Maura and Josh. "I just don't have the time."

Now she was sharing Luke's chair. They were both laughing at something he'd written.

Back to her and Josh. "And I don't have, like, the mental capacity? I've got to focus on dance and the show. *Not* on guys."

Back to Luke. "Sorry about you and Josh," he said.

"No big deal. We weren't right for each other."

"That," said Luke, "was obvious." They shared a meaningful look.

"He's pretty too," said Olivia.

Tabby looked at me. "Don't ask," I told her.

The show went to commercials.

"Well!" said my mom with a little shake. "I didn't realize this was quite so—sensational. Girls! Bedtime!" But she didn't move to herd them, and they pretended not to hear, and we all stayed in the living room and watched the show.

It was when Luke read a new section of his poem that I curled into the fetal position, where I remained all weekend. I avoided Jackson and Elizabeth. They said they were going to visit, but I made some oblique references to projectile vomiting to scare them off.

Lunch that Monday was the first time I'd seen them since the baneful Thursday of *Contracantos* III. They double-teamed me.

"Here's what we've decided, Ethan," said Elizabeth. "We have to do something."

"Yeah, that's what Luke said," I said wearily. I shoved my lunch bag farther away from me. I was still in that phase when you wonder why people eat food, anyway. "That's why we published the *Contracantos*. I don't want to do something. It'll probably backfire."

"Are you still sick?" she said. "This is not the Ethan I know."

She was just being nice. The Ethan she knew was just as spineless and depressive.

"He's not eating," Jackson told her.

"You wouldn't be eating either, if you knew what I've seen food become over the last four days."

"Anyone who can make vomit jokes is not sick," said Elizabeth firmly. She dumped my lunch on the table. "Eat. And listen."

I ate a corner of my PB&J. It wasn't bad. "Owamlihsin."

"I didn't tell you to talk. Or whatever that was."

I separated my tongue from my palate with some difficulty. "Now I'm listening."

"Plans, Jackson," said Elizabeth, all but snapping her fingers.

He got out his phone and started punching buttons.

"You guys have *plans*? What is this, a war mission?"

"Shut up and eat."

I took another bite.

"We don't have plans," said Jackson, holding the screen a few inches from his nose. "We have a list of things we're going to do."

"That's called a plan."

"Ethan Andrewhatever," said Elizabeth, "if I have to tell you to be quiet one more time, I'm . . . um. . . ."

"Threaten on," I said.

She grabbed my lunch bag.

"Hey!"

She looked inside. "Jackpot."

"Huh?" said Jackson.

"*Pot,* not son," said Elizabeth. "Except not pot. Better. I've got cookies."

"I'll stick to the sandwich. You can have those," I told her.

"Wait, really? Ethan, you're so nice."

"I know."

I didn't mention that the triplets had just discovered baking. I've seen the amount of spoon-licking they do. You'd have to list saliva as an ingredient, right up there with the brown sugar.

"I've been craving homemade cookies."

I decided not to inform her that Tabitha cracked eggs by holding them in her fist over the bowl and squeezing.

"Number one," said Jackson. "Get into Coluber's office."

"What?!" I yelped. I looked around nervously, not that anyone would bother eavesdropping on us. "Not this again."

"We have to. You remember that day I hacked into Brad-Lee's computer?"

"Of course." I wasn't senile.

"Remember how I said he'd set up a VPN-blocking agent?"

"Uh, sure." Okay, maybe I *was* senile. Technologically.

"Assuming that's the last barrier of encryption, his office computer may allow me to access his network files. I'm even more excited about the paper files, though. I wouldn't be surprised if he's savvy to the threat of hackers and/or subpoenas, and keeps anything incriminating in hard copy so it can be thoroughly destroyed."

"Why do you want to access his files?"

Elizabeth interrupted. "Ethan, I know you're touched in the head, but pretend you're smart. Briefly. It's all I ask. Jackson and I, we're like ninety percent sure he's getting money under the table from kTV."

"You have no proof of that."

"Exactly. That's why we're breaking into his office."

"But—" I ate a grape instead.

"Can we move on?"

"Just to tell you, my silence does not imply agreement. Nor that I'm going to help you with this cockamamie shit."

"We'll infer anything we like," said Elizabeth. "Son of Jack, go on. Number two."

"We're going to figure out why BradLee is Coluber's mole," said Jackson. "Then we shall either help him or destroy him."

"This isn't a video game," I said.

"Okay, not actually destroy."

"Why would we help him?"

"We like him."

"What if he's dating Trisha Meier?"

"Then he really needs help."

Maybe it was that I hadn't eaten anything solid for four days, but I had trouble formulating the questions I knew I should be asking.

Elizabeth came to the rescue. "He's the one who told Coluber about all of this. He's a pawn. But why? He's smart. So he's either secretly evil—"

"—in which case we destroy him—" inserted Jackson.

"—or Coluber has some hold over him."

"Blackmail?" I said.

"You've caught on. Congratulations."

"This is crazy. What if Coluber just wanted kTV at Selwyn for free publicity?"

"Right. Because he's so selfless and devoted."

"What if dumb old BradLee just thought we all *wanted* Luke on the show?"

"I thought you were obsessed with tricolons. Doesn't it bother you that we're stuck in the middle of one right now?"

Damn, she knew me well. I'd had that nagging sense of unease, like when you jump ahead on the page and you have to remember to read the paragraph you skipped.

"Number three," said Elizabeth. "The third thing we have to do is—"

"Luke," said Jackson.

"I am not doing Luke."

"Your juvenility is rank," said Elizabeth, but Jackson smirked and I felt validated. "We have to do something *about* Luke."

"Which is?"

They looked at each other. Jackson put his phone down. Elizabeth stuffed her dreadlocks into a gigantic ponytail.

"Which is?" I prompted again. They looked like I felt: uncertain and tired. Sad.

"We're in disagreement," said Elizabeth.

"Frankly, I'm angry," said Jackson. "I want to mess with him. I want to make him look like an idiot on-screen."

"I just don't know whether he should be blamed for all of this." Elizabeth shrugged.

"Of course he should be blamed," said Jackson.

I sympathized with both of them. Was he the villain or the

victim? I was angry enough to contemplate acts of violence that my skinny ass would never be capable of doing, but I also wanted to believe that it wasn't his fault. Because that was the only way we'd get him back.

"Problem is," said Jackson, "kTV's going to edit out anything that's not marketable."

"Right."

"But there are five episodes left. So we've got time. I bet I can get into their editing software if I read up on it. We could make him look like the asshat he is."

"We haven't even decided whether we're going to screw with him," said Elizabeth.

"Yes we have," Jackson mouthed at me.

"We. Need. More. Information."

"We're agreed on *that* count. We're learning everything about Snakeman and Avogadro."

"Jackson," said Elizabeth impatiently, "we discussed this. We're *not* doing code names."

"Avogadro?" I said.

"Because BradLee's the mole," Jackson explained, looking pleased with himself. "Ignore her. She'll come around."

Elizabeth folded a funnel into my lunch bag and tilted it to her mouth for the last of the cookie crumbs. "I draw the line at such nerdiness," she said, emerging.

"Hold still," I said. I brushed the crumbs off her cheeks.

"Did that just happen?" said Jackson. "Ethan? Seriously? That was *Elizabeth* you just voluntarily touched. *Elizabeth.*"

"I *am* a tangible being," she told him waspishly. The cheeks that I'd been touching three seconds ago were now the exact shade of her hot pink tank top. So were mine, I'm sure.

"Give me a second to wipe my memory card of that incident," said Jackson, fingers to his forehead, eyes closed. I glanced over at her. She was wearing overalls. Her shoulders had this endearing knobbly look, but her skin was as creamy as the flesh of a tree, its bark just peeled. She refused to look at me.

"Done," said Jackson. "Phew. Whatever just happened, I have the vague sense that it was highly disturbing. Anyway. Let's hatch a plan."

I leaned toward my friends. This was making me kind of excited. I know what you're thinking: I was being swept up again, just like when we published the *Contracantos*. I'd renounced "doing something," but that had lasted about four days.

But what can I say? I'm susceptible to a well-turned tricolon.

"Can I sit here?" said Elizabeth before English, gesturing toward Luke's abandoned chair. Now he sat across the room next to Maura.

"But what will your normal friends do without you?" I said. "Who will laugh at their normal jokes? Who will pass them normal notes?"

"Your absence will screw up their normal distribution," said Jackson.

"Ba-dum-*ching*!" I said, even though I only get like one per-cent of statistics jokes. (Ba-dum-*ching*.) Before she sat down, she gave us both the finger.

Our plan's name came to us that very class.

"You remember that Pound was an early proponent of Imagism," said BradLee. In Luke's face, not a muscle budged. "Pound moved on. His next movement was called Vorticism. He said, explaining the name, 'The image is a radiant node or cluster; it is a vortex, from which, and through which, and into which, ideas are constantly rushing.'"

VORTEX. I liked it.

"Isn't 'vortex' a Latin word?" I whispered to Jackson.

"Tornado," he said instantly.

"We shall be the tornado of justice," murmured Elizabeth. "The vortex of vengeance."

Across the room, Luke showed his notebook to Maura. She laughed.

Later in that same class, BradLee took us back to the lines I'd analyzed with her.

> *What thou lovest well remains,*
> *the rest is dross*
> *What thou lov'st well shall not be reft from thee*
> *What thou lov'st well is thy true heritage*
> *Whose world, or mine or theirs*
> *or is it of none?*

You know how you'll get obsessed with a song for a month or so? Then you hear it again, years later, and it's a nostalgia *ma-*

chine. You immediately remember what it was like back then, except everything's sodden with the golden goo of memory and looks a lot better than it really was.

Well, that's what happened when I heard those lines of the *Cantos.* All I wanted was to go back. *What thou lovest well remains. . . .* It hadn't remained, I thought. *What thou lov'st well shall not be reft from thee. . . .* That was wrong too. Luke had betrayed us, and it was painful to think of the soaring hope I'd felt when Maura had said, "I don't say these things to anyone else."

Ezra Pound had lied. What I'd loved had been reft from me, and I was bereft, and they were in their own world.

CHAPTER FOURTEEN

I think when I take up my quill,
"If I don't dare—then who else will?"
For what sets For Art's Sake apart
From other shows and other art?
This most of all: it's brave of heart.
                    — THE CONTRACANTOS

We planned VORTEX. "Might as well go tonight," said Elizabeth Friday morning as we drove to school.

"Tonight?" I howled. "I'm not mentally prepared."

"T minus fourteen hours," said Jackson.

Friday night, 9 p.m. The best time to ensure that anyone
and everyone involved with Selwyn would be occupied. They
picked me up in the Appelvan. It was just as dark as it'd been
that morning.

"Welcome to VORTEX," said Jackson. "A man. A plan.
A van."

"I'm the man," I said immediately.

"We're both men," said Jackson.

Based on the snorts and whoops that accompanied her laughter, it was going to take Elizabeth a while to recover. I asked Jackson, "Did you bring him?"

"Against my better judgment."

At the next red light, he handed Baconnaise's travel cage back to me. I took him out and cradled him in my hands. My nervousness instantly receded. Good old Baconnator. "Ready?" I asked him.

"Did your parents notice that you're wearing all black?" said Jackson.

I just laughed. Inside, the triplets were playing Don't Touch the Floor. My mom was a lava monster dozing on the carpet. My dad's back served as the bridge from coffee table to couch. My parents hadn't noticed anything I did for nearly five years now.

"Don't be nervous," I told Baconnaise. "You'll be in my pocket most of the night."

"Is that safe?" said Jackson. "Won't he get squished?"

"Ethan's pants leave plenty of space," said Elizabeth. "He's missing that thing called a thigh."

"But what about the tumor?" said Jackson. "Is he in pain? If you were in pain, would you want to spend the night in someone's pocket?"

"Stop calling it a tumor." I much preferred *benign lump*. "And it doesn't hurt him."

It had been getting bigger, but Baconnaise seemed supremely unconcerned. I was trying to imitate his attitude. Besides, we were at school. VORTEX was upon us.

We skirted the edges of the lot as we headed for the rear

of the school. I glanced back at the van. It was eerily alone, gleaming in dingy pedophiliac glory. I looked at Elizabeth and started to laugh.

"Silence," she said, giggling herself.

There were no shouts or footsteps as we approached the school. "No night watchman," said Jackson reassuringly. "I told you. He would have appeared on the master schedule."

"Good," said Elizabeth. "Alone to wreak our mischief."

"There should be an iron-grate-like thingy somewhere. According to the blueprints . . ." Jackson was pacing aimlessly, staring at his phone.

"Uh, Jackson? We are standing directly in front of an iron-grate-like thingy."

"Oh. Yeah."

This part of VORTEX was a Jacksonian contribution. Trawling Selwyn's blueprints in an idle moment on the admin server, he'd seen something labeled *Dumbwaiter*. It was as narrow as a grandfather clock. "Okay okay okay," he said nervously. "It should just slide up."

He grabbed a bar and heaved. Playing *Sun Tzu's Art of War* doesn't exactly develop one's upper-body strength, so I joined in. Turns out pencil-drawing and gerbil-training don't either. "Milksops," muttered Elizabeth. She squeezed between us. "One, two, three, *shove*."

There was a raspy squeaking noise that at first I thought was coming from Jackson's windpipe, but the grate gave way. It slid up into the wall and we stood on tiptoes, pushing, until we heard it lock into place like a garage door.

Behind it, there was another door.

"This is the true portal," said Jackson.

Elizabeth opened her mouth and then closed it again. One snide comment about the use of the word "portal" in a non-video-game context: suppressed.

Jackson was running his hands over the door with his flashlight in his teeth. "Doesn't seem to have a keyhole," he murmured. "Which is good, since the renovation notes indicated nothing of the sort."

"Why don't you try the obvious method?" said Elizabeth.

Jackson aimed his index finger at the door. *"Alohomora."*

Elizabeth walked up to the door and shouldered it. It gave way. *"That* obvious method."

We peered inside.

"It's tiny," said Elizabeth. It was maybe three feet deep and no wider than the entrance, eighteen inches or so. "It's going to be tough to fit all three of us in here."

"Maybe one of us should go down first," said Jackson.

We looked at each other. Nobody volunteered.

"Guess we'll have to squeeze in," he said.

It was definitely a squeeze. I took Baconnaise from my pocket and held him at my neck to protect him. "Why couldn't they have had the foresight to build this for three full-sized people?" said Elizabeth.

I spit. "Dreadlock in my mouth," I informed her.

"Gross," she said.

"My sentiments exactly."

"It's grosser for me than for you."

"Are you kidding? Your dead protein filaments were in my *mouth.*"

"My hair is coated with your *saliva*."

"Guys," said Jackson. "Squeezing into this thing is not the only item on our agenda."

Elizabeth snapped back to attention. "Does it move?"

"One would presume so, yes." Jackson was snippy, I knew, because he was beginning to think his brilliant plan would be foiled right from the start. If the dumbwaiter didn't move—if it was defunct, if it needed a key, if we couldn't figure it out— then we couldn't get into the school. We'd fail. We'd return to boring, betrayed life.

Jackson was playing his flashlight over the interior walls. "No buttons," he mused.

"It's not an elevator," I said.

"Think, think, think." He had his eyes closed. "Think like ink. Aha! I'm Mr. Ink Cartridge. I can't push buttons."

I always knew Jackson was going to crack one of these days.

"The signal to descend must be shutting the iron grate."

Oh. Shit.

"Oh," said Elizabeth. "Shit."

"Can we shut the door from the inside?" I said.

"I hate to say it," said Jackson, "but it's not very smart for all three of us to imprison ourselves on a Friday night in a dumbwaiter that hasn't been used for thirty years."

I had enjoyed the interlude. It'd been cozy, to be squished between Elizabeth and Jackson, to rub Baconnaise's soft fur against my neck, to wait for something to happen.

"We're going to have to split up," he said.

"I wish there were four of us," said Elizabeth. With three, one would always be alone.

"Get out," I said. "Let's get out so we can talk rationally."

Outside, our collective body warmth quickly dissipated. It was about fourteen degrees.

"Jackson," I said, "you're the only one who'll have a shot at fixing this thing if it breaks. You have to stay out here."

"We could both go," Elizabeth said to me.

I wanted to say yes. There was only one thing that sounded worse than descending alone in an antique dumbwaiter, and that was being stuck alone in an antique dumbwaiter.

"It'll be better if only one of is—is incapacitated," I said.

"Let me go."

"I'm going." I barely recognized my own voice. I never sounded that firm.

"This better not be some retrograde, anti-feminist, male-savior complex," said Elizabeth, but she stepped back.

"I've got Baconnaise. I won't be alone. And I've got my phone." Though I doubted the T-Mobile network covered dumbwaiter rides to hell.

"Send the dumbwaiter up empty if you can," said Jackson hurriedly, "and we'll know that it works. Otherwise, you'll have to let us in by the human back door." According to Jackson's research, that door only opened from the inside.

I stepped into the dumbwaiter. "See you soon," I said, trying to sound breezy.

Jackson was fumbling in his coat pocket. "Here." He gave me a baggie of trail mix. "Provisions. Just in case."

"That's so tactless, Jackson," said Elizabeth. "Though if you *do* get stuck, you could always pull a Donner Party—"

"And what, eat himself?" said Jackson.

"No, eat Baconnaise."

"Eighty calories max. Also lacking vital micronutrients. Not worth it."

They were still debating whether that'd count as cannibalism when I pushed the inner door shut. It was instantly pitch-black. "I'd never eat you," I said into the darkness.

Baconnaise wriggled in response.

I turned on my flashlight, but then I could see what a small cavern I was in. And I thought I should conserve my batteries, just in case. So I turned it off.

I'd been telling myself that it wouldn't be that bad. It was that bad.

1. I couldn't see a *thing*. My poor pupils couldn't find one particle of light. My whole body felt dilated, it was craving light so badly.
2. I couldn't hear anything either. Unless Jackson and Elizabeth were now bickering in sign language, the door was so solid that it blocked every sound.
3. I was suddenly aware that Baconnaise was a gerbil, not a human companion at all. (Just to clarify, that does not mean I was planning to eat him.)

I started to panic. I braced my hands against the walls, just to have something to touch, and I couldn't even feel them. I guess that was a side effect of the panic, but it felt like nothingness, as if I were a consciousness floating in a senseless sea, an out-of-body experience that made me realize how much I liked my body, how much I liked my eyes and my ears and my hands, and I'd never really thought about it before but it was very cool that they could bring the world into my head. I need to spend more time appreciating them, I thought. I would hold a Sense Appreciation Day. And then I thought I might scream.

But I didn't want to scare Baconnaise. I grabbed him and tried not to squeeze too hard—

And that's when he came to me. Ezra Pound came to me.

> *but that a man should live in that further terror,*
> *and live*
> *the loneliness of death came upon me*
> *(at 3 P.M., for an instant)*

I relaxed. It's just death, I thought, but it's *not* death. I could hear my breathing, and I could feel the metal walls with one hand, Baconnaise with the other. And I could see the glinting tabs of my zippers, which must have beguiled what unknowable light there was. I could see.

And there was a crank, the noise of machinery groaning to life, and the dumbwaiter began to move.

CHAPTER FIFTEEN

O kTV! Your dynasty
Lives on as far as we foresee.
All other shows? We sneer at them
And flip the channel to this gem
Each Friday night at 9 p.m.
                              – THE CONTRACANTOS

The trip down was rough. I was very happy that my tongue did not happen to be between my teeth at the moment of impact.

But Baconnaise and I both survived. And as soon as I clicked on the flashlight, I realized that the door had caught at the story above the printing presses, so the dumbwaiter was now open to the subbasement. The printing press seemed like a welcoming friend.

I turned on the lights. After I spent thirty seconds blinking and stumbling about like a wounded bat, I saw a button on the wall by the dumbwaiter. There was just one. I've had misgivings about pressing unlabeled buttons ever since watching a History Channel program about the random hiding spots for nuclear warheads, but I gave it a shove with my thumb. It worked. The dumbwaiter clanked upward.

When the dumbwaiter came down again, Baconnaise and I found ourselves stupidly grinning at an empty chamber. Then I saw Jackson's phone. He'd typed me a message. *Can't make it descend from the inside. Send us keys to real door. Key cabinet to your left.*

A few minutes later, I heard clattering on the stairway. Jackson seemed strung out.

"VORTEX is the Swiss cheese of plans," he said.

"He's been developing this metaphor for a while now," Elizabeth told me grimly.

"Uh, it stinks?"

"It's full of holes."

"Hey, man, cheer up. There was one hole. It's the doughnut of plans."

"Let's get to work." Jackson stalked over to the key cabinet. "Do they realize what a liability it is to have these keys out in public?" He grabbed a bundle, and another.

"We're not in public," said Elizabeth, shuddering a little. The subbasement felt even eerier at night. All that looming machinery made it feel like a mad scientist's laboratory, and I couldn't forget that we were a good forty feet below ground.

Jackson tossed Elizabeth one bundle of keys and stuck one in his pocket. "They've got a complete set in here, the morons."

"The janitors probably use it," I said.

"Duh," said Jackson. I was insulted until I realized he was talking to himself.

"Let's go," said Elizabeth.

We flipped off the lights and followed her up the stairs to the school. It was so shadowed and still that even the familiarity of the building was creepy.

"Here we are," said Jackson. This was where we would split up.

"We could stay together," said Elizabeth.

"We need to minimize our time in here," he said briskly. "Anyone could come back after the episode. There's a lot of kTV people running around with access."

We'd rehearsed all these arguments already. We needed to investigate two places, so we needed to break into two groups.

Elizabeth hesitated. I watched her. I would have barely shaded her high cheekbones, I decided. They were the brightest points of her face, two round summits topping angular mountains. I'd have thoroughly cross-hatched the shadows beneath her eyes. "Fine," she said. "Text if you'll be more than an hour."

"See you then."

Jackson began to spin away, but I grabbed him. I'd intended to hug him, but he was Jackson, and I was me, so instead I awkwardly slapped his shoulder.

"Waste of time," he muttered, but I noticed that he patted me back.

"Do you want Baconnaise?"

He considered it, which I took as a sign that he was more nervous than he was pretending. "Keep him."

Elizabeth real-hugged him. "Go," she whispered.

Resolutely, Jackson turned. Elizabeth and I went down the opposite hallway.

Jackson was heading for the art studio that had been taken over by the kTV production team. After school yesterday I'd chatted up Thomas, my cameraman pal, and in a fit of boredom he'd told me a lot about their editing software. I'd put my cell phone in my front shirt pocket, recording. After Jackson finished mocking me for my dumb questions, he'd said that he thought he could hack into their editing program from afar. But first, he'd need to familiarize himself with the real apparatus in their lab.

Meanwhile, Elizabeth and I would search the papers. Need you ask where?

In the Snake's lair. In Coluber's office.

Our goal was to find something incriminating. Something that proved Coluber was profiting from *For Art's Sake,* either as a kickback from kTV or because he was skimming off the top of what Selwyn got. Of course, Elizabeth and I couldn't do much hacking. I kid: we couldn't do any hacking. "It doesn't matter," Jackson kept saying. "He'd never store felonious files on his school computer's hard drive. We won't waste our time."

So instead, we were kicking it old-school, searching his files in the grand tradition of Mrs. Basil E. Frankweiler. We'd take photos of anything interesting so we could analyze it later. Jackson called this real-life hacking. I called it breaking and entering, but somehow, I still found myself outside his office, watching Elizabeth jiggle a key in the lock.

"Shh," I said as she gave a *pfft* of frustration.

"Don't you *shh* me."

"Stop making noise then."

"It fits. I can tell it fits. It's just not turning."

"It has to work. Jackson said it would work."

"Ooh, and whatever Jackson says is—oh." The tumblers fell into place, smooth metal sliding against smooth metal. I could almost feel the rightness as the key finally turned.

"Wait, wait," I said, fumbling in my pocket for the supplies Jackson had handed me.

"I don't want Baconnaise—" she hissed.

"No, he rides in the other—here they are." I handed her a pair of latex gloves and put another pair on myself.

"Thanks." She opened the door. We stepped in. Before she turned on the lights, she closed the door again and locked it.

"At least we'll have some warning if someone comes."

The very idea made me shiver. "It's Friday night," I said. That had been our nervous mantra all week. Nobody would ever show up at the school on a Friday night.

I watched Elizabeth as she began to open drawers. After a minute she jerked her head at me. "Why are we here again?"

"What?"

"We're looking for files, Ethan."

"Right."

I'd used up all my guts on that dumbwaiter descent. If I'd been alone, I'd probably have curled up and rolled under Coluber's desk like a frightened pill bug. I opened a file drawer and looked at the stacks of papers. I had no idea what I was doing.

Elizabeth said, "Budget items, kTV items . . ."

We'd been over this. I had no excuse. I thumbed through the dry, sharp manila folders.

"I got a paper cut! It tore right through the glove! My pinkie is bleeding!"

"Yeah, so's my heart. Don't you get DNA on those files."

"I'm in *pain*."

"Why don't I just halt our mission and find you a Band-Aid. You take pictures of these documents." She spread them over the expanse of Coluber's desk.

"You found something?"

"I found something that could be something. Here's my camera. Will your wound prevent you from pushing the button?"

"I'll manage."

The documents were too mathy to understand. And the few bits of English were words like "deduction" and "voluntary withholding," which might as well be math.

"Finished." I gathered the papers back into the file. "Uh, Elizabeth?"

She was hunched over the file cabinet. I couldn't see what she was doing. She grunted.

"Did you ever find that Band-Aid?"

"Shit, Ethan, you made me slip. No, I'm not finding you a frigging Band-Aid. *This* is what I'm doing." She brandished an untwisted paper clip in my face. I thought she was threatening to de-eye me until I realized she was using it to pick the lock of the file cabinet.

"Wow, you know how to pick locks?" Flattery is useful in such moments. Plus, I was actually impressed.

"My babysitter taught me when I was like six. Though I admit file cabinet drawers are the extent of my ability."

"I'm amazed."

"Laying it on a bit thick, aren't you?" But even from behind her, I could tell she was smiling. Her cheekbone was higher than usual, protruding from her mass of hair just enough that I could see its rise.

"Not at all. I'm truly dumbfounded."

"Dumb, maybe. Ah!" The drawer slid open.

"I thought people used hairpins."

"Hairpins are ideal, but who carries around hairpins anymore?"

How was I supposed to know the state of the American hairpin? How else did girls keep their hair out of their faces? I looked at the back of Elizabeth's head as she thumbed through the files. I'd never really looked at dreadlocks before. I'd always considered them one of those things it's rude to stare at, like a scar or a massive suppurating zit. But she was turned away and so I stared, and I realized that I liked dreadlocks. I'd thought I liked shiny, controlled hair, like Maura's high bun, smooth enough that if there hadn't been a color change you might have thought she was bald. (Well, bald with a large knob growing out of her crown.)

But dreadlocks were pretty. They were pretty in the way of things that weren't supposed to be pretty: not pretty like a sunset, but pretty like undergrowth, like an English muffin, like the mottled surface of an old car's bumper. And when she had them gathered into a ponytail, as she did now, they had this frightening power. The band was stretched around them just once, and they looked like they were threatening to burst it, thick and heavy like a roiling pot of cheese. She had a few beads stuck into them at points. And although Elizabeth was half black, her hair wasn't all dark. There were different shades of brown, and some of gold.

"What are you doing?" she said without turning around.

Falling in love with your dreadlocks, I'd have said if I were honest.

Why did I have this tendency to stare and stare and then to fall in love?

"This is definitely kTV related."

It wasn't because I was into art. I spend a lot of time staring at Herbert, but I haven't started crushing on him. (Not yet, anyway.)

"Hand me my camera, would you?"

It was so hard to rip my eyes from her hair that I expected a Velcro noise when I did. I found her camera. She accepted it over her shoulder, still combing through the file.

That was how the trouble with Maura had started. We'd been in the same Algebra II class freshman year. She'd sat in front of me. I'd stared at her neck, and once I memorized it, I no longer knew what life meant when I didn't stare at her neck.

Necks are highly underappreciated body parts, I decided, finding Elizabeth's underneath the mantle of dreadlocks. They were the connection between mind and body, the symbol of this strange combination of physicality and soul that makes us human. Ugh, I thought. Here I go again. Whenever I'm under stress, I have these pseudo-philosophical daydreams. It's a huge liability. During the PSAT I got so worried about free will that I skipped half the math section just to prove I wasn't a robot. (And also because I suck at geometry.) You'd think that natural selection would have eliminated that trait long ago. There was probably only one philosophical Neanderthal who didn't get crunched by a woolly mammoth, and that guy was my ancestor—

"Ethan! Earth to Ethan!"

"Oh, hi, yeah." I riffled some papers. "Just engrossed in the files. What's up?"

"Can you make any sense of—"

We looked at each other.

We looked at the door.

Footsteps.

Not Jackson's footsteps. Jackson went to Indian camp as a kid and he says he can walk, and I quote, "like a deer through the forest." These were heavy, hurried footsteps.

"Cat-piss," Elizabeth mouthed.

CHAPTER SIXTEEN

They came here from the land of sun,
Where all is light and sand and fun,
And granted to our dismal state,
By some amazing twist of fate,
This newfound fame! And gosh, it's great!
                                    — THE CONTRACANTOS

I was paralyzed.

Elizabeth wasn't. She stuffed the folders back in the drawer and eased it shut. I was all set to dive under the desk, but Elizabeth climbed on top of it.

She hissed at me. I followed. She clambered on top of the armoire. I followed.

The footsteps were getting louder. Sure, they might have been going to another office. But were we going to risk that? I was shot through with adrenaline. Elizabeth pushed a ceiling tile aside and scrambled up. From inside, she held the hole open for me. I'm a klutz but fear made me graceful, or at least quick. I even remembered not to squish Baconnaise in my pocket.

We'd made it out of the office. There wasn't much vertical space between the ceiling and the next story's floor, but there was enough to sit up straight.

"Stay on the strut," she breathed. She'd rotated to face me. Still holding the tile aloft, she motioned down and I saw how the ceiling worked. There were parallel beams every five feet or so. We were both on one now, and it easily held our weight. Bridging these struts were thin metal channels that supported the lightweight fiberboard tiles. You wouldn't want to put your weight on those.

She looked at me questioningly, and I nodded back. She let the fiberboard fall. It settled almost soundlessly, betraying its flimsiness. For the second time that evening, I was plunged into blackness.

But it wasn't truly dark this time. We'd left the office light on, and the ceiling was perforated with tiny holes. My eyes adjusted quickly and I could see her moving away from me.

"Come on," she whispered. We could hear somebody fumbling with the lock. She was scooting backward along the strut, straddling it with her legs straight as if frozen in a gymnastic vault. I followed her. She was right: it would be much better if we weren't directly above Coluber's office. Particularly if our visitor, still waggling the key in that blessedly uncooperative lock, was Coluber. I sure hoped Elizabeth had stuffed her camera in her pocket.

The door opened. We froze. We'd moved about eight feet down by then, and I was very close to her, facing her. We weren't quite touching, but if I'd leaned forward, I could have put my nose to hers.

She looked into my eyes. We could hear someone breathing underneath. The noise traveled straight up. The sounds were so distinctive that I could imagine exactly what he was doing: picking up folders, flicking through papers, heaving open drawers, ruffling through files.

Unfortunately, if sound traveled so easily up through the ceiling, it'd travel down as well. I knew I couldn't move, even to bend my cramping legs or dislodge my slight wedgie. What I wanted most in the world was to remain undiscovered, sure. But coming in a close second was the urge to take off those blasted gloves and wipe my hands. They were disgusting. The gloves had been shoved half off, and the dust from the beam had combined with my copious palm sweat to make a sort of paste.

But I tried to hold still, relax, listen. The visitor was look- ing for something, I thought. Some specific item. He was moving quickly. Every so often he'd let out a hum or sigh of exasperation. Then he paused. He said, "Aha." He opened the office door—

—when I made the mistake of looking at Elizabeth.

Her eyes were bugged out. Her mouth was full of air, clamped shut. She was grasping the strut with both hands, and she was on the verge of a cataclysmic giggling fit.

I clapped my hand over her mouth, dust be damned. This was no time for delicacies. I mustered the most threatening look in my repertoire. I'd been there, plunging through space and hurtling toward the giggles. It was a free fall. Everything depended on my face. A look of sympathy and she'd hit bottom. A mugging expression, a lifted eyebrow, and she'd hit bottom sooner. And all would be lost.

Down below, he'd opened the door and flipped off the light, but now he halted. He must have been standing on the threshold. It was the light, I thought. When he turned it off, he'd remembered that he hadn't turned it on.

My eyes adjusted to the new darkness. I stared into the distance, trying to look angry. This is not funny, I repeated to myself as if I could beam her the thought. This is not funny.

Of course, it *was* funny. In fact, it was knee-slapping, side-splitting, aisle-rolling, ass-off hilarious. I could feel a tiny muscle in my cheek begin to twitch.

I could not allow that to happen.

And he shut the door.

We heard the tumblers fall into place and we heard his footsteps recede down the hallway, and soon, we heard nothing at all.

I took my hand off her mouth. I expected a deluge, but instead she let out a long, shaky breath. She looked surprised too. The fit had passed like a storm.

"*Sky's clear,*" I said.

"*Night's sea,*" she said, and I looked at her—*shone from the unmasked eyes in half-mask's space*—and I thought how she'd quoted Pound right back at me, and how her eyes did look like a night's sea in the half gloom of the crawl space. The darkness was sapping the world of color, and I thought that dark eyes look better than light ones in the night, because they become a deep gray, full of tides and pools and waves. Those eyes met mine. I was going to kiss her. I cupped my hand to her chin again, and she tilted her face slightly upward, and—

CAT-PISS AND PORCUPINES.

PISS OF WELL-HYDRATED FELINES, PORKIEST PINIEST PORCUPINES.

WHY DOES THIS ALWAYS HAPPEN TO ME.

I'd lost my balance.

And one of my legs had crashed through the fiberboard ceiling.

Thankfully, Baconnaise was in the other pocket. He stuck his head out to investigate the sudden motion.

I had grabbed the strut with both hands and wasn't falling any farther, but there was no way to take this back. "No backsies," as Lila would say after she'd swindled me in a trade. And the earlier discomfort was nothing compared to this: one leg desperately pretzeled around a strut, the other dangling down into an office. Not Coluber's—we'd moved too far. Whatever office was next door. The fiberboard was cutting into my leg and I was clutching the strut with both sweaty hands and my face was very near the dusty beam and Elizabeth—

You know that giggling fit that I'd thought wasn't going to happen?

It happened.

But I will say that Elizabeth, despite needing frequent breaks to wipe away tears of laughter, eventually helped me out. First she found her flashlight to inspect the scene of the accident.

"Is Baconnaise okay?" she said.

"I'm the one you should be worrying about."

"Can't you pull yourself up?"

201

"Does it"—pant—"look like I can pull myself up?"

"Hold still."

I held still. I grimaced. I wish I could say I was feeling pain and humiliation in equal measures, but I was definitely more humiliated, even with the rough tile scraping my leg and my muscle-cramping, tendon-stretching position. To distract myself, I reviewed that third thought.

Why does this always happen to me.

There is no question mark, because that's not a question. It's a wail. I don't want to suggest that I'd already destroyed ceilings in pursuit of kisses, but I do submit two incidents:

1. Fifth grade. Chasing Laurel Roberts across the monkey bars. It'd just rained and the bars were slippery and she fell, so I fell after her. We each broke an ulna. There was no romantic tryst in the emergency room. She never let me chase her again.

2. Eighth grade. Playing Seven Minutes in Heaven at one of those experimental middle school parties. I was in the closet with Mischa Bettelheim, and as I leaned toward her I bumped a mop. It conked her on the head. Heaven turned into a purgatory or perhaps even a hell.

But, I thought, at least now I have a tricolon of botched romance. What rhetorical flair. Plus, I figured that this would have to be the last one.

Meanwhile, Elizabeth braced her legs against the strut and grabbed me at the armpits.

"Ready?"

She tugged. With difficulty, and pain, I extracted my leg and collapsed. Now the beam was what I wanted to kiss. Firm land! The joy!

"Andrezejczak," she said. She began to giggle again.

"Don't talk to me," I groaned.

Still laughing, she pulled up the destroyed tile, shone the flashlight down, shrugged, and lowered herself by the beam.

"Big clear desk below the hole," she called up to me. "Even you should make it okay."

I didn't have much of a choice. The crawl space had not been kind to me, and I wanted to leave it behind. She flipped on the overhead light just as I gingerly lowered myself onto the desk. The mauled fiberboard settled into place.

We looked around. Two things struck us immediately.

The office was blanketed with bits of ceiling, sprinkled like pixie dust from on high.

And the office belonged to Willis Wolfe, Principal, Selwyn Academy.

It wasn't hard to tell. Framed photographs, hundreds of them, covered all available wall space, waist level to ceiling. They featured Willis Wolfe smiling his toothy smile with Beyoncé, with George Bush I, with other people too shiny not to be famous.

"He's an egomaniac," I said.

Elizabeth was perched on the edge of the desk, still letting out intermittent spurts of laughter. I tried to distract her.

"Well, Baconnaise is doing fine." I had him on my palm. Even he seemed to be regarding me with a smirk. "We have to meet Jackson in twenty minutes. And we need to repair, um, the accident."

She looked in the closet. "Ha. I knew Willis Wolfe would have one of these." She'd found a miniature vacuum cleaner.

"Yeah, he's a bit OCD, isn't he?"

"Could explain the whiteness of his teeth." She began Dirt-Deviling. "Don't just stand there. Do something. The outline of your leg is immortalized in the ceiling."

I inspected the hole. "Uh, Elizabeth? Do you see any, like, tubs of wet plaster?"

"No, Ethan. Would Scotch tape do?" She was being sarcastic, but it gave me an idea.

"Actually . . ."

I grabbed the tape, pinched some computer paper from the printer, and climbed on top of the desk. I couldn't quite reach. So I heaved the swivel chair up first, but I couldn't bring myself to climb onto it. One mortifying fall per night was my limit.

"Uh, Elizabeth? Want to hold the chair?"

She rolled her eyes, hard, but she held the chair, and even took over tape-tearing responsibilities. Then I saw it.

"Holy crap."

"Are you referring to the ceiling? Because I'd call that a crappy hole."

"Too soon. And seriously, Elizabeth, look."

She must have heard the urgency in my voice, because she clambered up on the desk and looked at the photograph. It was high on the wall.

"Holy crap indeed," she said.

Willis Wolfe is freakishly timeless, but you could tell this picture was fifteen or twenty years old just by the mottled quality of the light. On the other side of the photograph was a guy whom I immediately recognized as Coluber. He looked like himself with more hair.

In between them stood a little kid, ten or eleven years old. Chubby. Familiar. Red-blond hair. I had no doubts, and neither did Elizabeth.

"It's BradLee," she whispered.

"It has to be."

"Look at that baby face." BradLee was essentially unchanged from his ten-year-old self. It was as if a fifth grader had grown stubble.

Elizabeth started snapping photographs of the photograph. "Meta," I told her.

"We need to show Jackson. We might not be able to get into this room"—she glanced at the hole in the ceiling, half-covered with flapping computer paper—"the proper way."

"No wonder he spies for Coluber," I said. "He's known him for years."

"He lied."

How many times had BradLee told us he had no link to the school? How many times had he joked that he'd chosen Minnesota with a dartboard?

"Let's get out of here," I said. The bald-faced lying was creeping me out.

"That looks like a kindergarten art project. Finish first."

I did a crummy job on the rest of the hole and clambered down. "Not bad," said Elizabeth. "I wouldn't have even tried."

The patch was approximately the same color as the ceiling tiles, but the join was obvious if you were looking for it. I climbed back up, rubbed my hands on my shirt, and transferred some dust onto the paper so it wouldn't shine as much.

"Getting perfectionistic, are we," muttered Elizabeth.

Too bad the dust would waft down over the next few days. Probably right onto Willis Wolfe's gleaming blond hair. Or onto the hair of anybody who was in here having a clandestine meeting. Like BradLee.

"Tell me there's a way out that doesn't involve going back into that ceiling," I said.

"You don't want to go back up there?" she said innocently. She tested the office door, and it opened. Thank goodness. She clicked the lock on the inside of the knob and flipped the lights off. We were out in the hallway.

"I hope Coluber actually left," murmured Elizabeth. I was thinking the same thing. In the ensuing brouhaha, I'd almost forgotten why we'd had to hide in the ceiling in the first place. Now, alone in the hall, the darkness encroaching, I was suddenly scared. Was he still around? Had he suspected something? Was he lying in wait to trap us?

Then we heard footsteps. Loud. Hurrying. In mutual terror, Elizabeth and I clutched each other. We couldn't move. We didn't even try to get away.

This all lasted about a second. Because then the footsteps turned the corner and we saw Jackson.

"Fricking deer in a fricking forest my ass," said Elizabeth very quickly.

"I didn't anticipate a reason to be quiet."

"You caught us at a bad time," she said.

"I can see that."

We dropped each other as if we'd been transmogrified into hot potatoes. "Not like that," said Elizabeth scornfully. She gave Jackson a brief recap while I tried to rewind to the moment I'd been too scared to appreciate at the time: what it felt like to hold Elizabeth in my arms, to be held in hers. I'd brushed a chunk of dreadlocks. They were surprisingly soft. That's all I could remember.

CHAPTER SEVENTEEN

We never knew how life would shine,
How sweet it'd be to ride cloud nine.
Now FAS has blessed us with its presence,
A king descending on the peasants,
Regaling us with grace and presents.
— THE CONTRACANTOS

You pretty much have to go to Dinkytown if you want to go anywhere after eleven in Minneapolis, so we went to Annie's Parlour. We nabbed a corner booth and watched trashed U students inhale greasy food. I had a chocolate-banana malt. Jackson got a half order of fries. Neither one of us could finish. Elizabeth had claimed she wasn't hungry, but she polished off both orders by dipping the French fries into the malt.

Girls are so weird.

The waiters were too busy to notice, so I let Baconnaise hang out on an empty plate. He had a French fry as a personal salt lick and seemed very pleased with life. Meanwhile, we shared the results of our investigation.

REPORT FROM ELIZABETH (abridged): "We photographed Coluber's financial documents. Ethan fell through the ceiling. [Here I redact their mocking repartee. It went on for ages. I sucked industriously at my malt and did my best to ignore them.] BradLee has known Coluber and Willis Wolfe since he was about ten. And Ethan is a wizard with Scotch tape."

REPORT FROM ETHAN (unabridged): "What she said."

REPORT FROM JACKSON (reported as I heard it—i.e., as gibberish): "I found the external drive that stores the RAM terabits of the X-Pro Lotus footage, but unfortunately, given their inaccessible plaintext software, it'd be difficult for an adversary to access the data even from the room itself much less from a cold-boot non-authenticated elsewhere locale."

"Explain that in regular-person language," said Elizabeth.

"Sure. A basic port scan revealed—"

She cut him off. "You are so irregular you don't even know what regular is. Skip the details. You can't get into the footage from afar, correct?"

"Correct."

"Damn."

"Indeed."

"There goes that idea."

"It wasn't really an idea," I pointed out.

"It was the seedling of an idea," Jackson said.

"An idea-fetus," I said.

"More like an idea-embryo."

"An idea-zygote."

"True. Just diploids."

"Does that have anything to do with dipshits?" That was a

disgusted Elizabeth. Jackson and I grinned at each other. And I missed Luke with a sudden pang that hit me right in the gut.

Though maybe that was just the load of chocolate-banana malt.

Jackson started perusing the images on Elizabeth's camera, using the arrows and the zoom with the deftness of someone who's devoted years of his life to video games. Elizabeth and I picked at fries, and watched the college kids stumble and guffaw, and said things when there was something to say.

"Did VORTEX even do anything?" she said at one point.

I hadn't let myself ask that, yet.

"We don't know anything more than we used to."

"Yeah we do."

"Nothing useful."

Then Jackson lifted his head. With a glassy stare at a guy with pumped-up pecs and a Sigma Pi shirt, he said, "Idiot!"

"He may not be terribly smart," I said in a quiet rush, "but you shouldn't antagonize that type, Jackson."

"I'm an *idiot*!" he said with the same intonation, still gazing at the frat-ass. "He encrypts the bite-protocol VWD with app-safe Norton anti-RAM Intel Duo PGP public key!"

Or something like that.

Jackson's eyes refocused. He saw us staring at him. "I can get into Coluber's files now."

"What are we waiting for?" said Elizabeth. She slapped a twenty on the table. "Pay me back later. Let's get to the Appelden. And I'm driving."

*　*　*

Of course, after all that brake-slamming and going up on two wheels at every sharp turn, Elizabeth and I had to wait around for Jackson to de-RAM the bites or whatever. He was working on one monitor and using the other to research problems. I'd briefly attempted to watch, but he was tabbing so spastically that it made me seasick. I sunk into the couch and let Baconnaise run free. After spending a long evening in my pocket, he was more energetic than Elizabeth and I put together.

"Want to see his circus tricks?" I asked her.

"Nothing sounds more appealing," she said, but she didn't have anything else to do.

"You can choose," I said magnanimously. I love captive audiences. "Tightrope walk? Yarn choice? Or a new one."

"Although it *is* fascinating to watch a gerbil always choose green yarn, I feel like I could do that myself. Let's mix it up. New one."

"I give you: Baconnaise the Tumbler! Doo-doo-*doo!*"

"What was *that?*"

"Somersault!" I ordered Baconnaise as I surreptitiously pulled his tail. The command was all for show. I'd discovered the link between "tail-tug" and "gerbil somersault" through pure serendipity, much like when Fleming discovered penicillin.

"Can he cartwheel?" said Elizabeth.

I was miffed that she wasn't appreciating his somersault, which was extremely endearing. "Can *you* cartwheel?"

"Of course." She did a nice one, although she almost kicked Jackson in the head. He didn't notice. "Can *you?*"

She'd made it look easy, but that's what always happens

211

with those impromptu gymnastics meets. Then you're the guy who's like, "I did it! Perfect ten!" while everybody else is like, "Your feet did not even clear your head."

"*Ha,*" said Jackson.

Elizabeth shot to his side. I scooped up Baconnaise and followed.

"Exhibit A," he told us. "Electronic check from kTV."

The screen was full of tabs and slashes and those < > things. The font was ancient. Jackson started pointing at various figures.

"See? Fifteen thousand. That's what kTV is paying for each episode. Paying to Selwyn—via Coluber."

"But," said Elizabeth, "according to the budget—"

"Yep, Selwyn gets ten," said Jackson. "Coluber is embezzling five thousand dollars per episode. That's ninety thousand for the season. Tax-free."

"I can't believe this file is just out there," said Elizabeth.

Jackson cackled. He was practically rubbing his hands together in maniacal glee. "'Out there' is an inaccurate description of the original location of this file."

"Huh?" I said.

"I had to use some sophisticated black-hat stuff. Packet sniffing, SQL injection."

"Are you taking drugs or hacking his files?" said Elizabeth.

"I wish I could see his personal bank account. I've got a new theory. Ninety thousand isn't all that much. And if he's only getting a flat fee, why would he be so invested in making the show a hit? But say he gets a percentage of the revenues."

"So the better *For Art's Sake* does, the better Coluber does?"

Elizabeth slammed her body against the den wall. "But it's making a fortune!"

"Correct," said Jackson darkly. "And I dare say Coluber is too."

"We have no proof," I reminded them.

The spell broke. Elizabeth sat down, and Jackson took off his glasses to wipe them clean. "And we're not going to get any," he said. "I could land in prison if I tried to invade the system of an accredited financial institution. More importantly, we don't know where he banks."

"We could steal his checkbook," mused Elizabeth.

"That's a terrible idea," I said.

"Sadly, he's right," Jackson told her. "Would a guy like Coluber carry a checkbook?"

"Can you get into any of his other files?"

"Not at the moment. Take a look. There's his main folder. I sent out a worm to get his password, but it hashed up most of the files."

"Try that one," I said. It was named "Schema."

"I already have."

"So you can't?" said Elizabeth.

She knows Jackson. The word "can't" vexes him. His shoulders shot up to his ears and he said, "Let me just try a rewrite."

I'd been up since six-forty-eight. It was almost two in the morning. I closed my eyes on the couch. Baconnaise had had a long day too, and he cuddled up in my neck-knoll.

"Shit!" said Jackson excitedly.

I breaststroked through the thick waters of unconsciousness.

"Shit what?" murmured Elizabeth, curled into a ball on the floor.

I finally surfaced. My limbs felt heavy and used.

"Shit this file."

"Shit what file?"

"Shit this 'Schema' thing."

"Shit it's like 4 a.m."

"Shit," I muttered drowsily. I closed my eyes again.

"No," said Jackson. "No, no, no." I could feel myself sinking down into the sweet—"Ethan and Elizabeth, come the shit over here."

"Don't wanna," said Elizabeth, but she unfurled herself and crawled over to the monitors. I was watching through half-closed eyes. "Ethan. I moved. You move too."

She'd looked ridiculous crawling, but I soon realized there was nothing I wanted less than to stand fully upright. At the level of Jackson's knees, we looked up at the screen.

"It's a schema for *FAS*," said Jackson.

"What's a schema?" That was me. I swear I know what a schema is in ordinary life.

"A plan, an outline, a model," he said impatiently. I was stuck on trying to remember what a "plan" was—the word sounded so familiar—but I nodded docilely. Then I started reading the words on the screen, the ones between the brackets, weirdly spaced in that typewriter font but with a meaning that was all too clear.

It was the future of *For Art's Sake*. It was a plan of Episode 15, which had aired during VORTEX. It was a plan of Episode 16, for next week, and 17, and—

"Stop scrolling so fast!" I said. I was trying to figure out what would happen between Maura and Luke.

"The details are unimportant," said Jackson.

"Uh-huh," agreed Elizabeth, but she was fixated on the document too. It was like finding a novel about your life. Not your life up to this point. Your *life*.

Jackson stopped scrolling. "There's dialogue in here."

"'MAURA: I told Miki I'd meet him after school!'" read Elizabeth. "Wow. Coluber knows how to make her sound as brainless as she really is."

"She has a brain!" I said hotly.

"'MAURA: And Miki's going to be so mad when he finds out about—about us—'"

"You're just reading it in a Valley-girl voice. She does not sound like that."

Jackson gave an irritated huff and scrolled all the way to the end of the document. Episode 17 broke off, unfinished, after only a few lines. "No Episode 18," said Jackson. "That could mean they don't script the finale—"

"It *is* live," said Elizabeth.

"Or they haven't written it yet."

"Go back to the part where Maura's talking to Luke," I said.

Jackson held down the brightness button. Twilight and then night fell onto the monitor. I was annoyed.

"*Jackson.* I have to see how bad it is."

"No. It's time to discuss the implications."

I collapsed from my knees onto my stomach. There was no use arguing with that tone.

"He's scripting it," said Jackson.

"He's a screenwriter."

"It's not a reality show at all." That was me.

We sat there in silence for a few minutes. Jackson had been right to turn off the screen. Now we could see the obvious.

"Cat-piss, we *knew* this already," I said heavily. "I *saw* this."

"I guess I just didn't believe it," said Elizabeth.

"I saw it, when I was in that locker. And that's the way these shows work. Everybody knows that. We didn't need to do all this investigation."

"I really believed it stopped with the frankenbiting," admitted Jackson. "I thought the contestants lived their lives like normal, and then the genius editors took over."

"You know what?" I said. I'd relived my conversations with Maura in the dance hallway so many times that they'd become like chewed gum; the substance was still there, but I wasn't getting any new flavor. But now I remembered something new. That shot of detail was enough to put me back there, back in that empty hallway, looking into those green eyes—

"Speak, Andrezejczak," said Jackson.

"Right. Well. Maura? You know how I talked to her?"

"Might have heard about it once or twice," said Elizabeth.

"She said, 'We're like marionettes.'"

"You told us that."

"And she was like, 'I say what I'm supposed to say, I do what I'm supposed to do. . . .' But I thought she meant she showed up on time to the challenges, or whatever. I didn't get it."

Elizabeth was looking at me with a strange expression. "Luke got it."

"He did," said Jackson, staring at the ceiling. Here comes

Señor Total Recall. "He said that maybe they got direction beforehand. Then he started talking about Coluber's personal incentive."

"Now quantified at five thousand dollars per episode," said Elizabeth.

"Not to mention the hypothesized percentage of *FAS* revenues."

"Rat dung," I said angrily. "We *knew*. Maura told us. Luke told us."

"VORTEX failed," said Elizabeth.

"Just a lot of self-indulgence," said Jackson. He killed the other monitor as well. The ceiling light blared down upon us.

Elizabeth fell dramatically onto the floor as if she'd been stabbed in the gut. "We were just searching for what we already knew. Knew, but didn't want to admit." Her dreadlocks were splayed out on the carpet like a halo, surrounding her head with dark gold, but I couldn't even stare.

CHAPTER EIGHTEEN

Before this time, before this era,
School was an eye with no mascara.
It lacked excitement, had no thrill.
Like Sisyphus, we trudged uphill.
Our practice time was time to kill.
                        — *THE CONTRACANTOS*

I knew Luke was avoiding us. He always came into English orbited by groupies, like a sun with a bunch of ditzy planets, and when he deigned attend calculus, he'd sit way in the back so he could zoom out as soon as the bell rang. Fine by me. I was avoiding him too.

But neither one of us could hide Monday morning, when I entered what I thought would be a pleasantly deserted bathroom and saw him.

He gave me a nod. If I'd been the unzipped one, I wouldn't have said a thing, but you know how urinal power plays go. I clearly had the upper hand.

"I saw the latest episode," I told him.

"Oh, really?"

This annoyed me. "Yes, really." Then I started quoting him. "'I've always loved how words can inspire imagination.' That was you, Luke. 'How they can capture emotion.'" Luke had spewed the sappiest garbage you could imagine, all about how *special* language is, how *close* he feels to words. He'd sounded like Miki F.R.

He stuffed his stuff back into his pants. "Yeah."

"Yeah?"

He sighed.

"I mean, what *was* that?"

"I know."

"You're following a script."

He shrugged. Under the fluorescence, he looked tired and pale: basically how a Minnesotan teenager ought to look at 7 a.m. in February. This bucked me up.

"What do you want from this?" I asked him. "That's all I want to know."

"The national exposure, the chance at the scholarship—"

"Come on. Be honest."

He ran a hand through his hair. "It's a really good opportunity for my writing career—"

"Luke."

There was a lot I could have said. There was a lot I wanted to say. We used to be best friends, Luke. We could sit on opposite sides of a classroom and have a whole conversation just by twitching our eyebrows. When you wondered whether it was possible to drive the entire Minneapolis–Saint Paul beltway in the space of one skipped lunch period, I came along. When I was obsessed with the badminton world championships, you barely made fun of me at all. You taught my sisters how to use a can opener. Then you helped me deep-clean the living-room rug. We drank your parents' *Kirschwasser* together, and I lied to your mom when she asked me why you were sick. We know each other's secrets. Last summer, you told me that in middle school you thought you might be gay because you liked our social studies teacher so much, and I told you I could be a repressed sexual deviant because I had that dream about—well, never mind.

We had each other's backs, Luke. I know how much you hate it when Jackson says "negatory" instead of "no." You know that I've always thought Elizabeth is sort of hot. Ever since seventh grade, we've scooted along on parallel tracks. We've had all the same references. We've lived the same life.

But instead, I just said, "Why?"

"I know. I betrayed all my convictions. Believe you me, I know. But I've been thinking, Ethan, and I don't think they were really my convictions. I don't think I believed in them."

"You didn't believe in the *Contracantos*?"

"I thought I did. But I'm not sure I wrote the *Contracantos* for the reason I said. I think I just wanted to be different. To do something cool."

"You didn't believe in—" I almost said "us," but that sounded like a bad rom-com. "You didn't believe in the Appelden?"

"I wanted something exciting. And the *Contracantos* was exciting, sure. But then kTV asked me to be on the show. And I knew you guys would be mad, but, Ethan, I couldn't look away. It was like, Finally! Something *awesome!*"

Then I knew nothing I said would matter. He'd always loved that word. And if he thought that kTV was more awesome than we were, we'd lost him. He'd always wanted to be awesome and to do awesome things, and we, apparently, had never been awesome enough.

English class did nothing to lift my spirits. Every time I looked at BradLee I could see his ten-year-old self, one baby face laid over another as if someone were fooling around with overhead transparencies. Luke was quiet. Maura spaced out. Elizabeth slept. Jackson let out the occasional chirp of victory when he estimated a square root within 0.001.

I tried to take notes on the end of Ezra Pound's life. You already know he was a fascist. But at the very end, BradLee told us, he took it all back. This is what he told Allen Ginsberg:

> [My work is] a mess . . . my writing, stupidity and ignorance all the way through. My worst mistake was the stupid suburban anti-Semitic prejudice, all along that spoiled everything. . . . I found after seventy years that I was not a lunatic but a moron. . . . I should have been able to do better.

How can you not feel sorry for him? I know, I know. He was a bigot. He supported people who did terrible things.

But. *Not a lunatic but a moron,* he said of himself. Can you imagine looking back at your entire volcanic life, always committed to one cause or another, spewing out energy and ideas like a vortex, only to think *that?*

He'd tried so hard his whole life. *I should have been able to do better.*

I listened as hard as I could to BradLee's lecture.

"Does anyone feel relief that he recanted his anti-Semitism?" There was a smattering of hands. "I'm sure we all do. But we need to be cautious about being relieved. Why?"

Nobody answered.

"Because, class, we argued that an artist's life doesn't matter when it comes to an evaluation of his work. And if Pound's fascism doesn't matter, his disavowal of that fascism doesn't matter either. Not in terms of our critical appraisal of the *Cantos.*"

I've experienced my share of depressing winter Mondays but that day was something else. I'd already been shattered, but the Pound quotation took my porcelain shards and pulverized them, drove a heel into them and ground them to dust. I kept thinking of that old man. He realized that he'd been wrong and—here's the kicker—he shouldn't have been wrong. Like every one of us, he had the burden of existing as a moral being, and he'd worn it wrongly. But he didn't stop caring. He didn't excuse himself. He looked back on his life—which he could not do over, which could not be edited or frankenbited, which was simply, tragically, *almost over*—and he said, "I should have been able to do better."

                              *   *   *

On Tuesday, I waded out of the slough of depression and
straight into the fires of anger. It was all BradLee's fault, I decided in Latin class. If the *Contracantos* had stayed secret, Luke
would still be our friend. I had a delectable daydream about
confronting BradLee, and I'd convinced myself I was going to
do it. But by the time Ms. Pederson released her prisoners,
Elizabeth was waiting outside the classroom.

"Ugh, I can't today," I said.

"You promised. And I got my dad to let me have the car." She
dangled the keys. That weekend, I'd made the foolhardy vow
that I'd accompany Elizabeth to the Science Museum of Minnesota to do our Advanced Figure Drawing assignment. "Get
down to the bones," Dr. Fern had said. "Literally." I'd planned
to draw the squirrel skeleton that the triplets had found in the
backyard, but Elizabeth said dinosaurs would be better.

"But I wanted—"

"To go home and play Candy Land and sink into a morass
of depression and calc homework on your bed?"

I did not deign to respond.

We got out our sketchbooks in front of the colossal triceratops. I'd loved this place as a kid. "Did you see the posters out
front?" said Elizabeth.

"Nope."

"*For Art's Sake* is filming here next Thursday."

"So that's why you wanted to come!" I didn't want to be
reminded of kTV.

"I'm just in it for the art grade."

"Did you know beforehand that they were filming here?"

"Dr. Fern told our class."

"Not ours," I said darkly. Unless I'd missed it when I was chatting with Herbert.

I always find sketching in public awkward. You can just feel all those people judging you. Now, it wouldn't have been bad at the museum—it was nearly empty except for some toddlers and their moms—except that Elizabeth's drawing was so much better than mine. Hers actually looked like a triceratops. Mine was more like a sweet potato with ears.

"I'm off to the diplodocus," I told her.

"The what? Ooh, are you finished? Let me see."

"No," I said, jerking the sketchbook to my chest. "The diplodocus is my true artistic calling."

It was peaceful back there. The toddlers weren't into Jurassic herbivores. "Diplo," I said, "you know what it's like not to be at the top of the food chain. You see why I couldn't draw next to her." I found a bench and got into a groove. I was thinking how nice it was to be somewhere other than school. The world was a big place. Not everywhere was contaminated with kTV.

Then I saw BradLee.

It's always a shock to the system when you see a teacher who's ventured out of their territory. They're so out of place, and they don't even seem to know it. It's cute. BradLee came over to me. He was wearing the same thing he'd worn to school—khakis and a button-down with his threadbare purple sneakers—but there was a lump in his pocket where he'd stuffed his tie, like a kid at a wedding reception.

Wait. This was the guy who'd betrayed Luke to kTV, who'd lied about his connection to Coluber and Wolfe, who had been known to hug Trisha Meier. I stood. I shut my sketchbook and dropped—no, *hurled*—it to the ground.

"You betrayed us," I said.

BradLee looked around nervously.

"We need answers," I said. "You told kTV about Luke's poem. You knew that wasn't what we wanted."

This wasn't one of my trademarked daydreams, full of the courage and comebacks I'd never have in real life. This was real.

"And now Luke's betrayed us too, and it's your fault. And he's screwing up his life." I heard footsteps and I knew Elizabeth had come to join me. "I know you keep saying that life doesn't matter, only art matters, but his *art* isn't good anymore. I know you've been watching the show. I know you've read the new *Contracantos*. It's crap. It's not a tale of the tribe at all."

"Ethan, this isn't a good time—" said BradLee.

I held up my hand like a crossing guard. It worked, which was most satisfying. "The *Contracantos* has been kTVed. It used to be genuine but they've made it fake. They're not making art at all. They're just making money."

"Stop, Ethan. I need to—" said BradLee.

"And you know what kills me?" Elizabeth was tugging at my sleeve, but I shook her off. This was the best part. "Ezra Pound said, 'I should have been able to do better.' And now, that's what *Luke's* going to think. That's the worst thought you can think, and when he comes to his senses, he'll think it."

225

"Oh. My. *God,*" squealed someone behind me.

I'd been so focused on delivering my oration before my courage crapped out that I'd had tunnel vision. If this were a movie, this part would be slo-mo. Ethan spins. His world shakes. He brings his hands to his face in shock and terror.

"I was just showing Trisha the dinosaurs," said BradLee weakly.

"We're filming here next week, did you know?" said Trisha Meier. "The ambience is amazing. It'll be an all-night challenge. Lots of dark corners for dark deeds!" She let loose her heinous laugh: *henc! henc! henc!* "But Brad, honey, you must introduce me to this young man."

Trisha looped her arm into BradLee's, and I looked around for the young man.

"Because that speech? That. Was. Incredible. I cannot believe we didn't catch that on camera. Phone, Brad." Elizabeth and I watched in dismay as BradLee disentangled himself and fetched Trisha's phone from her purse, which was on a row of stools in front of my diplodocus. Trisha kept talking even as she sent a text. "But you'll just have to do it again. We'll polish it up a little—we'll cut that last bit; I didn't get that at all—but the possibilities! The controversy! Why didn't we think of this ourselves?" She gave her phone to BradLee, turned to me, and slapped her hands flat against her thighs. "Now. Who *are* you? Tell me about yourself."

"Um—"

"Because you are a *cutie* and this could go so far. The voice of the common man! I can just hear the voice-over. 'Luke

226

Weston has many fans'—we'll pan to Maura—'but even the most charismatic writer can be the target of jealousy.' Fabulous."

Trisha grabbed my hand and led me to the row of stools. I was so horrified I could do nothing but follow. "Sit. I can *see* it." Elizabeth looked at me, agape, and sat on my other side. BradLee, looking at the floor, sat by Trisha. "You'll have to confront Luke, not Brad. Yes. Yes. And we'll throw in the romantic jealousy angle too, pretend that you have a thing for Maura. Or maybe that you and Maura—eugghh." That's my best shot at transcribing the suggestive waggle that came out of her mouth. "Sweetie, you do watch the show, yes?"

"Unfortunately," I said.

Her laughter pealed. "I cannot wait to get you on kTV! Let's get some reactions here. I'll prep you for your big interview." She crossed one pleather leg over the other and beamed ahead at an imaginary camera. "Tell me. What did you think of the last episode?"

"I hated it," I said. "Ow."

Elizabeth had poked me, hard.

"Was that an 'ow' of unrequited love?" said Trisha.

"Um. Not sure."

Trisha turned to BradLee. "How long have you known this darling child?"

"Get boring," Elizabeth breathed into my ear. "Get super boring. Make her forget about you." I got it. Luckily, I was an expert at being forgettable. I'd been practicing my whole life.

"Let's see," said Trisha. "We know what you think of Luke.

Pure, wild jealousy. And we know how you feel about Maura. Who wouldn't have the hots for Maura? But what about Miki? Miki Reagler?"

"Uh," I said. And it hurt, and a piece of my soul withered and died, but I said, "I like Miki."

"Really," said Trisha. "Even though he's Maura's most consistent partner? Now, we all know she'll probably end up with Luke. But you can't discount the tension between Maura and Miki. It's a physical thing. You can smell it. Very, what's the word?"

Revolting?

"Primitive," she said, her eyes narrowed in pleasure.

"Miki's cool," I said. I let my mouth hang open. My eyes drifted toward one another.

"Hmm," said Trisha, disappointed. "I can handle the truth."

"Urg," I said.

"How much should we feature Miki these next few episodes?" Trisha mused.

"Glug."

"He's obviously a crowd darling, but we don't want to play favorites."

"Wurg."

"That is the true woe of the reality TV producer." She was gazing at BradLee now, though gesticulating so wildly I feared for my safety. "It's an art form, really. So many characters! And we have to create the story line."

Elizabeth said, "So you look at the characters you have, and then force them into a cohesive narrative?"

Trisha seemed surprised that Elizabeth could talk. "In a

way. I wouldn't want you to get the impression that we create the story line."

I made another digesting-caveman noise.

"Isn't that right, Brad? Very different from a sitcom, isn't it?"

I heard BradLee's intake of breath, but Trisha turned to us and cut him off. "So. What's it like to learn English from a celebrity? You must have been starstruck—"

"Glugga," I said. "Ouch!" Elizabeth had jabbed me again. Apparently the strategy had changed again, though I wished she'd inform me without inflicting bruises. "Um, a celebrity?"

"Don't tell me! Brad! You didn't!"

I craned over Trisha. BradLee's mouth was moving, but words weren't coming out.

"You're so modest! That's what I love about you. Purse." BradLee stood as if dazed, found her purse, and handed it to her. She chucked him under the chin. "Cutie-pie! Now. Brad didn't tell you that he starred on *Mind over Matter?*" That was Willis Wolfe's old show.

"Trisha—" said BradLee.

"YouTube. Thank God for eighties nostalgia. Half the show's up on the Internet."

She tilted her phone's screen toward me. Elizabeth leaned in. I could feel her dreadlocks, her soft soft dreadlocks, dandelion-fluff soft, Selwyn-auditorium-chair soft, brushing against my neck.

"Hysterical!" Trisha shrieked. "Look at you!" She grabbed BradLee's arm and stared avidly at the screen.

A chubby redheaded boy was sitting in a beige kitchen, his

head supported in one hand while the other dug into a carton of ice cream. There was no doubt that the boy was the same one who'd appeared in the photograph in Willis Wolfe's office.

"*Mind over Matter,*" said Elizabeth.

"Duh," said Trisha. "Petey! Oh. My. God. So adorable. And he grew up to be just as adorable an English teacher!" She pinched BradLee's cheek. "Though why you chose teaching over acting is beyond me," she cooed. She turned expectantly to Elizabeth and me. "Who wants to see more?"

We didn't, but she wasn't really asking. She played clip after clip, and we watched them, and everything began to click. BradLee had known Coluber his whole life. He'd come to Selwyn to help with *For Art's Sake*. Of course he'd told Coluber about the *Contracantos*. "You knew that wasn't what we wanted," I'd yelled at him, but now I knew that he didn't care. He had never cared what we'd wanted.

Trisha's phone rang. "This is *the* most incompetent crew," she said. "Yes. Come on. Use a hair double. It's lighting. How tough can it be?" She hung up unceremoniously and stood. "I am so sorry to cut this short," she said to BradLee, "but they tell me I'm *essential.*" She gave him a triple-barreled kiss. "Mwa. Call me!" We watched as she threaded her way through the dinosaur fossils and left the gallery.

CHAPTER NINETEEN

We shudder to recall the days
Before the show. What drear malaise!
What somber clouds loomed overhead.
A new day's dawn filled us with dread.
Pathetic were those lives we led.
                            — THE CONTRACANTOS

"So she forgot about you," said Jackson in the Appelden an hour later.

Elizabeth guffawed. "Ethan, I must hand it to you. You can disappear like no one else."

"Yup." I knew she was offering an olive branch, but I was still peeved about the drive home.

"He's such a liar," she had fumed as soon as we'd shut the car doors. "The dartboard! Yeah, right. He's Coluber's right-hand man."

I leaned my head on the window. "Do you think Maura's going to end up with Luke?"

"*That's* what you care about?" She took a left turn so aggressively that I got a seat belt burn on my neck.

"Just wondering."

We were silent as Elizabeth drove along the Mississippi, the trees barren, the water gray and choppy and cold.

"I've got a prediction," I told her.

"What," she said. No question mark. I should have known at that point to shut up.

"Maura's going to hook up with Luke underneath the triceratops."

"*God,* Ethan. Somebody needs to tell you what's what."

"What? What's what?"

She took a deep breath and I thought she was going to launch into a major tirade. Instead, she exhaled. "Nothing."

"Oh, come *on.* What's what what?"

"Go have a heart-to-heart with Baconnaise, why don't you."

"Huh?"

"Forget it," she said. "Okay? Forget it. Forget I ever said anything at all."

When Elizabeth was in the bathroom, I convinced Jackson to pull up the *For Art's Sake* schema so I could figure out whether my prediction was right. I'd just started to skim through all the intro crap. Baconnaise was in my lap. Elizabeth was now lying like a corpse on the floor and doing her best to snootily ignore us both.

"One loose end," said Jackson. "Yes, BradLee's working for Coluber. As suspected. But what's in it for him?"

"Yeah, I was *trying* to work through all that in the car," said Elizabeth. I could tell she was glaring at me, and I tried to look innocent as I rubbed noses with Baconnaise.

"Why would he quit high finance to move to Minneapolis?" said Jackson. "To be the flunky of some corrupt producer he knew twenty years ago?"

"Maybe he likes teaching," I offered.

"Who would like teaching?" muttered Jackson. "Improbable."

"BradLee likes teaching," I said. I turned from the screen with the script, in which they were still explaining the rules of the museum challenge. "He likes *us*. You know how there are some teachers who obviously hate kids?"

"Pederson."

"Wyckham."

"Garlop."

There was a moment of silence, kind of like after you mention the name of someone who's recently dead.

"BradLee likes us. He's not just doing this to screw with us."

"Ethan said something worth listening to," Elizabeth told the ceiling. "Shocking, is it not?"

So much for that olive branch.

I went back to reading Episode 16. My prediction was right. O triceratops, when you roamed the earth, was there an inkling in that thick Cretaceous skull of yours that your bones would one day serve as the backdrop to a scripted, filmed make-out session?

> **LUKE:** This is so romantic.
> **MAURA:** I know.
> **LUKE:** Maura, these bones—this dinosaur—do
> you think he knew love?
> **MAURA**, *gazing up at the Triceratops:* I hope so.
> Because love is awfully sweet.
> **LUKE:** So are you.
> [They kiss.]

Now I needed to make sure she wasn't going to hook up with Miki F.R. too.

I scrolled through a scene where Miki F.R. chases Andy through the Human Body Gallery, trying to steal his cello. "All in fun!" Miki F.R. chortles.

I scrolled through a scene where Kyle's practicing a monologue from *Othello,* and Miki F.R. sneaks up and stabs him with Andy's bow.

I scrolled through the hosts' wrap-up banter. Apparently at least some of Damien Hastings's idiocy was scripted.

> **TRISHA:** What a night in the museum! Look at all
> the things that came to life.
> **DAMIEN:** The brachiosaurus?
> **TRISHA:** It's a triceratops.
> **DAMIEN:** It came to life?
> **TRISHA:** Rivalry. Anger. Love.

Did you see that?

Or perhaps I should say: Did you *see* that‽

I'd have missed it myself if I hadn't slowed down to feel sorry for Damien, who, despite the mousse, always seemed like a nice guy.

Nobody else uses that punctuation mark. Nobody.

"He writes the script," I whispered.

Elizabeth was now trying to talk Jackson out of attempting to make root beer in the extra basement bathtub. "It'll turn into real beer," said Elizabeth. "Your ass is gonna be dragged right into juvie—"

"He writes the script," I said louder.

"I've read up on fermentation," said Jackson irritably.

"INTERROBANG!" I shouted. That got their attention.

"I love interrobangs!" said Elizabeth.

"So does BradLee," I told them, pointing at the screen.

"That's pitiful," said Jackson. "Does Damien truly not know the difference between brachiosaurus and triceratops?"

"We should have seen this one coming," said Elizabeth. "He writes the script."

"For one, they lived eighty-five million years apart."

"Concentrate!" she shouted. "BradLee is the scriptwriter for *For Art's Sake!*"

My mom was picking me up, but I couldn't bear to rip myself away from Baconnaise.

"Jackson, come on. He needs some one-on-one attention. Let me borrow him."

"He's not a library book."

"Think of this as a sleepover. You'd let your kid go on sleepovers, right? To his cool uncle's house?"

"I guess. Ugh. Fine."

I set up Baconnaise in his travel cage and carried him out to the car. My mom didn't notice, but my sisters did.

"Is that a *rat*?"

"Mom! Ethan has a rat!"

"He's not a rat," I said with disdain. I held up the cage for their inspection. A mannered introduction would go far toward establishing a relationship of mutual respect. "Girls, meet Baconnaise. Baconnaise"—I turned solemnly toward him—"this is Olivia, this is Tabitha, and this is Lila."

Baconnaise nodded courteously. As I've mentioned, he's a genius. The triplets squealed.

"Baconnaise is a *gerbil*. Gerbils are the noblest of rodents, and Baconnaise is the noblest of gerbils."

"Is he really noble?" said Olivia. "Like King Arthur?"

"Yes. You can call him Sir Baconnaise if you want, but he's an informal dude. Baconnaise is fine."

They were intrigued. "Can we hold him?"

"Once we get home." I had a sudden image of Tabitha swinging him by the tail. "If you are very, very careful."

When we got home, I sat down cross-legged on the living-room floor and the triplets gathered around me. I opened the door of Baconnaise's cage. He'd shown during VORTEX that he was good with new situations, but I was worried he'd bolt. I'd underestimated him. He stepped out daintily and sniffed.

"He's so cute!" said Lila.

"He doesn't like that word," I informed her. "It's demeaning. Just because he's small doesn't mean he lacks feelings."

"I like his nose," she amended.

"Me too."

"What's *that*, Ethan?" said Tabitha in horror.

"What?" I couldn't figure out where she was pointing.

"That—that *thing*. Is he going to have a baby?"

"Hes can't have babies," Lila advised her.

"I think he ate a marble," said Olivia.

"It's not that big," I said defensively. "It's not as big as a marble."

"Yes, it is," said the three of them together.

"A shooter," added Olivia.

I put my head to the floor so I could see it better. How had this happened? It *was* as big as a marble. A large marble.

"Will he poop it out? When Tabitha ate Mom's earring, she—"

"It's called a tumor," I told them. "It's a product of cell mutation." That sounded too ominous. "It's benign. It's fine. They happen to people too, but we get them cut out in surgery."

"Why can't he have surgery?"

"He's too small."

"Is he going to die?"

"Of course not." I had to change the subject. "Want to see some tricks?"

"I want to hold him. Let me hold him. Please, Ethan. Please." That was Tabitha.

"Sit still and see if he'll climb on you."

He sniffed me out and ran toward me, sprinting up the

incline of my leg. I held still, to be a good example, and let him climb all the way to my shoulder. He perched there, for all the world like King Arthur surveying Camelot.

"He really likes you, Ethan," marveled Lila.

"That's because I'm very *gentle* with him."

"I'm gentle," said Tabitha.

"Baconnaise?" I said. "Can my sisters hold you? They're very *gentle.*"

He shrugged, so I showed the girls how to make a bowl with their hands.

"Who's first?" I said. Bad plan.

"ME!" all three of them shouted.

"I have a better idea." I'd wanted to test this theory anyway. "Sit in a circle. Baconnaise will choose."

They stuck their legs out straight and formed a circle, and I put him down in the middle. Olivia was wearing a green shirt. "Baconnaise, you stud," I murmured. I snapped my fingers.

Sure enough, he ran straight for Olivia, his tumor bouncing along beneath his stomach like a saddlebag. He scampered up and sat on her shoulder.

"Wow," said Olivia, barely breathing.

"Wow, Baconnaise," I said. He really did know his colors. Or at least green.

"Can I hold him?" said Olivia.

"*Gently,*" I said. She plucked him from her shoulder. I could tell by his splayed feet that he was scared, but he relaxed when she cupped him in her hands. Lila and Tabitha leaned over her, jealous as all get-out.

"The tumor feels funny," said Olivia. I was about to point

out how soft his fur was, and how that meant he was healthy. Then Tabitha grabbed him.

"Hey!" yelped Olivia and I in identical high voices.

Tabitha had him fully enclosed within her small hands. He must have been terrified. She stood. "You were being piggy."

"He chose me!" shrieked Olivia.

Like a psychopath with a loaded gun, Tabitha needed to be approached with care. "Tabby, you can hold him. Just give him some air," I said soothingly.

"How?"

"Open your fingers a chink—"

I'd neglected to notice that an indignant Olivia had risen behind me. She pounced. Tabitha hit the ground.

"Baconnaise!" I shouted. "Watch out!"

Tabitha had kept her hands cupped, and he hadn't gone flying through the air. But now Olivia was on top of her, prying her fingers open one by one. Tabitha, understandably, squeezed.

"BACONNAISE!" I joined the fray. I peeled Olivia off Tabitha and tossed her aside like a yogurt lid. I was sitting on top of Tabitha now. "Give. Him. To. Me."

Tabitha succumbed instantly. She'd rarely heard me use that voice. Heck, I'd rarely heard it myself.

He was very still.

"Did he get tilled?" said Lila.

I stroked his spine with my pinkie finger. He lifted his head and gave me a resentful look. I had to turn away. The guilt was overwhelming.

So I took it out on the girls. "This gerbil," I told them, "is riddled with cancer." I'd never spoken it aloud. "He's a sweet, fragile, sick, tiny animal. And this is how you treat him?"

"I didn't do it," whispered Lila. Tabitha was still fuming, but Olivia was tearful.

"He could have *died*."

I left. That had been my fault, not theirs, and the fluttering gray miasma of guilt kept reminding me of that. "Baconnaise," I said, "I'm so sorry." He was still in shock, I think, because he was slothful, making no chipper little gestures with his head or tail. "Let's get you away from human touch."

I gave him some cardboard in his cage, and within a few minutes he was happily gnawing. I watched him. I didn't study for my monster bio test. I just watched him.

CHAPTER TWENTY

We barely knew we wanted more.
We felt some discontent, but swore
That it was natural, just a stage.
We ne'er took action to assuage
Our restlessness, our guilt, our rage.
              — THE CONTRACANTOS

"One line of investigation remains," Jackson whispered to me in Latin the next day. "If it fails, I'm prepared to give up."

I was already prepared to give up. However, dactylic hexameter was kicking my butt and I needed distraction. I said, "What is it?"

"We need to figure out how they use the script. If the contestants parrot it verbatim, that's our target. We hack it, we write new dialogue, we make Luke sound like a dumbass—"

"I assume you're telling me this because you want me to do something."

"Gather some intel on the issue."

Ms. Pederson walked behind us to monitor our progress

on the scansion assignment. When the enemy became other-wise occupied, I said, "How?"

"Ask Maura Heldsman."

So the next morning, I returned to the dance hallway. It'd been a while.

"He's back," she said.

"Why do you always get here so early?"

"It's my only time for homework." She flipped shut her binder. "Not that homework is a major priority of mine. But if I start failing anything, Coluber's going to kick me off the show."

"Would that be so bad?" I plopped down beside her with-out an invitation.

"Uh, Juilliard?"

"I knew that. I really did."

"I'm so stressy." She curled her legs into her giant purple sweatshirt. She looked like a turnip, and she was still cute. "The deposit deadline's the day after the finale. If I win, I can go. If I lose, it's the U."

"Aren't you worried they've already chosen the winner?"

"God, what are you trying to do? Turn me into an even big-ger stressball?"

"But it's all scripted, right?"

"Not exactly."

"What's that mean?"

"I shouldn't tell you this, but whatever. You're probably the only person I trust. How sad is that? Sure, it's scripted. But if you can come up with something that works better, they'll run with it."

"Oh."

"The other contestants don't get it. But that's like the secret to my success. I do everything I can to make my character, my scenes, work better than everyone else's."

"Like what? What do you do?"

"Dance my heart out."

"Well, yeah. That's practically *in* the script."

"And hook up with every guy on the show." Her green eyes looked right into mine. "Which is practically in the script too."

I almost asked her how long it'd been in there. Which had come first? Had she given the idea to BradLee, or had BradLee written it for her? But then she'd have to answer, and I guess I knew which way it went, and I didn't want her to have to say it aloud.

"This is when you tell me you'll do anything to help me win," she said.

IMAGE. VORTEX. They'd both failed. And hacking the script wouldn't help, because kTV wouldn't necessarily follow the script.

"You alive?"

I'd never wanted to lie so badly.

"Ethan?"

"I don't think there's anything left to do."

She sighed. "I know. The *Contracantos*—that was you, right?"

"Yeah." She trusted me, apparently, so I'd trust her. "Me, Jackson, Elizabeth. And Luke. It was really Luke's idea. We were just following orders. Our great ideas were always his."

"I doubt that. He's not as awesome as you think he is."

"No, it's true. He is."

"Neither am I." She laughed. "We're messed up, Luke and me. People are always messed up when they only want one thing."

I looked into her eyes again, but she looked away.

"If you want lots of things, you can be happy when you get a few of them. But I only want one thing."

"What do you want?"

"I want to make it. You know that. I want to go to New York. If I don't go now, I'll never go. I'm a ballerina and I'm eighteen and I've got maybe ten years before my body starts to give out on me. This is my life, Ethan Andrezejczak. My one and only. You know how you'll have some great dream and you wake up and it slips off? It's gone?"

"Yeah."

"Then you forget the dream was even that good. It just slides away. And there are lots of sad things in this world, but the saddest thing I can think of, Ethan, is becoming some happy soccer mom with a coupon binder and a jogging stroller. And I'll be like, 'I used to dance.' But I won't even know. I won't even remember how much I wanted this."

After school, we saw BradLee leaning against his old Volkswagen, smoking. He guiltily stubbed out his cigarette when he saw us.

"Yo," said Elizabeth.

"Hey," he said.

Jackson and I kept walking to the Appelvan, but she stopped. She said to BradLee, "Why do you write the script?"

He twitched.

"We just want to know why. Is Coluber blackmailing you? Is that it?"

"For the record," he said, "I don't write the script. I have nothing to do with *FAS.*"

"And for the record, we don't believe you." Jackson and I were lingering awkwardly behind her. She twisted and gave us an exasperated look. I moved to her side.

"Why?" I said. "Why do you do it?"

BradLee checked over both shoulders. At this time of afternoon, the lot was full of teenagers backing out of parking spaces, so any adult with a healthy instinct for self-preservation stayed far away. "For the record," he said again, "I don't write the script."

"And off the record?" said Elizabeth. "Why?"

He checked over his shoulders again. He needed to stop doing that; it made him look like a bush-league crook. "Let me first remind you that selective colleges consider junior-year English grades to be of paramount importance—"

"Screw you, BradLee," snapped Elizabeth. She spun and started to walk off.

"Wait!" he said.

"I cannot believe you're threatening us. Considering what we know about *you*—"

"Look, off the record—"

"We could destroy you. We could make your life a living hell."

"I don't doubt it—"

"We're talking full-out rebellion. You'd never have control of your classroom again."

"Cyberwarfare," said Jackson.

"Spitballs," I said.

"As if we even care about any grades *you* give," said Elizabeth.

"Are you going to listen?" said BradLee. "Because I'll tell you. I'll tell you why I write the script."

"I'll draw an asterisk right onto my transcript," she muttered. "It'll be like, 'Note: grade issued by total d-bag.'"

BradLee sighed and pretended not to hear her. "Coluber asked me. I was waiting tables, trying to figure out what to do with my life, and Coluber called me up."

"So you lied," I said. "There was no job in finance."

"He remembered me from *Mind over Matter*. He knew I'd been an English major. But he wanted our relationship to stay under the radar so I could spy for him."

"There was no dartboard."

"After all, he needs to know who's glamorous, who should be on the show."

"There was no funny story about interrobangs."

BradLee looked wounded. "No! I have *several*—"

"We get it. He asked you to do it," interrupted Elizabeth. "But why say yes?"

"Either you're evil, or he's blackmailing you," said Jackson.

"No. Neither one. It's more complicated than that. I do it, well, for the reasons people do things. I get paid. I'm good at it. I thought it'd be cool to have a secret life."

More complicated, I thought, but also more bland.

"And because I think in the long run, the show's a good thing for Selwyn. Also that."

He was sagging against his dirty car, the snuffed cigarette limp in his hand. He was wearing those awful old purple sneakers, and he'd never shaved that half-witted beard. He was a good teacher. He didn't have to be a good teacher. Coluber wanted him to spy and write, and he'd have kept the job even if he'd sucked at teaching high school English.

"I'm sorry about Luke," he said. "Coluber was adamant that we try to get him. And even then, I didn't think Luke would go for it. Not completely. I didn't think he'd drop you guys."

"But you'd have told Coluber about the *Contracantos* anyway," said Elizabeth.

"You know?" His mouth hung open as he stared into the parking lot. "I'd have told him anyway."

"You're just like Ezra Pound," I said.

BradLee nodded, his eyes drooping. "Like Pound," he said, "I should have been able to do better."

Nothing changed. We had seen the sordid underbellies of Selwyn and BradLee and *For Art's Sake,* but there was nothing to do about it. It was a dark time.

So we kept going, and school kept going. Mrs. Garlop taught us Euler's method. Ms. Pederson cattle-prodded us through Book II of the *Ars Amatoria*. I realized that there is really only one pose of defecation, but I kept forcing Herbert into it, and Dr. Fern would appraise my sketchbook, her finger on her cheek, and say, Hmm, perhaps his legs are too short, perhaps his torso is too long. I'd brush off the eraser turds and squint at Herbert and try again, but it never came out right, and neither Dr. Fern nor I could ever figure out why.

Giselle went up. Elizabeth and I went together, presumably to watch Jackson's adroit manipulation of the lights. Maybe that's what she watched. I watched the effortless effort that was Maura Heldsman dancing. One leg would pop up as if it had a string attached and she would smile euphorically, but her other leg was planted, her calf muscle bulging. She danced freely, her dance was freedom itself, but by seeking that freedom she had been enslaved.

At the same time, I thought about putting my hand over Elizabeth's.

I didn't do it, but I thought about it.

CHAPTER TWENTY-ONE

But then the show: renown and fame!
Though once obscure, we found acclaim.
We Selwynites extend our most
Wholehearted thanks to the West Coast's
Best network, kTV, our host.
                        – THE CONTRACANTOS

When the museum episode aired, we watched it in the Appelden, Elizabeth and Jackson and I. We roused ourselves to make
derisive comments, but when it was over we sank back into
the hazes that had become our default states ever since we'd
realized that we knew everything but could do nothing.

Jackson was liquidating Mongols on *Sun Tzu*. I was half sitting, half lying on the couch, my chin on my chest. Baconnaise
was lolling on my stomach. He too had been listless lately. He'd
always been a sensitive guy. Our moods must have been rubbing off on him.

And hauling around that tumor probably didn't help. Have

you ever chewed three or four sticks of gum simultaneously? That's what it felt like. A clod. Ungainly. Squishy, solid, too big.

I thought Elizabeth was zoning out on kTV, but she suddenly grabbed the remote, flipped off the TV, and sat upright.

"GUYS."

Baconnaise swiveled his head toward her and flicked his tail. With a percussive snap of keystrokes, Jackson paused his game. I shoved myself upright and turned to Elizabeth.

She looked surprised. "That worked? I'm honored."

"It sounded urgent," said Jackson.

"It is."

"Talk, then." I could already feel my attention waning.

"We need to *do* something," she said.

Now I'd lost all interest. "How many times," I asked Baconnaise, "have we heard that?"

"Twice," Elizabeth responded. "*Twice,* Ethan. Before IMAGE and the *Contracantos.* Before VORTEX and the break-in."

I wasn't going to be sucked in by a tricolon yearning to be completed. I'd matured. "Whatever," I said. "It doesn't work. 'Doing something.' Like that does anything."

"It'll be different this time," she said. "We know so much more."

"We know everything. We can't do anything." I let my butt slide forward again so my head was the only vertical part of me. It gave me a crick in my neck, but that was preferable to expending the energy required to sit up. Baconnaise was sprawled apathetically on my chest. He was lying like a pregnant zebra, on his side with all four legs akimbo, the tumor between them. He must be exhausted, I thought. So was I.

"You're so negative."

"Why wouldn't I be negative?" I knew she was baiting me. "I've had enough of plans. Plans never go according to plan."

"Our plans do go according to plan," said Elizabeth, who had clearly been thinking about this. "They've just sucked as plans. We didn't formulate our goals correctly. We didn't know what we wanted. We could have anticipated all the problems with VORTEX."

"Except the ceiling part," Jackson said thoughtfully.

"I am not interesting in planning again," I said. "I want to sit here. It's March. Two more episodes of the show, two more months of school. It'll be over soon."

"*FAS* will have another season," said Elizabeth.

"So what? That's senior year. We'll choose to ignore it. Then we'll go to college and we'll never have to think about any of this again."

Elizabeth was looking at the remote mournfully. She was wearing her typical blinding clothes: green scrubs, a wide pink top, bowling shoes that were so smothered in sparkles that it looked like she'd stepped in unicorn dung. But the clothes seemed out of place in the camel-colored Appelden. "Maybe so."

"You're right," said Jackson. "It's a choice."

I thought he was backing me up. I thought I'd got them. That I, Ethan Andrezejczak, had actually won an argument.

Then Jackson stood up, and his voice became fervent. "We could choose to stay here. We could lie around the Appelden and let people sell their souls. Compromise their ideals. Act like harlots so they have a chance to live their dreams."

He took a step forward and almost tripped over Honey Mustard, but he wasn't derailed.

"These are people we know. This is something we could change. If we don't, if we choose this life"—he gestured to the TV, the twin monitors, the couches and the dog kennel and the gerbil cage, the beigeness of it all—"we're going to live with this choice forever."

Honey Mustard barked.

"And every time we think about high school or *For Art's Sake* or Maura or—or Luke—every time, we're going to hear a voice whispering, '*You should have been able to do better.*'"

"Hell yeah, Jackson," said Elizabeth after a moment.

"Seriously," I said. "I can't believe the words 'live their dreams' crossed your lips."

"Me neither," said Jackson, dropping back into his chair, his pale cheeks flushed. "Desperate times call for desperate measures."

"You got me," said Elizabeth.

I didn't want to admit that I was feeling the old fires stirring too. "You were already on his side," I told her.

"But if I hadn't been, I would be now."

"You can't know that. That's the most fallacious thing I've ever heard."

"You sound like Luke," said Elizabeth.

"Shut up about Luke." Now I was angry, angry that I'd almost been conned into throwing my heart and soul into some dumb plan that would only fail at the end. "I sound like myself."

"Are we going to choose ignominy or glory?" said Jackson. "Will our lives be dull or packed with adventure?"

"You've been reading too many fantasy novels," I told him.

"We need to do something," said Elizabeth. "We need a plan. But first we need to answer the all-important question."

"What have you two been smoking?" I muttered.

She glared at me. "What do we *want?*"

"Glory," said Jackson.

"Justice," said Elizabeth.

"Luke back," said I.

"Okay," she said sternly. "Get over it."

"What?" I yelped. "Luke is *dead* to us. That's not something you get over."

"You're wrong."

"Your best friend betrays you, the best guy you've ever met, and you move right on?"

Elizabeth sat up sharply. "I've wanted to say this for like a month now."

Uh-oh, I thought.

"Luke is not who you thought he was. Luke's not who any of us thought he was. He told you that himself. He had a price. Maybe everyone does, maybe some people don't, but Luke did, and that's that. You're mourning a person who never existed at all."

I grabbed Baconnaise. He woke up and trotted sleepily up my arm. I watched him and didn't meet Elizabeth's eyes.

"You're all about the people who don't exist, aren't you, Ethan?" she said. "Your best friend was a guy you didn't know.

You idolized a teacher you didn't know. You're in love with a girl you don't know. Now all you want to do is play with a gerbil who doesn't even have a personality *to* know. You think he does, but Ethan? Hello? Baconnaise is a rodent."

Baconnaise is so much more than a rodent, I thought. But she was too angry to interrupt.

"That's what you're trading in for us. Look. I'm an actual girl, sitting beside you, and over there, look, it's your best friend. And you treat us like drones or droids or something. We're the things you have to deal with until you make it to your *real* friends. But guess what? Maura's not even a person to you, just some dancing goddess. Luke wasn't a person either. He was this ideal, telling the tale of the tribe or revising the mythopoesis or whatever your big theory was. That's the only reason you like them, because you don't know them at all." She flopped back onto the couch. "It's sick."

"I'm leaving," I said. "You—you—"

I wanted to call her a bitch. I almost did. But I couldn't get the word out. I started wondering whether that'd be sexist, and then I started thinking about how many thoughts could squeeze into the tiniest pause between words, and *then* I started thinking that now I was thinking about my thoughts, and also thinking about the fact that I was thinking about my thoughts, and how that could go on forever, as if my first thought had been placed between two mirrors and now there was an infinite, recursive series of thoughts. And then I thought about how everyone else probably thought about thoughts too, and how there were so many *thoughts* out there, an oppressive consciousness ladled over the globe like a thick, congealing sauce.

I felt *mise en abyme*. Tossed into the abyss.

"Cat-piss and porcupines," I finally said. "I'm leaving."

But I didn't stand up. It sounds superbly lame, but I didn't want to leave Baconnaise. Maybe Elizabeth was right, I thought. Not about all of it. But about him. Him and Herbert. I spent a lot of time having conversations with Baconnaise and Herbert. I knew they didn't have real personalities, but it was exhausting to be around real personalities.

"It's too complicated," I said. I put Baconnaise down again. He immediately went back to sleep. I looked at Elizabeth. She had flushed a bright, beautiful red. "Real people are too complicated. I'm not equipped to handle it."

"*Nobody's* equipped to handle it," said Elizabeth. "But you have to."

"No." How to explain? "I'm singularly unequipped. I can't deal. That's why I've been crushing on Maura for years. That's why I hang out with Baconnaise and Herbert and a bunch of four-year-olds."

"Who's Herbert?" said Jackson.

"Andrezejczak," Elizabeth said, "you're doing it again. 'I'm singularly unequipped.' You think you're the only real person. You think you're the only one who's amazed and scared and freaked by how complicated everyone is."

"You are?"

"Of course I am."

"You are?" I said to Jackson.

He shrugged. "This is between you two."

Typical Jackson, I thought. Then: but Jackson is complicated.

"Everybody else has unattainable crushes too," she said.
"And imaginary friends. Some part of their mind that they
talk to when they can't deal with talking to real people. You
just happen to name yours."

"Is the therapy session over?" said Jackson. "Because we've
got plans to plan."

"Ethan," said Elizabeth, "Luke was wrong. He wanted an
awesome, complicated life, and he thought he had to go on
kTV to get it. He didn't know that sometimes, the most awesome and complicated thing you can do is just stick around."

For the rest of that evening, we discussed what we wanted
and how to get it.

"We need to take control of the discourse," said Jackson.

The word "discourse" always makes me feel dumb.

"We need to be the ones speaking. So we need to do something *on* the show. We can't let them report it. They're experts
at spin."

"But that's impossible," I said. "They'll twist anything we
do. They'll frankenbite it until it supports their message."

"Not something they can't edit," said Jackson. "Not the live
finale."

He was a genius. Or I was a dimwit. There was a gulf between us, that's all I knew.

"But before we proceed," he said, "we've got a problem.

The name. We had IMAGE and VORTEX. But Pound went from Imagism to Vorticism to fascism. To anti-Semitism. Do we call our plan NAZI? ADOLF?"

I cut him off before he said something politically incorrect. "How about EZRA?"

"This is for you, Ezra," said Elizabeth.

"We're doing what you should have done."

There were notes on BradLee's whiteboard, notes about long poems. Our test was coming up. The unit was almost over.

> Long poem = haven to voice identity, resort of
>   the oppressed.
> A way for those who've been denied a voice to
>   find that voice again.

CHAPTER TWENTY-TWO

"Curses," said Jackson. "The schema's gone."

"Do you think BradLee told him?"

"Nah. You know when I rewrote the file with the Merovin-gian protocol? And did the Bonaparte programming scan?"

(I have made the executive decision to replace all com-puter terminology with French monarchical dynasties.)

"Well, I think the Capet bot left traces. They must have run a Carolingian-Bourbon test."

"We can't read the script anymore?" said Elizabeth.

"Nope."

"I don't really mind watching the episode," I said, turning on kTV.

I saw Elizabeth's mouth open in the exact shape required for a snarky comment about how I meant to say that I didn't mind watching Maura Heldsman. Then I saw it close.

"We don't have a choice," I said, smirking at her.

It took a second, but she finally smirked back. "You win. Give me the remote."

"She *is* the remote-meister this month," Jackson reminded me.

I tossed it over to her. "Don't mute anything but commercials," I said. "Or Miki Frigging Reagler. You can always mute him."

"I think that's Maura," said Elizabeth, pointing at the screen.

Maura was not usually hard to recognize, particularly for such an expert as the honorable Ethan Andrczcjczak. But the thing on the floor of the dance studio looked more like a small earthen mound.

"That is an *intense* fetal position," said Jackson. "That's the kind of fetal position that saves your life in an earthquake."

"Maura?" said Luke, entering the studio. "Let me help, okay?"

"No," said the lump.

"We can talk through your ideas. Like last time."

"No."

"What's wrong? You're not upset about us, are you?"

"Close your eyes!" I shrieked as triceratops make-out footage aired. Violins swanned.

"It's over, Ethan," said Elizabeth. I cracked an eye. They were back to the studio.

"I know what's wrong," said Luke. "You're thinking about the future, aren't you?"

Maura gave a violent nod.

"As our season draws to a close," said a voice-over, "so does senior year. Are our contestants pumped, or panicked? Fired up, or freaked out? Find out—right after this."

The show reopened on the Selwyn stage. Trisha and Damien and Willis Wolfe joked about the cold. They hyped up the prize. Then they announced the challenge.

"Tell us, through art, what's next for you," said Trisha. "What does your future hold? You have five days to prepare your piece, but take care: only three contestants will advance to the finale!"

Elizabeth muted the commercials. "I hate to say it," said Jackson, "but it'll be very difficult for us to take action if Luke gets kicked off."

"It's going to be Kyle," said Elizabeth as she turned the sound back on.

As if on cue, Miki F.R. said, "Hey, Kyle? Buddy? I hope you're choosing your monologue carefully, because you, my friend, are the underdog."

"Uh, thanks, Miki," said Kyle. "What are you singing?"

"Oh, I've got some ideas," Miki F.R. said airily. In the next shot, he was surfing the Internet. "Just checking what's out there," he told the camera. The shot zoomed to his Google search bar, which displayed *song musical theater hot guy college turning point awesome*. Jackson sunk to his knees, clutching his forehead and whimpering. I thought he had a migraine, but he started shouting, "Keywords! Keywords! Woe is the state of Googlage in America!" Elizabeth threw slobbery dog toys at him until he shut up.

"It'll be Kyle," she repeated. "Unless someone else totally hashes up the performance."

"Which could happen," said Jackson, pointing at the screen. Maura was standing at the barre, absentmindedly doing calf raises and staring into the mirror.

"Maura!" said Luke, entering the studio. "I thought I'd find you here."

"Doesn't he have a long poem to write?" I muttered.

"Point in favor of the argument that he's not writing it," said Jackson.

Maura tiptoe-ran to Luke and gave him a kiss. "Close your eyes!" I shouted, but it was already over.

"How's the writing?" she said.

"Let's just say my theme is uncertainty."

"Mine too." She sat down with an audible plop. It was the most ungraceful Maura move yet. "I haven't even started. That's how uncertain I am." Her voice was trembling.

"You want me to leave you to it?"

"Soon," said Maura. "But——" She grabbed Luke's hands and pulled him down too.

"Close your eyes!" said Elizabeth.

"Gross," I said. I could hear the slurps.

"There's one thing I *am* certain I want in my future," murmured Luke.

"*You,*" all three of us said with him.

"BradLee, BradLee," said Elizabeth. "You're letting us down."

"Dialogue doesn't get much more predictable," said Jackson.

"Can I open my eyes yet?" I said.

After the commercials, there were interviews with Kyle and Miki F.R. Kyle was deciding between Shakespeare and Tennessee Williams. He sounded far too intelligent to be featured for long, so we had to suffer through a lot of Miki F.R.

"You know how some people need less sleep than others? Well, I need less rehearsal! But this is different. Not because I need the practice, but because it's just so much *fun*."

"This can't be scripted," I said. "He's this douchey in real life too."

"The song is a lovely lagoon," he said, "and I just want to dive in."

Fetal Maura came back. Now she was sobbing.

"I don't *know* what my future is. And we've only got two days left and if I don't figure out something I'll be kicked off—"

"Can you use that urgency?" said Luke. "The uncertainty? How you're pulled between two different lives?"

"Luke, just go away."

"Yes!" I shouted.

"Wait," she said. "I didn't mean that."

"No!"

"Well, actually, you should go away."

"Yes!"

"But I still love you!"

"No!"

"She puts you through the wringer, doesn't she?" commented Elizabeth.

I sunk back into the couch, exhausted. "Baconnaise," I moaned, like a guy crying for water in the desert. Elizabeth scooped him from his cage and handed him over. "Hey, little man. Want to do some tightrope walking?"

Elizabeth rolled her eyes, but she didn't say anything.

"Welcome back to *For Art's Sake!*" said Trisha. "These five days have been jam-packed with preparations, and personally I am *thrilled* to see these performances."

"We'll start with Luke Weston!" said Willis Wolfe.

"Unlike my co-contestants, I'm just a junior," said Luke, "and my 'future' is filled with uncertainty. That's a theme you'll hear in this week's installment of the *Contracantos.*"

"The *Contracantos* is Luke's epic poem," Trisha reminded us.

"Not technically an epic," said Luke.

"I'd call it epic!" said Damien.

"I'll just go ahead and start," said Luke.

Baconnaise was looking up at me expectantly, but I knew I had to listen.

Luke read his verses.

"He didn't write that," said Elizabeth.

"He could have," said Jackson.

"He's not who we thought he was," I said. "But—"

"No," said Jackson. "I don't think he could have written that."

"Me neither," said Elizabeth.

They looked at me.

Had he written the new *Contracantos?* It was crappy and clichéd. It was un-Luke. Then again, he seemed pretty un-Luke too. He looked more kTV every episode, with longer hair and cooler clothes. I didn't know whether I'd ever seen beyond his surface. But I needed to. The success of EZRA, the chance of vengeance, of justice for Maura and for all the casualties of kTV's corruption: it all hung on our ability to tell whether Luke still wrote the *Contracantos*.

"I'm unspeakably impressed that you can do such things with words," Trisha was saying.

"He didn't write it," I said slowly.

"Are you sure?" said Elizabeth.

"No," I said. "But sure enough."

We looked at each other and nodded. Our plan was clear. We'd chosen. We were betting that Luke didn't write the *Contracantos*. We were betting that we knew him well enough to know.

Kyle went with a monologue from *Macbeth*. "It's about uncertainty and doubt," he explained, "ambition and indecision— all emotions that are very familiar to me, and to most Selwyn seniors."

"Hmm," said Trisha. "Go right ahead."

"*If it were done when 'tis done,*" said Kyle, "*then 'twere well it were done quickly. . . .*"

"We'll be back after this break," Trisha said when he was finished. Elizabeth muted it.

"I'm nervous, guys," she said.

"What, is your future full of uncertainty and doubt?" said Jackson. "Ambition and indecision?"

When Elizabeth unmuted the show, Trisha cried, "Miki Reagler, come on down!"

"This last semester at Selwyn is a bittersweet time," said Miki F.R. "I adore this school."

The camera panned to a smug Willis Wolfe.

"My time here has gone by so fast," said Miki F.R. "Time flies."

"Oh, barf," I said. Baconnaise looked revolted too. "Where's your dad's knitting basket, Jackson?"

"He moved it because you kept stealing his yarn. But he left the tightrope." Jackson threw me a hank of Baconnaise's favorite green yarn.

"Bacon-Bacon-Baconnaise!" I said, dangling the yarn near his head. He perked up. Even with the tumor, his steps were as light as a ballerina's. He was a joy to watch. Plus, he helped me keep my eyes off Miki F.R.

"And so, I present the best song in *Rent*," he was saying, "one of the best songs of all time—'One Song Glory'!"

Damien was hyperventilating with excitement. Trisha gave him a shut-up-or-else glare as Miki F.R.'s pianist started into some arpeggiated rock-opera chords.

"One song," sang Miki F.R. *"Glory. One song. Before I go."*

I looked up long enough to see the starry-eyed judges, the head-bopping musicians, the agape audience, and Miki F.R., whose eyes were squeezed shut with passion.

"You are an expert," I told Baconnaise, who had crossed the green tightrope six times now. "I love you just as much as I hate Miki Frigging Reagler."

"Every time, Miki!" Trisha said, blinking tears out of her eyes. "Every time!"

"Thanks, Trisha," said Miki F.R. in an ethereal, faraway voice. "Thanks, everyone."

"Glory!" sang Damien. *"From the soul of a young man! A young mannnnn!"*

"I am so fricking grateful to have been on this show," said Miki F.R.

"Wow," said Trisha, somehow managing to gaze at Miki F.R. while simultaneously glaring at Damien. "Wow." She gathered herself. "And finally, ballerina Maura Heldsman!"

Maura walked onstage. Instead of wearing a leotard and pointe shoes, she was in all black: leggings, a tank top, sneakers. She could have been going to the gym.

"Maura! You must have something different for us. Tell us about it."

"I'd prefer to dance first," said Maura.

And so she danced. The music was atonal. I usually couldn't interpret dance, but even I could tell that she was expressing Luke's idea of being pulled between two lives. On stage right, there were exuberant leaps and spins. On stage left, there was nothing. She ran maniacally between the two, and when the music ended—"stopped" would be a better word, because no chord resolved—she sprawled, as if falling, onto the middle of the stage. She stayed there.

There were at least fifteen seconds of silence. All I could do was stare at her. That was all anyone could do. Slowly, the audience began to clap. The applause built until they were standing, and the camera panned to the judges and they were standing too. It was the weirdest dance I'd ever seen, and the most remarkable.

Maura slowly got to her feet and gave an embarrassed smile and a curtsy. Finally, the applause stopped.

"That was—"Trisha began.

"I have to win this show," Maura said.

"But—" said Damien.

"I have to win this show," Maura said again.

The judges figured out that they should be quiet.The camera zoomed in on Maura. She was dripping with sweat. It lingered, but she didn't say anything else.They finally cut to commercials.

Elizabeth hit mute. "You know what?" she said after a minute. "This sucks."

"It really does," I said.

"I don't even like Maura. But I can't stand the thought of her not winning."

"Commercials over," said Jackson.

"Well!" said Trisha. "This last challenge has been *intense.*"

"I got goose bumps when Maura said that," said Damien.

"Me too," I said.

Jackson glanced at me, and I swear that if he didn't have an image to uphold, he would have said, "Me too."

"'I have to win this show,'" Damien was quoting.

"But will she even make it to the finale?" said Trisha. "Contestants, let's chat."

"I'm nervous *for* them!" said Damien.

This whole agreeing-with-Damien-Hastings thing was making me uncomfortable.

"Luke. Kyle. Miki. Maura," said Trisha. "You all have impressed us so much. With your talent, with your dedication. But one of you has to go. Maura, please step forward."

Maura did so, with a defiant jut to her chin.

"Maura, you are—invited back for the finale!"

She closed her eyes and exhaled. So did I. So did Elizabeth and Jackson, and maybe I'm thoroughly deluded, but I think Baconnaise did too.

"Miki," said Trisha. I'd never seen Miki F.R. nervous before. "You are—invited back!"

He punched the air with one arm. "Yeeee-ah!"

"And we're down to Kyle and Luke," said Trisha. "This was a tough, tough decision."

"This isn't about who's less talented," said Damien. "It's about who's not *as* talented."

"And the decision, ladies and gentlemen. Your three finalists will be Maura Heldsman, Miki Reagler, and—"

The camera, of course, went to Kyle and Luke.

"Luke Weston!"

Kyle shrugged, smiled, and shook Luke's hand. Luke pulled him into a man-hug.

"You're going to go far, Kyle," said Trisha.

"Though not any farther on this show!" said Damien.

"And it's sad," said Trisha, "but compared to Luke's eloquent poem, Miki's heart-wrenching song, and Maura's unbelievable dance, your monologue—well, Kyle—"

All the judges spoke together. "THAT WASN'T ART!" What a lovely catchphrase. Kyle was whisked away.

"Be sure to tune in next week!" said Trisha. "We'll start at eight with an hour-long recap of the season: the highs, the lows, the drama, the art. And at nine, our live finale!"

"I'm so psyched!" said Willis Wolfe.

268

"And we'll be bringing back all the original *For Art's Sake* contestants for special interviews and unique insights into the show."

"All that *plus* performances from our three finalists!" said Damien.

"And then, a winner! From kTV's hit reality show, *For Art's Sake*—see you next week!"

Elizabeth zapped it. "Our imperative is clear," she said.

"Now for the details," said Jackson.

"Listen up," I said. "I've got an idea."

What we needed for EZRA, scheduled concurrently with the live finale, one week from that day:

1. The printing presses.
2. A voice.
3. Baconnaise.

CHAPTER TWENTY-THREE

The Serpent Vice lives to be just.
In Coluber we put our trust.
He's made a choice so cool we flipped:
That no contestant should be skipped.
The whole lot should be scholarshipped!
— THE CONTRACANTOS

"*Cantos?*" I said, shoving a newspaper into a freshman's hand.

There wasn't much shoving involved, actually. Everyone welcomed having something to do. It was 7 p.m. on Friday, March 23, and the live finale of *For Art's Sake* would air in two hours. They'd forced the student body, the studio audience, to come early for some technical sound-check reason. The details mattered little to us once we realized how it would work to our advantage: when you're facing two hours without entertainment in a dim, crowded auditorium, any distraction is welcome.

We were wearing the balaclavas again, and we'd made *Selwyn Cantos* shirts for the pretense of authority. We distributed a newspaper to every student within ten minutes flat. I'd just furtively looked around to see whether it was safe to de-mask when one last group approached.

"*Cantos!*" said Elizabeth brightly. She stuffed a newspaper into Coluber's face. He was with some kTV guys, the ones in blazers and fancy jeans who always hung around the set looking arrogant.

Good thing he's a self-centered tool: he didn't even notice that she was wearing a ski mask. He didn't even glance at her face. "Okay," he said. Cramming the newspaper under his arm, he held the auditorium door for the producers.

He had no idea what he was holding.

But he'd know soon enough. He'd hear the rustles, or one of his minions would, maybe even BradLee. If he couldn't find the newspaper Elizabeth had given him, he'd stick out his forked tongue to nab another copy. He'd peruse the front page, where he'd see nothing of interest. It was just the *Selwyn Cantos*, just the school newspaper in a special Finale Edition with in-depth reporting on the show: FOR ART'S SAKE TO CLOSE SEASON WITH SUSPENSEFUL CLIMAX, we'd headlined the article.

Then he would open the paper. And inside, it was *Contracantos*. Pure *Contracantos*. Not the bastardized, bowdlerized version that Luke read on kTV, but a poem Elizabeth had lettered, I had illustrated, and all three of us together had written. It wasn't a work of genius, but, I'd realized, Luke's original *Contracantos* wasn't a work of genius either. I'd once thought you had to be a genius to write a long poem. It turned out that you mostly just had to try.

Coluber would read the poem. He'd get angrier with every

word, but he would follow the instructions therein. He would have to. He'd have no other choice.

Assuming everything went to plan.

Shizzit, I was nervous. I gave Baconnaise a little squeeze in my pocket, and he nipped my finger reassuringly.

The lobby had emptied, so we peeled off our masks and *Cantos* shirts, leaving all-black techie clothing. "Lead the way, Jackson," said Elizabeth. He was already heading up the stairs that led to the balcony, and we followed him through an un-marked door, around the winding passageways that girded the auditorium, down another flight of stairs and through another door and down more narrow stairs until he raised his finger to his lips and, his hand on a metal doorknob, whis-pered, "Backstage."

We knew our respective tasks.

"One hour, forty-nine minutes until go time," said Jackson. "Godspeed."

"You text us when you've done it," Elizabeth told him.

"Roger."

"How many times do I have to tell you? Just because this is a covert operation doesn't mean you have to say roger."

"Roger."

Elizabeth *pff*ted and Jackson disappeared back up the stairs. She pulled the door open. We were in the wings. It was a mess of kTV cameramen and lackeys and officious twenty-somethings with clipboards and walkie-talkies, and nobody noticed as we walked confidently to the rearmost side cur-tain, drew it open, and stepped behind it.

The curtain settled over us with dusty grandeur. I knelt down and brushed off some floor. "Milady, a seat?"

Elizabeth gracefully sunk into a lotus position. "Roger, milord."

This was a weird time. We were nervous but we had an hour and forty-eight minutes to kill. And if the plan was working—*if if if*—then it was working as we sat behind the velour curtain, bored and overwrought all at once.

I'd taken Baconnaise out of my pocket, and he was languishing on my lap. He didn't move much these days.

"We can talk, right?" I whispered.

"This must be soundproof," said Elizabeth, poking at the curtain. "It's sure airproof." She fanned herself with her hands, but that just stirred up dust. She broke into a coughing fit.

"I hope it's soundproof."

"I'm sweating already," she said between hacks.

"I've been sweating for like a week." And I couldn't believe that the time had come, that EZRA was happening now. I patted Baconnaise, and he gave me a lazy, appreciative peck.

"They're all reading it now."

We were silent as we imagined what it was like to be in the auditorium with nearly every other member of the student body. They'd all be digesting the announcements in our *Contracantos*. The whispers would start softly, and then they'd rise to the point that the kTV sound engineers would have to yell for silence. Then the whole cycle would start over again.

It was big news, after all. And they'd want to debate where it came from, and what it meant, and whether it was true.

                              *   *   *

What our *Contracantos* told them:

1. That the Parent Board and Student Council
   would be reviewing whether *For Art's Sake*
   would return for a second season. The presence
   of kTV had a huge impact on life at Selwyn,
   and it was an oversight that the parents and
   students hadn't been consulted in the first
   place.
2. That a large fund would be extracted from
   "the school's coffers" (which meant, of course,
   "Coluber's personal bank account") to fund
   scholarships for all the contestants who *didn't*
   win. After all, they'd greatly contributed to the
   glory and reputation of the school, so it'd be
   a shame if they weren't able to pursue their
   dreams of an artistic career. Coluber himself
   had championed their cause, the *Contracantos*
   said. Some people had tried to talk him out
   of it, but he'd triumphed over the naysayers. It
   would be unjust any other way, he'd told them.
3. That Coluber would announce the nineteen
   new scholarships to a nationwide live audience
   directly after Luke's performance in the finale.
   Therefore, the studio audience should be sure
   to pay lots of attention to Luke, and to applaud
   Coluber's announcement with vim and vigor.

Of course, none of this was true. Yet. By presenting it as true, it would become true. That was our hope: that art would become life.

We figured that Number 1 would be the easiest, because the Parent Board and Student Council, two perpetually power-hungry organizations, would immediately be like, *Yeah!*

Number 2, of course, was more difficult. Coluber would read about the new scholarships. He may have been reading it that very second, while we inhaled dust and sweated behind the curtain. And he'd rack his brains for a way to get out of it, and—we hoped—he wouldn't think of anything. He'd realize that he had to give the scholarship money. If he didn't, the students would boo, rebel, call him out on live national TV. Even if he exposed the issue as a fake, the students would still demand scholarships for their classmates. We hoped.

And Number 3. Our plan hinged on Number 3, because Number 3 was a lie. We weren't going to wait for Coluber. If he decided to brazen it out and not make the announcement, the students *might* call him out—but it was more likely that they'd be confused and the show would move swiftly onward and before they realized they needed to do something, everything would be finished, the cameras off, the season over. Coluber would have slithered out of everything.

So that's why the scholarships weren't going to be announced after Luke's performance by Coluber. They would be announced during Luke's performance. By Luke.

We *hoped.*

It all depended on Luke.

Which meant that it all depended on Jackson, who, at that

very moment, was alone in the deserted kTV editing studio, hacking the scripts and the teleprompter.

"Nothing," said Elizabeth, checking her phone. She'd last checked about a minute ago, but we'd started to feel panicky.

"He said it would take him forty-five minutes," I said.

"It's been almost an hour."

"I know that."

"Don't snap at me."

"I'm not snapping."

"You're snapping."

Baconnaise was agitated. He shuddered and made the arduous climb from lap to shoulder. "Look, Elizabeth," I said, trying to sound calm for his sake. "I'm nervous. I'm sorry."

I could hear her sigh, her slump. "Me too. I wish he'd text us progress reports."

"He said they would interrupt his creative flow."

She snorted. "Great, now I have dust up my nose. Yeah, well, I'm freaking out here."

I almost put my arm around her, and then I wondered whether she'd think it was weird, and I remembered crashing through the ceiling, and I thought about Maura. By then, it was too late. The moment had passed.

No word from Jackson. It'd been another twenty minutes. "Do you think Luke and Maura are really together?" I said.

Elizabeth heaved a sigh heavy with dust and exasperation. "Why are you asking me?"

Oops. Now I wished I hadn't. I'd just been bored, and Baconnaise had not been forthcoming.

"Because, Ethan, I have no insight into the matter."

"Oh. Sorry. I thought you might. Because—"

"Because I'm a *girl*?"

I'd forgotten how irritable Elizabeth gets when she's nervous.

"News flash. *Girls* have no more understanding of *love affairs* than *guys* do," she said. She hissed it, actually.

"What about, like, those magazines?"

"It's not something you *learn* from *magazines*." Still quite hissy.

"How do you learn it then?" I was curious. Maybe she knew something I didn't.

"Try using basic human sense."

"I'm not very good at that."

"Oh my frigging God, haven't we had this discussion already? Nobody is good at it."

"So why are you telling me to use it?"

"Because that's the point. You have to *practice*."

How do you practice? Can I practice with you? Is this conversation over? I didn't know what to ask, and I didn't want to unleash another slew of italics, but she kept talking.

"You're an art major. You know what people say when you tell them you can draw."

"Well, I'm not sure 'can' is the word I'd use."

"Stop pretending you suck at everything, Ethan. What do they say?"

"They say, 'Oh, I can't draw.'"

"Exactly."

"'I'm terrible at art.'"

"Yeah. And I'm always thinking, it's not like they'd pick up an instrument and expect Mozart to flow forth. But when they can't draw on the first try, they give up. It's like they're expecting too much of their hands. Hands need practice drawing. Eyes need practice seeing."

"Okay," I said. "I think I see where you're going."

"Shut up. I'm reaching my dramatic conclusion. Ethan: you need to practice love too. It's hard, it's really hard, and if you don't practice, how can you expect to be any good?"

"Selwyn should add it as a major. The art of love."

She giggled, which I took as a victory.

"Everyone would graduate *so* well adjusted," I said. I was getting into this idea. I could imagine the intro class: What Is Love? It'd be interdisciplinary, philosophy and literature and biology all working together. (No math. Math has nothing to do with love.) And the final project would be a field study. Once you'd passed, you could move to the intermediate-level classes: Love in Film, or Practical Applications of Love, or Coping with Crushes—

"I don't think they're really together."

Right. Luke and Maura. "You don't?"

"Nah." She was quiet for a minute. "But does it matter?"

I looked at her in the gloaming, and she'd never looked so pretty, the lines of her face exaggerated by the harsh faint light of our cell phones, her eyes fluid, her wild hair melting into the shadows of the curtain, and behind her face the unknowable thoughts, tangy and smart and unexpected, awesomely complicated. I almost—almost, again!—let my hand drift toward her head to touch a dreadlock. I remembered how soft they were.

"I don't know," I said.

"Does it matter to you, I mean."

That question was not about Luke and Maura. I may have been an amateur in the study of love, but I knew that much. But I still didn't know what I wanted: to be with Maura, to be with Elizabeth, to be alone, just me and the Baconnator. This was where my course would help. It would help you figure out what you wanted. Then she shook her heavenly head and her dreadlocks bounced and she said, "It matters, Ethan. To you, it matters."

CHAPTER TWENTY-FOUR

While millions watch the finalists,
We'll hold our breath for final twists.
For after Luke, dear Serpent Vice P
Will offer each contestant nicely
Fifty thousand bucks, precisely.
  — THE CONTRACANTOS

"Cat-piss," cursed Elizabeth as she looked at her phone.

"Porcupines," I said as I looked at mine.

Jackson had sent us the same text: *Circumstances have con-spired and I'm unable to access the scripts. Still working on tele-prompter. Mobilize for backup plan on Phase C.*

"I had a dream," said Elizabeth, "and it was that we wouldn't need this particular backup plan."

"Same," I said grimly.

"Let's get it over with."

We staggered our escape. As before, the backstage area was so hectic that nobody noticed a thing. We met in the hallway and scuttled down to the green room.

"Hide here," said Elizabeth, pulling me into a niche in front of the set-storage room. She checked the time. "We should see them file out in about two minutes."

They were true to the schedule that Jackson had found on the admin server. The seventeen students who'd already been kicked off *For Art's Sake* came out and turned to go onstage. Then came Maura and Miki F.R. and Luke. Then Trisha Meier and Damien Hastings and Willis Wolfe. Then a few techies. The door clanged shut.

"Get 'er done," Elizabeth muttered, and she shot out of the niche and into the green room as soon as the last techie turned the corner. I grabbed Baconnaise and tried to take deep breaths. I didn't envy her her job, but mine was nerve-racking too.

It was five till nine. The show was about to start. With everyone onstage during the introductory scene, Elizabeth was sweeping the deserted green room for scripts. She'd remove one page from all of them; in Luke's script alone, she'd replace that page with something else.

It was my task to create a diversion should anyone try to get into the green room. I was equipped with the following:

1. My powers of persuasion. We'd brainstormed several stories that would cause a delay long enough for Elizabeth to escape. In most of them, I'd pretend that I'd had a mental breakdown and needed professional help ASAP.
2. Baconnaise. I could engage the would-be intruder in a conversation about Baconnaise's awesomeness. I could show them some tricks.

Or I could drop him; they'd think he was a rat
and start screaming.

3. A hammer. Not for violence, although if it was
Miki Frigging Reagler I'd be sorely tempted.
But to break the glass on the wall-mounted fire
extinguisher and evacuate the building. This was
a last resort for two reasons. First off, it would
ruin the live show and EZRA as well; we'd have
to start planning all over again. Furthermore, it
was a felony.

You know me. I do not handle nervousness well. I had to dissociate, or else I really was going to have a mental breakdown.

So I started thinking about that major. The art of love.

The intro class, I decided, would have a unit on Ezra Pound. They'd analyze those lines I'd read with Maura and in BradLee's class:

> *What thou lovest well remains,*
> *the rest is dross*

I'd always misread them. I'd looked at Maura, I'd looked at Luke, and I'd had stirring thoughts about how they'd remain. And I'd liked "the rest is dross," because it gave me permission to stop looking at anything or anyone else. This doesn't matter, I'd said about Elizabeth, and Jackson, and kTV, and so much else. It's dross.

But I'd missed the word "well." You have to love something

well, to keep it. And I had not loved well because I had not known how.

That would be the point of the major, I thought. Everyone knows how to love, but not how to love well. The mistake is too easy. You call her a goddess and you think he's perfect and suddenly they're not people anymore. You've betrayed them. Instead of being in awe of their complexity, you've swept it away.

This class would not be pleasant. I can tell you that it's painful to have the rosy gauze ripped from your eyes, the halos dashed from their heads. You cling to your idols. But I can also tell you—not from experience but from the glimpses found in daydreams and books and cold hard thought—that once you've recognized a person as a person, you can start to love that person *well*. It's an awful thing to learn, but it's the best thing in the world to know.

Both Baconnaise and the hammer remained in my pockets. Elizabeth made a fast sweep of the green room. She exited with a stack of the pages she'd torn from the scripts.

"Do you think you got them all?"

"I have no effing idea." I thought she'd be adrenalized and happy, but she sounded even more irritable than before.

"What do you mean?"

"I got all the ones I could find. And realized in the process how—how tenuous this all is. If I missed one, if somebody took their script onstage, it's all over."

I declined to think about that. "Did you get Luke's?"

"I got his *main* one. In that black notebook he uses onstage. Who knows. He could have another." She waved the sheaf of pages. "I got a full script too."

"You didn't."

"I wasn't going to tell you, but—" She shrugged. "Maura was wrong. They've chosen already. Look."

I grabbed the script from her, scanning pages and flipping toward the end.

> **TRISHA:** We'll take a short break, but we've got so much more left!

Flip, flip.

> **DAMIEN:** And seriously, nobody knows what's going to happen.

Flip, flip.

> **MIKI:** I'm so *incredibly* honored.

No.

> **MIKI:** This is literally a dream come true. Thank you, Trisha! Thank you, kTV! Thank you, America!

"We have to keep walking, Ethan."

I hadn't even realized I'd stopped.

"We can't get caught back here. God, this is why I didn't want to show you."

"Miki Frigging Reagler," I said.

"Put them in here." She'd taken the lid off a garbage can.

"Ew."

"Now." You don't mess with anyone who says "now" like that. The scripts were duly placed underneath the remains of the kTV dinner and adorned with globs of mustard and shreds of turkey. Elizabeth dumped a half-full Diet Coke over them and I replaced the lid.

"I can't believe she's going to lose."

"This is why EZRA has to work," said Elizabeth. She grabbed my elbow. "We've got to get that scholarship for her."

"And for the rest of them," I said, trying to be fair.

"I just care about Maura." She looked at me, and I couldn't tell whether she was going to laugh or cry. "Oh, Ethan, what's happened to us?"

"We have to do everything we can," I said. We'd reached the fork in the hallway.

"Yes. *Everything.* Sacrifice *everything.*"

"I will." I didn't want to split up, but that was the plan, and I was fully committed.

"See you when it's over." She dissolved down the other hallway. I went on alone. We'd decided, way back in the era of rational thought, that Elizabeth and I should disband, one going to stage right, the other to stage left. If they discovered only one of us, that person could possibly pass as some kTV obsessive who wanted to get as close to the action as possible. But if they found two, they'd think *plot.*

Why not just go back to the auditorium? That was tempting. But the sound guys probably had it on lockdown. And besides, being in the wings would allow us to troubleshoot. We'd entered uncharted waters, the part of Jackson's timetable that said, "Resolve problems on an as-needed basis." Which meant, "Improvise." And that was terrifying. Terrifying with a trumpet, terrifying now.

• • •

Standing behind a side curtain, I mouthed to Baconnaise, "So far, so good."

Elizabeth and I were hidden much more openly than we had been earlier. I couldn't see her, but I knew she mirrored my position. It was weird to watch the show from the wings. Trisha and Damien and Willis Wolfe looked orange and plastic, like low-quality action figures. The stage was hung with cameras, and I knew that the entire Selwyn student body was in the audience. But all that betrayed their presence was a rustle, an undulation, like the sea at night.

The performers, presumably, had a direct view of me. For a while I blanched every time somebody looked in my direction. But their eyes always seemed blank and unseeing, like those of slightly manic zombies, and I started to believe what Jackson had kept promising: the lights were so bright that the performers couldn't see *anything* that wasn't under the same degree of illumination. In my black clothes, ensconced in curtain, I was darkness to them.

And so I watched the show.

"A thousand welcomes to you from chilly Minneapolis, Minnesota," Trisha cried.

"Here we are," said Willis Wolfe. "It's the live finale of the show that's stolen the hearts of the nation—"

"*For Art's Sake!*" said Damien.

"Tonight is a celebration," began Trisha. She introduced the seventeen students who, as she put it, *used* to compete on the show. They'd serve as one of the judging panels for the finalists. "They'll have one vote," said Trisha, "the studio audience another, and we three judges the third. And with those three votes, we'll choose the inaugural champion of *For Art's Sake!*"

I wished I could talk to Elizabeth. I was alert for any sign that they'd read our *Contracantos,* that something was different, but I hadn't picked up on anything yet.

"And now," said Trisha, "the trio you've been waiting for— our finalists!"

"First," said Willis Wolfe, "the newest addition to the show, poet extraordinaire, budding man of letters: Luke Weston!"

There was Luke. He was wearing these snazzy dark jeans and a white V-neck T-shirt. The Luke I knew did not wear V-necks.

"And next, everybody's favorite actor," said Damien, "the guy who can dance like Fred Astaire, act like Brad Pitt, and sing like Pavarotti." He only stumbled a little bit over Pavarotti. "I give you: Miki Reagler!"

Miki F.R.'s entrance will be seared in my memory forever. He walked in all nonchalant, but then he recoiled at the sight of the audience. He clapped his hand over his mouth and widened his eyes in this hideously fake moue of surprise. Then he recovered, winked, and handsprang across the stage. Yuck.

"And now," said Trisha, "the prima ballerina. First in the company, first in the hearts of men!" She raised an eyebrow until everyone, even Damien, got her stupid joke. "I present graceful, gorgeous Maura Heldsman!"

Maura just walked, but her walk looked about ten times more elegant than Miki F.R.'s gymnastic cavorting.

"Thank you! Thank you!" said Trisha. "Just look at your three finalists! Aren't they incredible?" You have no idea how much applause I'm omitting. This finale was straight-up thirty percent clapping. "We'll be back soon with interviews, performances, and a special, surprise announcement that will make you *all* very happy."

A special, surprise announcement.

They'd read it.

EZRA was up and running.

CHAPTER TWENTY-FIVE

Fifty K is a shitload of zeros!
So give our Serpent Vice a hero's
Welcome when he comes on-screen
To tell the world of the nineteen
New grants he's adding to the scene.
                    — *THE CONTRACANTOS*

It only took one boring commercial break for me to realize that Trisha's claim of a special, surprise announcement meant absolutely nothing. It was a buy for time. They had read the *Contracantos,* but now they would scramble to find a way to sidestep it. I could imagine the frantic conversations. "I'm not going to do it," Coluber would say. "I simply refuse."

"You have to," Blazer Guy would respond. "Look at this audience. They're going to rebel otherwise."

"These children can't force me to do anything," Coluber would say.

Blazer Guy would be the sort to nurture a secret fear of teenagers. "They could form a mob. They could kill us all."

"Better death than generosity."

During the break, the stage crew had brought in some couches, where Trisha Meier sat with several former contestants. All her interview questions were designed for controversy. Tears were an obvious goal. I kept one hand in my pocket, wrapped around Baconnaise, and paid only intermittent attention.

I had to look when they played that odious bush-shaking footage again, back from the Landscape Arboretum episode.

"Josh DuBois," said Trisha, "you *clearly* enjoyed your time with Maura. Are you rooting for her to win?"

Josh was sitting all akimbo on the couch, just as he did in Latin class. "I'll go out on a limb here and say no. No. Maura Heldsman does not deserve to win."

Trisha feigned shock, but she was loving it.

"The champion should be a great artist, sure, and nobody's saying Maura can't dance. But they should also have, like, character."

"Come on, Josh," inserted Kyle Kimball. I always knew I liked him.

"I've been waiting a long time to say this," said Josh. "Maura doesn't care about other people. She's sold herself to win this show."

"Wow," said Trisha. "I see some true emotion coming through here."

That only tightened my resolve. "kTV is the wrong side," Jackson had said once in the Appelden. "They're wrong. Usually I don't even believe in right and wrong, but they're wrong."

*   *   *

"Here we go, Baconnaise," I whispered half an hour later. "The moment of reckoning."

The orchestra had set up in the pit, and the stage was ready for the three performances.

"We're ready for our first finalist!" said Trisha.

"What about that special, surprise announcement?" said Damien.

Trisha ignored him. "Willis Wolfe, tell us. What's the challenge this week?"

"The challenge is that there is no challenge." You could tell Willis Wolfe thought this was vastly profound.

"The finalists have simply been told that they have three minutes," said Trisha. "Three minutes, for the performance of a lifetime. Miki Reagler, you've drawn the first slot. Miki, come on down!"

Miki F.R. jogged out to wild applause. He grabbed the handheld mike. I shot him beams of animosity.

"I am performing one of my favorite show tunes—and that's saying something!" he said. "This song speaks to the amazing, crazy time I've had on this show, a time I'll never forget." What a suck-up.

Trisha made a heart shape with her hands and pushed it toward him. "Love ya!" she cooed.

"I present the anthem of lovers everywhere. From *A Chorus Line*, 'What I Did for Love'!"

Damien leapt to his feet. "OH MY GOD, THAT'S MY

FAVORITE SONG!" He *had* to be going off script. "Best. Song. Ever."

The orchestra launched into it. Miki F.R. crooned, and then he belted. He could sing, I'll admit. I took Baconnaise out of my pocket so he could watch.

"Kiss today goodbye," sang Miki F.R., *"and point me toward tomorrow. We did what we had to dooooo!"* Baconnaise was not won over. *"Won't forget, can't regret what I did for love!"*

"Miki, you make me cry every time," said Trisha.

Miki F.R. was shaking his head. "Trisha, honey, I make *myself* cry." Baconnaise and I rolled our eyes at each other.

"And now for our second contestant!" said Trisha. "Maura Heldsman!"

"Here she is," I told Baconnaise. "Here's the girl." He'd never seen her, except on TV.

Maura entered in a leotard and pointe shoes. "Hi, everyone. I'll be dancing the part of Odette from *Swan Lake.*"

"Classic," murmured Trisha.

"Using a variation on the Petipa-Ivanov choreography."

"Also classic."

The orchestra swept into the piece, and Maura danced. There were only a few feet between us, but it felt like miles. She'd become otherworldly. It was alien, what she could do with her body, the concentration on her face. When it was over, she had to bow about eight times before the audience would shut up.

It was impossible to believe that she would lose.

"Maura," said Trisha, "that was virtuosic. How are we ever going to choose among our three finalists?"

"Yeah, that was awesome," said Damien. "And I wish I had calves like yours."

"Thank you *so* much, Maura," Trisha said quickly. "We'll take a short break, but we've got so much more left! Our third finalist's performance. That special, surprise announcement. And at last, the winner will be crowned! Stay with us."

Now I really wondered whether they were just dangling the special announcement to pacify the schemers out there. Maybe they'd keep mentioning it, and then suddenly conclude the episode. Coluber was probably persuading Blazer Guy. "We can give them kTV backpacks," he'd tell him. "However, we cannot make this announcement on national television."

"But they could ruin our episode," Blazer Guy would say.

"This announcement will ruin my *life*."

But Luke was up next, and he would make the announcement for Coluber. That was why Elizabeth had replaced the scripts. That was why Jackson was hacking the teleprompter. They did *have* a teleprompter, right? I took a few wary steps, craning as far forward as I could without betraying my location. They had to have one. Sometimes Damien sounded downright intelligent.

Ah, there it was. I could just see it. It was strung up in a makeshift fashion, hanging from the ceiling with unconnected wires dangling down. There was only one bundle in use, a couple of green wires that made a circus-awning swoop to where they were tacked at the top of the curtain. TV looked so crappy from the inside, the glamour as jury-rigged as that ceiling I'd Scotch-taped back together.

I retreated back to my hiding spot, and that's when the physical nervousness hit me. My knees went all loose, as if my patellas had liquefied. My left thumb started spasming and my heartbeat was quick and light and the only thing keeping me from melting into a gormless, formless mess was Baconnaise, cupped in my right hand.

Because it was then I realized I hadn't heard from Jackson. He'd never responded to the update about the green room. And he had said he'd text us when he accessed the teleprompter. I didn't dare check my phone; the light would be a dead giveaway. I hadn't felt a buzz, but maybe my nervousness was dulling my senses. I reached into my pocket and grabbed the phone. Baconnaise vibrated, but the phone was still. I wished I could look at it. It was surely holding that text message, I told myself.

"I am overjoyed that it's time for our third finalist's performance," said Trisha. "His work just blows me away. Luke Weston, it's your turn!"

I put Baconnaise back in my pocket. He didn't want to see Luke. He felt betrayed by Luke, who had always pretended to like him.

The cheers rose as he came onstage. Luke had always had an admirable walk. It was the only fast walk you could ever describe as a saunter; it was confident and eager and athletic. He was holding the black notebook that disguised his script.

That was what Elizabeth had found in the green room. She'd said so. So why was I so nervous?

"Looking good, Luke!" said Damien.

"Hi, everybody!" said Luke with a grin.

And he opened his notebook, and he froze.

He'd hit our poem. Jackson had wanted to type it with the same font and formatting that kTV used for their scripts, in case Luke glanced at it beforehand. But Elizabeth and I had prevailed, symbolic force over logic: she'd written it out and I'd illustrated it, just as we'd done with the first two issues, just as we'd done with the issue we'd distributed today. It was unmistakable, and we knew he'd recognize it immediately.

But—and this was our biggest gamble in a plan full of them—we hoped, we believed, that he wouldn't be able to re-cite his true lines from memory. Luke knew every word of the *Contracantos* that he actually wrote. But we had bet he hadn't written these lines. It could have been Coluber, it could have been BradLee, it could have been some other kTV screen-writer. But it wasn't Luke.

Or was that giving him too much credit? Maybe he *had* brought himself to write it. Maybe he'd written that dross.

But by the way he tensed, staring at the notebook in dis-belief, I knew that we'd bet right. He'd never written anything that appeared on *For Art's Sake*. He'd just parroted their lines, going along with the scripted reality. I thought it'd be worse if he turned out to have written the crap that he'd read on the show, but as I watched him fumble with his artsy notebook and shoot a panicky smile to the audience, I felt a wave of loathing for him, for his duplicity and weakness.

But I had to pay attention.

Luke gave a desperate look to the judges' table.

Trisha beamed at him, but I could see the ire in her bared teeth: *Start talking, Luke, or live to regret it.*

Luke gestured to his script.

I saw Trisha surreptitiously flip a page on her desk. Then she grabbed Damien's script. But they'd have the versions with the missing pages, the pages Elizabeth had destroyed. Unlesses flooded my mind—unless she'd missed one, unless they had multiple copies, unless they'd printed out new versions—but Trisha's toothy grin didn't relax.

No hero jogged onstage with a new script. Twenty seconds of Luke in confusion had been broadcast across the country. I could imagine Coluber's face right now, hissing in anger, cursing the incompetence of his crew.

Then Luke's face cleared. He smiled, his old rakish grin, and the audience cheered.

"Hey there," he said. "Sorry about the technical difficulties." He was adorable. They cheered again. "I'm stoked to present the final installment of my long poem, the last section of my *Contracantos*."

I couldn't figure out why he felt so good. Was he stalling? But he kept glancing at his notebook as if the correct words had rematerialized.

"I can't let this opportunity go by without thanking the person who made it possible for me to stand up here. Ladies and gentlemen, let's give a mega hand to the beautiful, the talented, the great Trisha Meier!"

Trisha had relaxed too. She shook her head lovingly at Luke and pretended that she wasn't lapping up the applause.

I didn't get it. He wasn't reading from his notebook, because this stuff wasn't in the script we'd put in there. And Jackson had hacked the teleprompter. That was the whole plan.

I took a few steps forward. Then I understood why his glances down were so quick and fake, how he was able to face the audience so winningly and to speak with such assurance. It was indeed the teleprompter. Which was in perfect, working condition. The screen loomed balefully, flanked by the cameras with their Cyclopean eyes, and on it the words appeared like karaoke. It was mesmerizing to watch the confluence of the typed words and his speech, and I almost let my jaw go slack and watched the episode, just as I'd watched the seventeen before it.

"And now," he said, "my poem."

Luke started reading the poem. I watched the teleprompter. Verses were scrolling up from the bottom. Theirs. Not ours.

Jackson had told us that he'd be in touch. But he hadn't been. With sudden clarity, I knew I'd been fooling myself. If my phone had buzzed, I'd have felt it. There had been no message from Jackson. He must have been caught.

But if Luke's poem was read as scripted—

It had all hinged on Luke's poem.

If Luke didn't make the announcement, Coluber wouldn't make the announcement.

Nothing would be righted. Everything would stay the

same. Miki Frigging Reagler would win, and Maura Heldsman would stay in Minnesota, and her other life, the one where she went to Juilliard and danced in New York, would slip away.

Peter Martins. Lincoln Center. That is all. Period. I don't want anything else.

It would slip away like a dream upon waking. She'd forget how much she'd cared.

A mess. I should have been able to do better.

Coluber would only get richer. So would kTV. They'd do another season, and another, pressing students through the mangle of hope, goading them to dream big because big dreams make better TV when they're crushed. BradLee would keep spying, and Luke—

Well, Luke wouldn't be our friend either way. That was over. EZRA wasn't about getting Luke back.

All these thoughts jostled for space in the five seconds of cheers that followed Luke's first couplet. I felt my phone buzz against my leg and I didn't look because I knew what it would say. *Ethan: DO something.*

Then there was a buzz against my other leg, and I grabbed him. Baconnaise. I never had gotten used to the tumor. It felt like a Ping-Pong ball.

He looked at me. I could have sworn he smiled.

"Baconnaise," I whispered. There had to be something I could do, something *we* could do. I looked around madly. Left. Right. Up.

Those wires.

"Baconnaise," I whispered again. "Baconnaise, you stud. Choose green."

298

I crouched and put him down and he took off with all the bravery I'd always known he had, climbing the curtain like he'd been trained in parkour. What character. What pure, thought-less courage. He made a little leap—he was above the stage now—he was at the bundle of green wires, the ones leading to the teleprompter. He looked back at me questioningly.

I nodded. I snapped my fingers. It didn't matter, now, if anyone heard.

He heard the signal and somewhere in his rodent brain it resonated, the same signal I'd given him so many times in the Appelden. He dove for a green wire and he took it in his mouth and he began to chew. And I couldn't watch but I watched, I watched the screen and Luke and my Baconnaise, and the screen flickered and the look of concentration on his little face was unbearable, I was so filled with pride and hor-ror and hope. The lines on the screen zigzagged and the words became illegible. I glanced at Luke—he'd abruptly stopped, mid-couplet—and I knew the end was near. So I turned away from the snowy teleprompter and my former best friend, and I looked only at Baconnaise.

He was still chewing. Twenty feet above the stage, still gnawing away. I heard Luke begin to speak again. He was reading from his notebook, reading our new words. Easily, winningly. He was a natural. And the audience rumbled with expectation and joy, and—

I knew it would happen.

Elizabeth said later, "You couldn't have known."

But I will always know this: I knew it would happen.

CHAPTER TWENTY-SIX

The power lay behind the throne,
But he'll discharge the long-held loan.
And we are awesome. Our art lasts.
The snake was hiding in the grass:
Poetic justice kicked his ass.
                    — THE CONTRACANTOS

Luke was almost finished.

"Poetic justice," he read with gusto, "kicked his *ass.*"

Baconnaise kept chewing and there was nothing I could do. I saw what I knew I would see. His entire body stiffened as if electrocuted—which it was—and his eyes bugged, his shape swelled as every hair stood upright. Even then he did not take his jaws off the wire. I had my arms outstretched like a suppliant, desperately gesturing for him to let go, to come back, but we hadn't practiced that part. I hadn't taught him to come back to me.

Luke finished his *Contracantos,* our *Contracantos,* to wild applause. The poem had announced the new scholarships. They wouldn't be able to get out of them now.

I thought it was over. I put my hands down. I almost covered my face. But the current must have stopped running, because Baconnaise lifted his head and jerked himself away from the bundle of wires. He flew through the air and landed on the stage with a catlike grace. I heard a faint shriek, and Baconnaise shot across the stage, moving with the mania of a madman, a madgerbil, and Luke held out his hands, and Baconnaise propelled himself into them. And there was a sudden stillness, and Luke looked down.

"Thank you *so* much, Luke Weston," said Trisha Meier, prancing toward him from the judges' table. Under her smile I could see the curl of revulsion toward whatever vermin had dared fling itself from the bowels of this Midwestern stage and die on her star's lap.

The audience took her cue and began to clap.

"And we'll be back with the final vote after this break!" said Trisha Meier. Her smile dropped with a thud the instant the cameras blinked off. She ushered Luke offstage, toward me. She started yelling at the pages running around with clipboards. Luke stood there, looking uncertain and alone.

I stepped out from behind the curtain. He wasn't surprised.

"Hi, Ethan."

"Hi."

"Here he is." He gave me Baconnaise's tiny body. The hairs had settled. I cradled him in both hands but his body was smaller than I remembered. He was almost weightless in death. I choked up. Baconnaise.

"He saved us," said Luke.

I didn't question that statement at all. I just nodded.

Luke reached out his hand but froze in midair, waiting for permission. I nodded. He stroked the little body. "I missed you." He was talking to Baconnaise.

I think he was talking to Baconnaise.

"When the mind swings by a grass-blade," said Luke, two fingers soothing his fur.

It took me a second to realize: he was quoting the *Cantos,* the real *Cantos.*

"An ant's forefoot shall save you. The clover leaf smells and tastes as its flower."

I stroked his fur too. And although I knew that the difficult, individualistic, dangerously intelligent Ezra Pound had never imagined his masterwork being quoted over the corpse of a gerbil named Baconnaise, I didn't think he'd mind.

And you know what? If he'd minded? Well, guys, key difference between life and art: *ars longa, vita brevis.* Art is long and life is short. Ezra Pound is dead. The *Cantos* are not.

"Welcome back to *For Art's Sake!*" said Trisha.

"You did it!" cried Damien.

"I did it!" Trisha addressed the camera. "I was telling them during the break, I was like, I'm not sure I'm going to be able to get through the last welcome-back without tearing up!"

"But there's still so much excitement left!" said Willis Wolfe.

"That's right. First, some very exciting news." She didn't look too excited. "The news that Luke Weston hinted at with that *memorable* poem."

The finalists and former contestants filed onstage, all twenty standing in a row.

"I'd like to introduce America to a very special someone," said Willis Wolfe. "He's my colleague, and he's my friend: the vice principal of Selwyn Academy, Sebastian Coluber!"

Coluber came onstage from his first-row seat in the audience. "Thanks, Willis. Yes, I do have an extremely exciting announcement." Nope, he didn't look excited either.

"Mr. Coluber has been essential to the production of this show," said Willis Wolfe. "He's been behind it all along."

"And it's been a pleasure," said Coluber. "So rewarding."

"Do the announcement!" said Damien, like a little kid.

"Ah yes," said Coluber. "As you've learned from Luke's terrific poem, we've been thinking about the fairness of the prize. The winner is set to receive one hundred thousand dollars of scholarship money. But what about the other contestants? After all, they gave so much of themselves to this show—so much heart, so much spirit."

Trisha was nodding tearily along. The contestants looked tense.

"And so," said Coluber, "to each of the non-finalists, Selwyn and kTV will work together to offer—" He swallowed. "Fifty thousand dollars, to be applied to any arts institution in the nation!"

The former contestants went wild. They danced, they screamed, they hugged. So did the audience. I was proud of my classmates.

"The winner was already set to receive a hundred-thousand-dollar scholarship," said Coluber, "as well as a trip to LA, a spread in *La Teen Mode,* and a guaranteed signing with an agent. However—"

He looked as though he might puke.

"To the finalists, who have devoted their school year to these eighteen episodes—Selwyn and kTV will present a one-hundred-thousand-dollar scholarship!"

The audience screamed even louder. Miki F.R. leapt up and clicked his heels in joy. Maura and Luke hugged each other, so Miki F.R. vaulted over to force himself between them. At last, when the audience calmed down, they separated. Maura was tear-stained and glowing.

"It's hard to keep yourself from smiling when something like that happens," said Trisha.

"Why would you want to keep yourself from smiling?" said Damien.

"It's heartwarming," said Willis Wolfe. "It's a lot of money. But it's heartwarming."

Trisha brandished three envelopes. "And now, I hold the fate of our three finalists."

The losers evacuated the stage. Luke, Maura, and Miki F.R. stood in a row, holding hands.

"One envelope holds the opinion of the seventeen former contestants," said Trisha. "One holds the opinion of the Selwyn student body. And one holds the opinion of the three judges."

"Nobody knows what's going to happen," said Damien. "Seriously."

"Each contestant will unseal one envelope," said Trisha. "Luke Weston, tell the world its contents!"

"The first vote says"—Luke grinned—"Miki Reagler!"

Miki F.R. clasped his hands over his cheeks. He was trembling.

"Miki, open that envelope," said Trisha.

"The second vote says—Maura Heldsman!"

Maura smiled, but calmly.

"Now, Maura. Maura, you hold the winner in your hands."

"Unless it says Luke!" That was Damien. Trisha ignored him. Of course there wouldn't be a three-way tie. The whole thing was rigged.

"Maura, make that announcement. Who is the winner of *For Art's Sake*? Who is America's Best Teen Artist? Who is the inaugural champ—"

"Miki Reagler."

"What?" said Trisha.

Maura waved the paper and beamed. "Miki! Miki, it's you!" She hugged him, all smiles, but Miki F.R. pulled away so he could start jumping up and down. He'd probably practiced this moment in front of his bedroom mirror.

"America, I give you the champion! Miki Reagler!"

You could already tell Trisha was ruing the decision to have the contestants announce the winner. The drama quotient was severely lowered. Now Luke was shaking Miki F.R.'s hand.

Miki F.R. grabbed the mike. "I'm so *incredibly* honored."

305

Even the judges were standing and clapping. Everyone was. Heck, I was.

"This is literally a dream come true. Thank you, Trisha! Thank you, kTV! Thank you, America!"

Minutes upon minutes of applause.

"And that is that," said Trisha. "It's been a great season, folks. Congratulations to Miki, our champion. Congratulations to Maura and Luke, our finalists. Congratulations to our judges and the other contestants! And one last note from your hosts—"

"THAT WAS ART!" they all yelled together.

The Selwyn orchestra struck up the theme music. That was EZRA. And that, as Trisha said, was that.

CHAPTER TWENTY-SEVEN

We learned throughout our show's long run,
As plans were planned and deeds were done,
That we aren't certain. We concede
That doubts may weaken any creed:
Is this art, this life we lead?
                                    — THE CONTRACANTOS

"One more day of Pound, guys," said BradLee.

I opened my notebook. I'd be sad to see him go. I liked the *Cantos*. Well, I sometimes liked the *Cantos*. I liked it when lines were taken out of context. I did not like dealing with the entire 824-page poem. It was too much for me. Too many thoughts.

"Much of the information we'll be using today is from a book by Eustace Mullins. A biography. It's called *This Difficult Individual, Ezra Pound.*"

What a boss title.

"We've touched on reactions to Pound before, when we

considered his anti-Semitism in the context of the distinction between life and art. I'm sure you all recall perfectly."

I looked around at the class. Lots of hooded eyes and blank faces. I turned back to BradLee, and our eyes met.

"A refresher, perhaps?" BradLee paused, longer than he usually does during lectures. "People are only people. People do bad things. Yes, Ezra Pound was a Nazi sympathizer. He was doing what he thought was right. Or maybe it was more complicated than that. After all, he was a person, and he was imperfect."

I was pretty sure—I still am—that he was talking right to me.

"But we need to separate his life from his art, as best we can. We've isolated art, carved out a space for it, claimed it's different. Now we have to live up to that claim."

BradLee, I thought, was sort of a shitty person. He was also a person I liked. He was also the best teacher I'd ever had.

"Critics have said a lot of things about Pound. We're going to look at a few, and decide whether they're right. With that, we'll conclude our unit on the long poem."

I bet Jackson would have been happy to hear that. "The best thing about poetry is that it's short," he'd said way back. Jackson, however, had not been in school this week. He was over at the U, undergoing a battery of psychological testing. That's what happens when you get caught in the kTV lab and claim that you were hacking the closed-captioning because it was so riddled with typos. And that you had been commanded to do so. By an angel.

"We don't even *believe* in angels," Mr. Appelman had said in horror.

Right in the middle of the finale, they'd had to drag him away from the lab as he kicked and screamed about the "loose"/"lose" mix-up. "God hates typos!" he'd chanted for the next six hours.

A disturbed, disturbed child. Either that or a hero.

"Here's our first critic," said BradLee.

You've sat through a bunch of English classes, so I'll spare you the details. I won't tell you what we thought of Hugh Kenner, who thought that no contemporary poet appealed more, through "sheer beauty of language," to those who would rather talk about poets than read them.

I won't tell you about my crazed hand-waving, seat-bouncing rebuttal to Philip Larkin. Thus saith Larkin: "Nobody criticizes E. P. for being literary, which to me is the foundation of his feebleness, thinking that poetry is made out of poetry and not out of being alive."

There's a lot of literary, difficult, meaningful crap in Pound's work. But thus saith Ethan: if you're looking, there's a lot of literary, difficult, meaningful crap in being alive.

I've got to tell you about my favorite, though. It's by Macha Rosenthal, and she wrote that it was "as if all the beautiful vitality and all the brilliant rottenness of our heritage in its luxuriant variety were both at once made manifest" in Ezra Pound.

Not to degrade Pound, but doesn't this also describe *For Art's Sake?* This horrible, compelling show? It *was* full of beautiful vitality. It was full of the kind of stories that could make a few million Americans solder their butts to their couches at 9 p.m. every Friday. Those stories were about people with purposes, people who wanted to get somewhere, and if that's not beautiful and vital I don't know what is.

But it was also rotten, brilliantly rotten at its very core. The show wasn't for art's sake. It was art forsaken. It was for money's sake, for greed's sake, and it was commercialized and fake. So there you go: the remarkable convergence of Ezra Pound and reality TV.

Beautiful vitality, brilliant rottenness, a luxuriant variety of both: that had been the whole school year. There had been perfect times, like when I was sitting with Maura Heldsman in the dance hallway and the printer cartridge of life had just been replaced so all the colors were bedazzlingly bright and I'd figured out how to live and how to love and nothing, ever, could possibly be more beautiful than the green of her eyes, the line of her back. But there were times when I'd been blinded by the rottenness of the world. When Baconnaise's hairs rose and I knew that I'd sent this conscious being to his death. When Luke waved to us in the cafeteria, and went to sit somewhere else.

But perfect? Rotten? Can I even categorize them? For underneath my memory of Maura's beauty is the knowledge that I never loved her well. And underpinning Baconnaise's death will always be his sacrifice. He didn't know what he was doing, he didn't believe in a resurrection, he didn't *not* believe in a resurrection; he just did what he had to do. He didn't think about things. He didn't write and write and write and imagine that there'd be answers at the end of it. He didn't know how confusing it would be to write so much and think so hard and still know nothing for sure.

I thought there'd be some resolution, I guess is what I'm saying. I thought I'd have some answers. Maybe the important thing is that there are no answers. There are only questions. And asking the questions is important, not answering them.

But that's an answer!

So in conclusion? This is what I've concluded. Not nothing, but only this, which is not at all the same as nothing:

I don't know.

ONE OF THE WAYS I COULD POSSIBLY END THIS THING

It was the last weekend before school ended.

"Ethan," said my mom, sitting at the kitchen table, "I just got a phone call from Mrs. Weston."

I'd just woken up. It was nine-thirty, barbarically early for a Saturday, but I had to go to this figure-drawing master class for extra credit. ("The Art of Excretion" made for a craptastic quarter grade.)

I was groggy, and it took me weirdly long to remember that Mrs. Weston was the mother of Luke Weston. "Okay," I said, shuffling over to the cereal cupboard.

"She told me something very strange about *For Art's Sake*."

"Yeah, I could tell you strange—AHH! DON'T DO THAT TO ME!"

"SURPRISE!"

I had bent down to open the cereal cupboard and found not Cheerios but two small girls, now raucously cackling.

"We knew you'd fall for it!"

"Because you're D-U-M-B dumb!"

"Who taught you about silent *B*'s?" I muttered. My heart rate slowly subsided. "All I did was open the cereal cupboard. That doesn't count as 'falling for it.'"

"It's not the cereal cupboard. It's the Secret Club cupboard."

"So where's the cereal?"

"In the pantry."

"I was congratulating her about Luke's performance on *For Art's Sake*."

"Congratulating?"

"That's what she said! She said—she said *darkly*—that it wasn't a matter for congratulation. That they'd exploited him."

"Did he tell her that?" I opened the pantry. "Because that's a little ironic—AIII! OLIVIA, I HATE YOU!"

"That *does* count as falling for it," pointed out Lila.

"Give me the Cheerios, or I spoon out your eyeballs," I said.

"D-U-M-B dumb!" chanted the girls. But they did give me the Cheerios.

"Now shoo," said my mother. "Ethan and I are trying to have a conversation."

"You could have said that like three minutes ago," I told her.

"You looked like you needed a shock."

"It's true that I am now fully awake."

"Mrs. Weston is up in arms. And I feel behind the times. So Luke didn't win?"

"Nope."

"And I lost her in the details, but they're apparently giving scholarships to all the contestants."

"Yeah."

"Well. After hemming and hawing for six weeks, they're saying Luke's not eligible. Because he wasn't on the show from the beginning."

"Ah."

That Coluber. That slimy Coluber. *To the finalists, who have devoted their school year to these eighteen episodes. . . .*

Take away the comma, and take away Luke's eligibility.

"And she's been calling the other parents to gather details. You know what Mrs. Weston is like when she's after something."

"A hungry bulldog?" I said helpfully.

"I wouldn't go that far. But——well, I see your point. She's learning some peculiar things about this show. You should have *heard* what she told me from Mrs. Heldsman."

Lurch. (That was my heart.)

"That sweet girl——what's her name, honey?"

"Laura? Maura? Something like that."

"I think you're right. Maura. She was portrayed as an absolute——*harlot.* It's unconscionable, what they've done to her reputation. And the whole thing is making Mrs. Weston wonder: why did the parents allow this in the first place?"

"Interesting," I said.

The principal and vice principal may think they're in charge of a school, but only until they have to face down an angry and mobilized group of parents. Because schools need kids. Arts schools need talented kids. And the people who spawn the talent and feed the talent and drive the talent around? Parents.

It was as if they had a list of everything we'd hoped to accomplish via IMAGE, VORTEX, and EZRA. Led by Mrs. Michelle Weston, the Parent Board achieved the following:

1. No more kTV at Selwyn. Rumor has it *For Art's Sake* is looking for another host school, but Mrs. Weston has publicly vowed to do everything in her power to stop it. (Who'd win in a fight, Mrs. Weston or Trisha Meier? It'd be a battle for the ages. Actually, it could make a good reality TV show.)

2. No more Coluber at Selwyn. Yes, he's gone. Strangely enough, the entire Parent Board received an anonymous email with grainy pictures of certain documents. And even though the email—kill.the.snake@gmail.com—was obviously not to be trusted, it prompted them to investigate financial matters, and Coluber's under-the-table money came out. Jackson was right: kTV was paying him fifteen percent of *For Art's Sake*'s revenues. He resigned. The Parent Board has engaged legal counsel, and they're deciding whether to sue.

3. Willis Wolfe, though—he managed to stay around. I think everyone accepts the fact that he's clueless. And besides, he's so pretty, with those teeth glistening against his tanned jawline.

ANOTHER OF THE WAYS
I COULD POSSIBLY END THIS

Shoot back a few weeks, to mid-May. We were in the Appelden. We'd spent the past two weeks taking APs, and even though I was convinced they were going to start issuing negative scores to quantify just how badly I'd done on bio, the exams were blessedly over. The Parent Board's wild rampage was yet to come, but kTV had packed up and headed southwest for the summer. Nobody talked about *For Art's Sake* anymore. It was back to the old debates: *Wicked* versus *The Producers*. Monet versus Manet. PBR versus Natty Light.

"Jackson," said Mrs. Appelman, "Honey Mustard needs to be taken out."

The windows were open, and the Minnesota spring was blowing in.

"We'll come," said Elizabeth.

But once we'd made it to the dark backyard we realized that the spring air was still wintry, and Elizabeth and I elected to shudder on the back porch instead of following Jackson and Honey Mustard to the rear of the big lot.

"What's up with Maura?" she said.

"No clue." I hadn't seen her since the day of the English exam, during which we'd been given two hours to write three essays. Maura wrote for thirty-eight minutes. Then she shut her test booklet, skewered her bun with her number-two pencil, and took a nap. I guess Juilliard didn't care about AP scores.

"Meaning that you're over her?"

"Well."

"Didn't think so." She skipped down the steps into the backyard and held out her arms. "Spring! Spring! You're not going to get over her, are you?"

"I don't know if I want to."

She chortled. "Too true."

"I'll get over her when she goes to college."

"You'll find someone else to idealize."

"Probably," I said vaguely. I was looking at the stars, which I hear are better in Minnesota than in, say, New York.

Sky's clear / night's sea.

"And once you've made New Girl unattainable, you'll fall in fake-love all over again."

"Yep. You've fathomed the depths of my psyche."

"Ethan the cretin," she said, but in a nice way. She did a few cartwheels on the grass. I started watching her instead of the stars. Then I hit rewind.

"Wait. *Made* her unattainable? These girls—they *are* unattainable."

"Not as unattainable as you think." She sat down on the top step, so I sat next to her. We could faintly hear Jackson exhorting Honey Mustard to poop. It was highly romantic. The dark of night, the gleam of stars, "come on boy push it out I'm freezing my ass off."

"What do you mean?"

"Good question. I'm being imprecise. I should have said: they're *not* unattainable. They are, in fact, attainable."

"Unattainable is my *type*."

"Maura Heldsman wasn't unattainable."

"If you Google Image 'unattainable,' you see Maura Heldsman."

"Come on, Honey Mustard, I know it's cold but you just gotta go, okay?"

"I think she had a bit of a crush on you."

"WHAT?"

"Just a theory." Elizabeth smiled. "I'm freezing. I'm going inside."

Ready for anticlimax? Guess who never talked to Maura Heldsman again?

Yeah, me.

If this were a show on kTV, we would have admitted our mutual affection. Although we tragically would have no future, we'd have had the bittersweet knowledge of what might have been.

Just kidding. If this were a show on kTV, we would have made out. Minimum.

But this is where real life will let you down. There was no

grand live finale. Instead, I went to graduation and saw her in a weird hat.

And although I was tempted to write it differently, that is the true denouement of the Maura Heldsman chapter of my life.

THE THIRD WAY TO END THIS, WHICH WILL REALLY BE THE END (I GUESS)

It was Saturday. The day after EZRA, the day after the *For Art's Sake* finale.

Early that evening, I went over to Jackson's. I had a chilly parcel in my pocket. It was Baconnaise.

Well, it was Baconnaise's *body*. It wasn't really him. You'd think that since I knew that, I could have brought myself to play a majorly satisfying trick on the triplets. "Would you like a Popsicle, girls?" "YES!" "Open carefully!"

But I couldn't. Baconnaise had done too much for me.

He had spent the night in a Ziploc body bag next to the fish sticks. I smoothed his fur, closed his eyes, and laid him in a stationery box atop a soft bed of wood chips and raisins. His arms weren't long enough to cross over his chest, but I tried.

Then I biked over to Jackson's. It was one of the first truly springlike days. Elizabeth was doing homework on her porch. After recovering from a fit of laughter—apparently I looked funny on a bicycle?—she walked after me to the Appelden.

Jackson led us out to the basketball hoop. I liked the continuity. Every pet the Appelmen had owned for the past quarter century was buried here, from the beloved thirteen-year-old golden retriever Honey to Pico de Gallo, the carnival goldfish who had begun floating upside-down a record six minutes after being released from his baggie. I liked that the bodies stayed together while the condiment souls went up to the great refrigerator door in the sky. I liked that it gave a weight, a history, to every pet, even the ones whose lives and deaths hadn't inspired any great love at all.

I gave the coffin to Jackson.

"I got the shovel," he said. "But I thought I'd wait to dig until you guys came."

"Let's take turns," said Elizabeth.

I shrugged and nodded agreement. I'd kind of wanted to do the whole thing. I'd had this vision of myself out there alone, digging the grave, drowning my grief in sweat.

But Baconnaise was tiny. This would not be an ordeal. Elizabeth bent down with the trowel and then Jackson did, and then he handed it to me, and the black loamy soil gave way easily to the blade. This was the most fertile land on earth. With those three swipes we had a grave, and I put Baconnaise's coffin inside.

"Say something," Elizabeth said to me. But I couldn't.

"Wait," said Jackson, and pelted inside. He brought out his edition of the *Cantos*. By the looks of it, he'd barely cracked the spine. He passed it to me. "Read something."

"Which part?"

"You think *I* know?"

Elizabeth looked at me. "You know."

I knew.

"What thou lovest well remains," I read, *"the rest is dross/What thou lov'st well shall not be reft from thee/What thou lov'st well is thy true heritage/Whose world, or mine or theirs/or is it of none?"*

Jackson lifted the trowel and began to cover Baconnaise with dirt. "He was an excellent gerbil."

"He was valiant," said Elizabeth. "He was a hero."

I was glad they were speaking, because Baconnaise deserved more than Ezra Pound. Philip Larkin's thing about the *Cantos* being too literary—that was bullshit. But even if Pound's poetry was made out of being alive, it was still art that came from life. It wasn't life. And when you die I bet that you want real life, pure real life, eulogies that are unpoetic and messy, smeared with tears and truisms, clichéd as hell, the kind of stuff a person means.

"He was good and kind and brave and true," said Jackson.

"He was loyal," said Elizabeth.

"He was a real friend," I said.

Then, over the rise that separated the backyard from the front, appeared Luke. We turned at his footsteps.

"I thought you'd be burying him now," he said. I couldn't tell whether he was sheepish or just keeping his voice down, his confidence at a low simmer, because of the circumstances. "You always bury your pets at sunset."

"Yeah," said Jackson.

Nobody else said anything. Luke came to stand with us, looking down at the small patch of disturbed earth. That was all there was. The next rainfall would merge that soil with the soil around it, and soon the grass and weeds would grow in their Minnesota riot, pushing into his body with their roots.

"Thanks, Baconnaise," said Luke.

"Thanks, Baconnaise," we echoed, and the four of us turned and walked back to the house.

ACKNOWLEDGMENTS

Much of the information about Ezra Pound comes from John Tytell's excellent biography, *Ezra Pound: The Solitary Volcano*. The Public Library of Cincinnati and Hamilton County provided essential resources; I am (literally) indebted.

I am grateful to many people for their generosity, patience, and good company. These include my parents, Ellen and Charlie Hattemer; my siblings and first readers, Spencer, Derek, Lucy, Emma, Rebecca, Peter, and Henry Hattemer; and my friends, colleagues, and students. Sorry, everyone, for stealing your lines. Many thanks to Heather Daugherty, Michael Trudeau, Artie Bennett, Kelly Delaney, and the whole team at Random House. And my deepest thanks to my agent, Uwe Stender, and my editor, Erin Clarke, who have offered such incisive suggestions and expressed such remarkable enthusiasm. I am surrounded by people as kind as they are smart, as insightful as they are funny, and I am very lucky.

ABOUT THE AUTHOR

Kate Hattemer, the oldest of eight siblings, grew up in Cincinnati, Ohio. She attended Yale University and taught high school Latin in Virginia before returning to Cincinnati, where she now works as a bookseller. *The Vigilante Poets of Selwyn Academy* is her first book. Visit her on the Web at katehattemer.com.